## "Getting hitched solves all your problems."

*Yep, she was JoBeth McCoy, problem solver to the world.*

Garrett circled the room and sank onto a chair before his empty dinner plate. "No. This is crazy." Elbows on the table, he cradled his head. "I'm sorry. I don't know what I was thinking. I'm not myself lately."

He was hiding something, she was certain. She had a feeling she knew the source of his reluctance.

No matter the personal cost, she'd pry the truth from him. "Would you say yes if someone else asked?" She fought the rough edge in her voice. "Because there are plenty of other ladies in town."

Marshal Cain bolted upright. "This is the rest of my life. You're the only one I'd even consider."

"Ooo…kay."

That was a decent response, right? He hadn't exactly explained why he'd choose her over someone else, but Jo guessed that was about as good an answer as she was going to get. While she might have hoped for something more revealing, at least he was still considering her suggestion. He hadn't outright refused her yet.

**Books by Sherri Shackelford**

Love Inspired Historical

*Winning the Widow's Heart*
*The Marshal's Ready-Made Family*

## SHERRI SHACKELFORD

A wife and mother of three, Sherri Shackelford says her hobbies include collecting mismatched socks, discovering new ways to avoid cleaning and standing in the middle of the room while thinking, "Why did I just come in here?" A reformed pessimist and recent hopeful romantic, Sherri has a passion for writing. Her books are fun and fast paced, with plenty of heart and soul. She enjoys hearing from readers at sherrimshackelford@yahoo.com, or visit her website, at www.sherrishackelford.com.

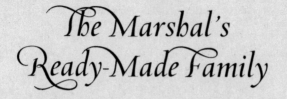

# The Marshal's Ready-Made Family

## SHERRI SHACKELFORD

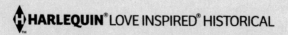

HARLEQUIN® LOVE INSPIRED® HISTORICAL

Recycling programs for this product may not exist in your area.

**LOVE INSPIRED BOOKS**

ISBN-13: 978-0-373-28251-7

THE MARSHAL'S READY-MADE FAMILY

www.Harlequin.com

Printed in U.S.A.

And above all things have fervent charity among yourselves: for charity shall cover the multitude of sins.
—*1 Peter* 4:8

To Barb, Jenn, Deb, Donna, *lizzie and Cheryl—
otherwise known as the Friday Night Critique Ladies.
Thank you for the friendship, the knowledge,
the occasional argument, the food and the laughter.
We always come back to laughter, don't we?

I'm a better writer for the group.

I'm a better person for knowing each of you.

# Chapter One

*Cimarron Springs, Kansas*
*1881*

JoBeth McCoy knew Marshal Garrett Cain's life was about to change forever—and all she could do was sit with his young niece until he heard the tragic news about his sister.

The towering double doors behind Jo and five-year-old Cora creaked open, and Reverend Miller cleared his throat. "You can send in the child now." He held out his hand for Cora. "Marshal Cain has been informed of his sister's passing."

Her heart heavy, Jo stood, then hesitated in the dappled sunlight. A soft breeze sent pear blossoms from the trees on either side of the shallow church steps fluttering over them like fragrant snow petals.

Cora rose and snatched Jo's hand. "Will you go with me?"

A riot of flaxen curls tumbled merrily around the little girl's face, but her Cupid's-bow mouth was solemn beneath her enormous, cornflower-blue eyes. Cora clutched a paper funnel filled with lemon drops in her left hand. Her battered rag doll remained anchored to her right side.

Jo met the reverend's sympathetic gaze, grateful for his almost imperceptible nod of agreement. He was a squat, sturdy man in his middle fifties with thinning gray hair and a kind smile.

The three of them stepped into the church vestibule, and Reverend Miller directed them toward his tiny, cluttered office. Jo paused as her eyes adjusted in the dim light.

Marshal Cain sat on a sturdy wooden chair before the desk, his expression grim. Her heart skittered, but she swallowed back her nerves and forced her steps closer.

His eyes were red, and the tail end of a hastily stowed handkerchief peeked out from his breast pocket. As though embarrassed by his tears, he didn't meet her gaze. Instead, he focused his attention on the petite fingers clutching Jo's waist. He didn't stand or approach them, and for that Jo was grateful, especially since Cora cowered behind her.

He caught sight of his niece's frightened gaze and blinked rapidly. "Hello, Cora. I know we've never met, but your mother and I were brother and sister."

Jo had only seen the marshal a handful of times, but he was an imposing sight sitting down, let alone standing. Well over six feet tall, he wore his dark hair neatly trimmed. Though he didn't sport a beard, a five-o'clock shadow perpetually darkened his jaw.

His face was all hard lines and tough angles, with a deep cleft dividing his chin. An inch-long scar slashed at an angle from his forehead through one thick, dark eyebrow. Other women might prefer a gentler face, but Jo found his distinctive features fascinating. *Not that she looked.* A woman simply couldn't help but notice things once in a while.

Cora took a hesitant step from behind Jo. "Mama is dead."

"Yes."

"Papa, too."

The marshal's knuckles whitened on the arms of his chair. "I know," he replied, his voice gruff.

Jo glanced between the two, her chest aching for their shared grief. From what little information she'd gathered, the girl's parents had died in a fire three weeks ago. As Cora's closest living relative, Marshal Cain had been assigned guardianship. Reverend Miller had just broken the news, and the poor man was obviously devastated by the loss.

Realizing the reverend had deserted them, Jo craned her neck and searched the empty vestibule. Everyone in town knew she had all the sensitivity of a goat at a tea party, and this situation definitely required a delicate touch.

She caught sight of Cora's dismayed expression and decided she'd best keep the two talking until the reverend returned. "Why don't you show Mr. Cain what you bought at the store this morning."

The marshal's gaze flicked up at Jo, then quickly returned to Cora as she dutifully extended her arm, revealing her precious stash of candy.

"Want one?"

"Uh, well, sure." He stretched out one hand and plucked a lemon drop from atop the mound. "Your mother liked peppermints," he added.

Cora nodded eagerly. "Me, too!"

Relieved by the girl's easy acceptance of Marshal

Cain, Jo spurred the conversation. "Cora rode a train all the way from St. Louis, didn't you?"

"Mrs. Smith wouldn't let me sit by the window." Cora fingered a dangling edge of pink ribbon circling the frilly waistband of her dress. "She was grumpy."

A shadow crossed the marshal's eyes. "Sorry 'bout that. I didn't know you were coming. I'd have fetched you myself."

"Would you let me sit by the window?"

"I guess. If you wanted."

The tension in Jo's shoulders eased a bit. They'd been frantically searching for the marshal since the day nearly two weeks past when Jo had transcribed the telegram announcing his niece's imminent arrival. He'd been escorting a prisoner to Wichita and had run into trouble along the way.

By the time they'd discovered his location and informed him that he was needed back in town posthaste, the poor little girl had already arrived with her grim-faced escort. Mrs. Smith had been terrified of Indians, and certain she'd never make it back to St. Louis with her scalp intact.

Since the skittish escort was obviously frightening Cora with her hysterics, Jo had cheerfully assumed responsibility for the little girl and hustled Mrs. Smith onto an eastbound train. Three days had gone by since then.

"When are we going back home?" Cora asked.

Jo's heart wrenched at the innocent question.

"Well, that's the thing." Marshal Cain cleared his throat. "I thought you could stay out here and live with me." The raw vulnerability in his expression touched Jo's soul. "We're the only family either of us has left."

Cora's solemn blue eyes blinked with understanding. "Don't you have a mama and papa, either?"

"Nope. Your mom and I lost our parents when I was fifteen and your mother was eighteen."

Though his expression remained neutral, Jo sensed a wagonload of sorrow behind the simple words.

Cora clasped her hands at her waist. "Did they die in a fire like my mama and papa?"

Stark anguish exploded in the marshal's gaze, and Jo took an involuntary step backward. His reaction felt too bleak, too powerful for an event that must be almost twenty years past.

Covering his revealing lapse, he absently rubbed his cheek. "Smallpox."

"What's that?" Cora asked.

"It's a sickness." The marshal angled his face toward the light. "It leaves scars."

Jo and Cora leaned closer, both squinting. Sure enough, the rough stubble on his chin covered a scattering of shallow pockmarks. Jo had never been this close to the marshal before and she caught the barest hint of his scent—masculine and clean. Her stomach fluttered. Once again she couldn't help but wonder how all his imperfection added up to down-right handsome.

Cora shrugged. "Your face doesn't look bad."

Jo glanced down at her own rough, homespun skirts and serviceable shirtwaist. Men's flaws made them look tough. But a woman who dressed and acted like a tomboy, well, that was another story. A woman without corkscrew curls and lace collars wasn't worth the time of day. She'd learned that lesson well enough when Tom Walby, the only boy she'd ever had a crush on, had mocked her for being a hoyden before the entire eighth-grade class.

Turned out men fell in love with their eyes first and their hearts second. Which was too bad, really. Nettles were far more useful in life than roses.

"Did you ride a train after your parents died?" Cora asked.

"I don't remember," the marshal replied. "That was a long time ago for me."

Cora nodded her agreement, her flaxen curls bobbing. "You're old, so that musta been a really, *really* long time ago."

Ducking her head, Jo muffled a laugh. Marshal Cain blinked as though her presence had only now fully registered through the haze of his grief. He hastily stood, knocking his hat to the floor. They both reached for it at the same time, nearly butting heads. Jo touched the brim first. As he accepted his hat, the marshal's rough, callused fingers brushed over hers, sending a scattering of gooseflesh dancing up her arm.

Jo met his dark eyes, astonished by the intensity of his gaze.

"My apologies for not greeting you," he said, sounding more formal than she'd ever heard him. "We met in church once, didn't we?"

"Don't be sorry, Mr. Cain." For some reason, she seemed to have a difficult time catching her breath when he was near. "You've been busier than a termite in a sawmill. I'm JoBeth McCoy."

The admission earned her a dry chuckle. "Seems like you can't turn a corner in this town without running into a McCoy."

Jo grinned. She had five younger brothers, and they never expected her to be anyone but herself. In fact, they'd probably clobber her if she started acting like a regular girl. "They're a handful, yes, sir."

"Reverend Miller says you and Cora have been inseparable."

Jo had taken a proprietary interest in Cora's plight from the beginning. The messages concerning her care had been clipped and chillingly professional. A child thrust into such turmoil needed more than a hired guardian like Mrs. Smith. She needed love and understanding.

Jo squeezed Cora's hand. "I work in the telegraph office. Part of my job is keeping track of unclaimed packages after the trains depart." She winked at Cora. "'Course this was a special case. Everyone needs a friend sometimes, right, Cora?"

The little girl returned the comforting pressure. "JoBeth sent twenty-six different messages trying to find you. I counted. JoBeth has five brothers. I counted them, too. I don't have any brothers. Do you have any brothers?"

"Nope."

The marshal and the little girl sized each other up like a couple of nervous spring foals. They were wary, yet curious, too. Suddenly, Jo realized how terribly unnecessary her presence had become. Cora didn't need her anymore—she had Marshal Cain.

Though he'd only been in town a few months, Jo sensed his unwavering resolve. He'd spent his time quietly and methodically cleaning up Cimarron Springs, a Herculean task. Their previous sheriff had been lazy and corrupt, and every outlaw west of the Mississippi had exploited his lax law enforcement. The marshal still had loads of work ahead of him, but he didn't show any signs of slowing.

And now that he and little Cora had each other, they didn't need her.

A band of emotion tightened around Jo's chest. Though she and Cora had known each other a short time, she felt a kinship.

A small hand tugged on her skirts. "How come you don't know Marshal Cain? You said you know everyone in town."

Jo glanced at the marshal and found him studying Reverend Miller's book collection as though it was the most fascinating thing on earth. She wondered if he was thinking about the deluge of invitations he'd received during his first few months in Cimarron Springs. Introducing a new man in town was like tossing raw meat into a pack of wolves. A pack of female wolves.

Warmth crept up Jo's neck. Of course, no one had considered her as a possible love interest. Not even her own parents had invited the marshal for dinner. Not that she cared, since she never planned on marrying. She'd pinched her cheeks and fluttered her eyelashes for Tom Walby and look what that had gotten her. He'd told her he'd rather court his grandfather's mule.

She wasn't about to make the same mistake twice.

Covering her unease, she fanned the tip of her thick, dark braid. "Marshal Cain has only been in town a few months. I guess he's never had call to arrest me. If I was a cattle rustler, we'd be on a first-name basis by now, I'm sure."

Cora giggled. The marshal sputtered, then coughed, and Jo immediately regretted her joke. A little ribbing always worked on her brothers when they were tense, but the marshal seemed embarrassed by her teasing. As the silence stretched out, the walls of Reverend Miller's office closed in around her, and the air grew thick.

Oblivious to the tension gripping the adults, Cora plucked a lemon drop from her paper funnel and popped it into her mouth. "Can I have a puppy?" she spoke, her voice muffled around her candy. "Mama said we couldn't have a puppy in the city. But you live in the country, don't you, Mr. Cain?"

Jo caught the marshal's helpless expression before he quickly masked his thoughts. He'd lost his sister and brother-in-law and discovered he was guardian of his five-year-old niece in the course of a few tragic moments.

He didn't live in the country. He lived in a set of rooms above the jail.

Cora spit the candy into her cupped palm. "The bears won't eat my puppy, will they? Mrs. Smith said Kansas was full of giant man-eating bears."

"Mrs. Smith was mistaken," Marshal Cain replied, his voice no more than a whisper.

Jo instinctively reached out a hand, but the marshal flinched. Flustered, she clenched her teeth and let a flash of anger douse the pain. "I was just being nice. It's not like I was gonna hit you, fool man."

For years after she'd socked Tom in the eye for humiliating her in public, the boys in town had made a point of shrinking away from her in mock terror.

The marshal gingerly touched his side. "It's not that, I bruised a couple ribs in a scuffle up north."

Jo mentally slapped her forehead. Of course he wasn't mocking her, he didn't even know about her humiliation. Why was anger always her first line of defense?

"I'm sorry," she spoke quickly. "Can I get you…a…a pillow or something?"

"No need. I've suffered worse."

Every time she tried to say the right thing with a

man, the feminine thing, it always fell flat. And how had Reverend Miller gotten lost in a two-room church?

She whirled and collided with the object of her ire.

The reverend steadied her with a hand on her elbow. "I see the marshal and his niece have gotten acquainted."

"No thanks to—"

A commotion outside interrupted her words. The reverend clasped his hands, his face pinched. "I believe you're needed outside, Marshal Cain." He glanced meaningfully in Cora's direction. "Tom Walby is in one of his moods."

Jo and Marshal Cain groaned in unison. Tom had grown from an adolescent annoyance into an adult bully with a nasty temper and a penchant for drinking. Every few weeks he got into a fight with his wife and took out his frustration on the local saloon. Jo flipped her braid over her shoulder.

Tom's wife never resisted the opportunity to smirk at her, still lording over her victory all these years later. Considering the prize had been Tom, Jo figured it was a loss she could endure.

"Can you look after Cora?" Marshal Cain directed his question toward Jo, and she eagerly smiled her agreement. "I'll take care of Tom as quick as I can."

The marshal knelt before Cora and enveloped her hand in his grasp. "Don't worry. We have each other now, and everything is going to be all right."

Jo's throat burned with rare emotion. They *did* have each other. They were a family. Not in the regular way, but a family nonetheless. If God had blessed her with a little girl as precious as Cora, she'd never let her go. Except she'd most likely never have a family of her own. Men didn't court girls who wore trousers beneath their skirts.

Jo shook off the gloomy thoughts. She had five brothers, after all. More family than one girl needed. With the boys already courting, she'd have her own nieces and nephews soon. She'd be the favorite aunt.

*Just as long as she didn't end up like Aunt Vicky.* The woman had fifteen goats and was known to dress them up for special occasions.

Marshal Cain slapped his hat back on his head. "Much obliged for your help."

He strode out the door, taking with him the crackling energy that surrounded Jo whenever he was near. While she didn't envy the marshal's task, she was grateful for the reprieve.

Surely by the time they met again, this strange, winded feeling would be gone. Besides, she liked him, liked the way he smiled at her, and she didn't want to ruin their camaraderie.

Cora tugged on her skirts. "You have something in your hair."

Ducking, Jo checked her disheveled reflection in the reflective glass of Reverend Miller's bookcase doors. She smoothed her fingers over her braided hair and released a scattering of pear blossoms, then threw up her arms with a groan.

She'd spent the entire conversation with white petals strewn over her dark hair.

Jo slapped her faded bowler back on her head. Even if she wanted to attract the attention of someone like Garrett Cain, she didn't stand a chance.

Garrett Cain closed the jail doors with a metallic clang. His prisoner, Tom Walby, paced the narrow space, a purple-and-green bruise darkening beneath his left eye.

Tom kicked the bars. "You don't understand, Marshal, it wasn't my fault."

"Not today, Tom."

Something in Garrett's voice must have penetrated the inebriated fog of Tom's brain. The lanky man groaned and braced his arms on the spindly table in his cell but kept blessedly silent. Dirty-blond hair covered Tom's head, and blood crusted on his chin. His blue-plaid shirt was torn, and his brown canvas pants rumpled. He'd given as good as he'd gotten in the saloon fight, but the whiskey in his belly had finally caught up with him.

Garrett spun the chamber of his revolver. Tom and his wife had two temperatures—hot and cold, love and hate. There was no in-between for those two, and their intensity terrified Garrett. He feared that sort of hard love because he'd seen the destructive force devour its prey with cruel finality.

He absently rubbed his chest. A hard knot had formed where his heart used to be after his parents' deaths. They'd been a fiery lot, too, and he and his sister had huddled together during the outbursts. The senseless deaths of his mother and father had wounded him—not mortally, but gravely.

No one in town knew the truth. That his father had killed his mother and then turned the gun on himself. The shame of his father's actions had shaped the course of Garrett's life.

Everything had muddled together in his brain…guilt, anger, fear. He'd wished more than once in childish prayers that he'd been born into a different family. Then God had taken his away. Garrett had corralled his emotions until the pain had passed, and when he'd finally emerged, he'd discovered his temporary fortress had become permanent. Nothing touched him too deeply anymore—not pain, not joy.

He was content. Good at keeping his emotions contained.

*Until now.*

The loss of Cora's mother, his only sister and last living relative, buffeted the walls around his heart like ocean waves. Horrors he'd spent a lifetime forgetting rushed back.

Tom paced his cell. "I saw that McCoy girl was taking care of your niece. You better be careful of that one. She'll have your little girl wearing pants and shooting guns."

Grateful for the distraction, Garrett considered his prisoner. "What's wrong with that?"

"Well, because…because it ain't feminine, that's why. I'd never settle with a girl who could outshoot me."

"Probably a good move on your part," Garrett retorted.

He didn't know why everyone in this town was blind to JoBeth McCoy's beauty. Her skin was flawless, her eyes large and exotic, and tipped up the corners. Her lips were full and pink, just made for kissing.

*Now, where had that thought come from?*

"The man should be the strong one," Tom slurred. "It ain't right when a girl can outscrap and outgun you."

"I don't think you give women enough merit. I've known women to endure things you and I couldn't even imagine."

Tom scoffed and spit into the corner.

Garrett shook his head. There was no use having a sensible conversation with someone who'd drunk away all his good sense. "You're making bad choices, Tom, and it's gonna catch up with you. One of these days you'll make a bad choice you can't sleep off or take back. What's gonna happen to your wife and your son when you're locked up for good?"

"What do you know about it?" Tom said sulkily.

"I know plenty."

Garrett stuffed his hands into his pockets and retrieved Cora's lemon drop. Pinching the candy between his thumb and forefinger, he let sunlight from the jail's narrow window bounce off the opaque coating.

His whole body ached from grief, as if he'd been thrown from a wild mustang. Why had God given him such a precious gift, a beautiful little girl to love and care for? He'd let his sister, Deirdre, down and now it was too late. He hadn't seen her once after she'd married, not even when Cora was born. Her husband was a good man, but visiting Deirdre brought back too many memories. Too many unsettling feelings from his youth.

Not that he'd purposefully stayed away. He kept meaning to visit St. Louis, but something would always come up. One year had passed, then two, then six—all in the blink of an eye. And now his sister was gone.

"Hey," Tom Walby said, gripping the bars with both hands and sticking his whiskered chin between the narrow opening. "Give me that candy."

"Nope." Garrett slipped Cora's gift back into his pocket. "Tom, do you ever pay attention in church?"

"Nah. I only go on Sunday when the missus forces me."

"Too bad. The reverend was preaching to you last week. He said, *Blessed are the poor in spirit, for theirs is the kingdom of Heaven.*"

"Ah, c'mon, Marshal," Tom garbled, squeaking his

sweaty hands down the bars. "You don't believe in that Bible stuff, do you?"

Garrett considered the question. *Did he?* Sometimes yes and sometimes no. At times like this, he wished he found comfort from God; instead, he felt only a deep and abiding sense of betrayal. "Why don't you sleep it off."

"If only it were that easy," Tom declared, stumbling toward the narrow cot lining the jailhouse wall.

He collapsed onto his back and threw one arm over his eyes. Surprised by the man's articulate response, Garrett paused for a moment. He leaned closer, but Tom was already sound asleep and snoring.

"Yep," Garrett muttered. "If only it were that easy."

Confident he had time before Tom awoke and recalled his earlier rage, Garrett walked the short distance to the boardinghouse where JoBeth McCoy stayed. He knew where she lived. Watching her take the shortcut to the telegraph office each morning while he fixed his coffee was the highlight of his day. Even from a distance her forest-green eyes flashed with mischief as she scaled the corral fence, a pair of trousers concealed beneath her modest skirts.

He caught sight of Jo and Cora and his heart thumped uncomfortably against his ribs. They sat crouched over a red-and-black set of checkers, their heads together. Jo's hair was dark and long and stick straight, while Cora's hair was a short blond mass of wild curls. Jo's eyes were vivid green, with dark lashes, and Cora's eyes were crystal blue with pale lashes.

They reminded him of an Oriental symbol he'd once seen in San Francisco—a black teardrop and a white teardrop nestled in a circle. They were opposite, yet somehow they complemented each other perfectly.

JoBeth McCoy was different from other women, and her uniqueness fascinated him. Not that he was interested in courting—a man with his past definitely wasn't husband material—but something in Jo sparked his interest. She didn't simper or flutter her eyelashes, and he was drawn to her unabashed practicality. Too many people created unnecessary complications for themselves, like his drunken prisoner.

Garrett paused on the boardwalk, grateful they hadn't seen him yet. His eyes still burned, and emotion clogged his throat. He pinched the bridge of his nose, not wanting Jo to see him like this—vulnerable and aching to cry like a baby.

After inhaling a fortifying breath, he clapped his hands, startling the two. "Who's winning?"

"I am," Cora declared proudly.

Jo winked at him in shared confidence, and his heart swelled.

"Reverend Miller has invited you two for supper," she said.

Her obvious compassion soothed him, and for a moment the pain subsided. The townspeople were all desperately trying to ease Cora through the transition, and he appreciated the effort. "What time?"

"Five o'clock."

"Five it is, then. Speaking of food, have you two had any lunch?"

"Nope."

"Not yet."

"Why don't we mosey over to the hotel and eat."

Jo rubbed her hands against her brown skirts. "You two don't need me anymore—"

"No!" Cora exclaimed.

Her face pinched in fear, and Jo placed her hand

comfortingly over the little girl's. The simple purity of the gesture humbled Garrett.

Pale blue eyes pleaded with him. "Can I stay with Jo until dinner?"

His stomach dipped. Of course Cora was terrified. Her whole world had turned upside down. She'd lost her parents, her home—everything that was familiar. Then she'd been placed on a train with a stranger and shuttled across the country into the care of yet another stranger.

Jo wrapped a blond curl around her index finger and smiled, her face radiant. "I suppose I could stay a tiny little while longer."

Garrett fought back the sting behind his eyes. Who wouldn't be terrified by all that upheaval? The little girl had been adrift and alone until Jo had sheltered her. Now they were connected. He'd seen that sort of devotion before over the years. He'd even been the recipient once or twice of a victim's misplaced allegiance. Those false attachments had quickly faded when people were reunited with their families.

Except Cora didn't have anyone familiar.

"I need you, Jo," Cora stated simply.

Garrett's gaze locked with Jo's. He couldn't mask his churning emotions, and he knew right then she saw him for what he was—exposed, terrified. Yet no censure entered her expression, only compassion and understanding. For a moment it seemed as if everything *would* be okay—as though she'd be strong enough for all of them.

*I need you, Jo.*

The truth hit Garrett like a mule kick. He needed guidance and Cora had taken a shine to Jo. He'd do everything in his power to foster the budding relationship—even if it risked his brittle emotions.

*If only his life had been different.*

He and Cora both needed Jo desperately. Yet only one of them was worthy of her.

## Chapter Two

The weathered boardwalk planks beneath Jo's feet rumbled. With Cora between them, Jo and the marshal paused beneath the hand-painted sign for the Palace Café. A group of young boys, blessedly minus any of her brothers, dashed around them, laughing and calling to each other. Visibly alarmed by the group's roughhousing, Cora latched on to Jo's leg.

"Don't worry." Jo ruffled her curls. "They're just full of energy. They have the week off while their schoolteacher is visiting her sister during her confinement."

Another baby, and the birth had been particularly difficult. Jo stifled a shudder. Her ma served as midwife around town, and Jo often assisted. Each birth she attended crystallized her fears and renewed her vow to stay single.

While there was joy, too often there was pain. She'd swaddled the tiny bodies of stillborn infants. She'd led distraught husbands from the room and sat with them while they wept. She'd felt the hand of a laboring mother go limp as the woman's exhausted body gave up the battle for life.

After all she'd seen, she'd never experience the innocent hope and wonder most expectant mothers felt.

Not that she had any prospects in the matter, but she didn't like this strange push and pull tugging on her emotions lately. More and more often she found herself lingering over the newborns, inhaling their sweet scent and wondering what it would be like to have one of her own.

Jo mentally shook off the disquieting thoughts. It was no use pining for things that could never be. She'd been rejected before and, while she knew she could survive heartbreak, she dreaded a repeat of the humiliating experience.

Cora peeked out from beneath her pale eyelashes. "When will I go to school?"

The marshal blanched. "I don't know. I'm not sure. Should she be in school now? What should I do?"

"There's no need for panic." Jo chucked him on the shoulder. "We'll talk with the teacher when she comes back next week."

"You're right." He mopped his forehead with a blue-patterned bandanna. "Of course you're right. There's no need for alarm. I'm just new to all this."

The marshal's dedication melted Jo's insides. Seeing a tough, hardened lawman reduced to a bundle of nerves over a tiny little girl was the most precious sight she'd ever seen. She didn't know whether to laugh or cry, hug him or chuck him on the shoulder once more. But she felt better about Cora's new living arrangements than she had all week.

She'd known the marshal was fair and levelheaded, but seeing him this vulnerable lit a warm glow in her chest. Anybody could be a tough lawman, but it took a real man to show his vulnerability.

Cora tipped her rag doll side to side, sending its yellow-yarn braids flopping. "I know some of my letters. But I can't read yet."

The marshal squinted thoughtfully. "I'll talk with the schoolteacher when she returns. Are you ready for lunch?"

"Nope." Cora glanced around. "I dropped Miss Lily's coat."

She dashed back a few paces, leaving Jo and Marshal Cain alone on the boardwalk beneath a cloudless, brilliant blue spring sky. Jo had been thinking about his rattled composure when she'd teased him earlier, and she wondered if he was embarrassed by female attention. She'd noticed the odd affliction with her brothers. They were as tough as buffalo jerky with their friends, but as fluffy as milkweed when it came to a pretty girl.

Testing her theory, Jo smiled coyly, her lips stretching with muscles she rarely used. The marshal returned the smile, his face turning pink.

To her shock, she felt her own cheeks warm.

She'd done it—she'd almost flirted with a man and he'd sort of responded. It was no wonder Mary Louise held court to all those besotted suitors in the mercantile like the queen of England.

"Hey, runt," a familiar voice sneered.

Jo's smile faded. Bert Walby sauntered up the boardwalk, his fingers hitched into his striped vest pocket. Tom Walby's brother never missed an opportunity to bait her. She stood up straighter, bracing for his verbal attack. Tom and Bert looked alike with their gangly frames and straw-colored hair.

Gritting her teeth, Jo faced her tormentor. "You're looking awfully fancy, Bert. You going before the judge?"

He scowled. "That's funny, runt, cuz you look the same as always. You get dressed in a barn this morning?"

Chuckling, he snatched the hat from her head, then reared back and cocked his arm in order to toss it onto the dirt-packed street. The next instant, Bert staggered into the marshal. Unsure what had knocked him sideways, Jo leaped back. The two men slammed into the jailhouse wall. Bert yelped and collapsed onto his knees. Marshal Cain bent, hooking his right hand beneath the man's shoulder, and hauled him upright. The marshal whispered something in Bert's ear before shoving him forward.

With a grumble, Bert circled his right shoulder and rubbed his biceps with his left hand.

The marshal crossed his arms and cleared his throat.

Leaning down, Bert plucked her hat from the boardwalk and dusted the brim against his thigh before returning it. "I was just checking on Tom. Heard you locked him up again."

The marshal braced his legs apart. "Tom's responsible for his own actions. You can pick him up before supper. He should be sober by then."

"It's nobody's business what a man does on his own time."

"Tom makes it my business when he goes smashing up property."

Bert tossed a glare over his shoulder as he beat a hasty exit.

Jo replaced her hat and frowned at Bert's retreating back. "That was odd. He usually doesn't back down that quick."

Marshal Cain shrugged, his expression deceptively

neutral. "Seems like Bert's got a grudge against both of us."

"We've been feuding since the eighth grade." Jo snorted. "Since I gave Tom a shiner. The Walbys are too afraid of my brothers to settle the score outright, but whenever Tom or Bert sees me alone... You get the idea."

"I do." A muscle ticked along the marshal's jaw.

Cora skipped between them with her doll. Miss Lily sported a red coat trimmed in navy blue rickrack.

Garrett yanked open the café door, clanging the bell suspended above them, his attention focused on the street. His gaze settled on the spot where Bert had taken up vigil near the jailhouse. Garrett looked between the two of them, and his eyes narrowed. Jo's shoulders sagged. So much for flirting with the marshal. Now he'd see her like everyone else in town did—a rebel who scrapped with the boys.

She set her jaw. It was best not to pine for something she'd never have. Over the years she'd grown wiser, more protective of her emotions. Loosening her resolve was a road paved with disaster.

It was best if Garrett thought of her as a buddy, because a friend couldn't break her heart.

The café bustled with activity. Plates clanked together and the low hum of voices surrounded them. The succulent aroma of fried chicken filled the air. Garrett pulled out a chair for Cora and Jo in turn, then caught the curious glance of a middle-aged woman in a burgundy bustled dress.

He touched his forehead in greeting and leaned nearer Jo's ear. "Is it all right? You and I eating together. I don't want any gossip."

Jo rolled her eyes. "Don't worry about it. We're fine."

For an instant he thought he saw a flash of disappointment. The moment passed so quickly, he shook off the odd feeling. Why would Jo *want* people gossiping about them?

Starched white cloths draped the wooden tables, and mismatched china covered the surface. The decor was a curious blend of faded elegance and homespun crafts. In the center of the table, a pint-size milk jug tinted a clear shade of blue-green held a posy of coneflowers.

Garrett kicked back in his chair and studied his surroundings. Most of the people in town were familiar by now, and they'd moved passed their initial wariness. A few gentlemen nodded in his direction, and Mrs. Schlautman flashed him a smile.

Jo rested her menu on the table. "How'd you end up here, anyway?"

He couldn't hold back a grin. "You sure are direct."

"Is that bad?"

"No, no. I like it." *Too much.*

Garrett planted his elbows on the table and fisted his hands. "I was bored. I needed a challenge. When I heard what I was up against, what the previous sheriff had let go on around here, I knew this was the perfect job for me."

"Will you stay? After you're done cleaning up the town and all?"

"Hadn't planned on it." His gaze slid toward Cora. "But things have changed."

Their waitress bustled past and took their orders, momentarily interrupting his troubled thoughts. Jo and the woman exchanged a few pleasantries, their friendship obvious by their banter. The woman returned a moment later with a pencil and paper, and Cora happily accepted the distracting items.

Garrett scratched his head. "I never even thought of that."

"You're new to all this. You'll learn." Jo pressed her thumb against the tines of her fork. "Do you have any other family? Someone who could help out for a bit?"

"Just a cousin and his wife." Garrett glanced away. "They won't be much help."

"I thought you said you didn't have any family."

"None that claim me." He ducked his head. "I guess that's different than no kin at all."

There was no love lost between him and Edward. For a time after his parents' deaths, Garrett had stayed with Edward's family. They'd been mortified by the scandal, and resentful of the added burden of two extra children. Especially Garrett, who bore a striking resemblance to his father.

He shook his head. "It must seem strange to you."

"I've never wanted for brothers, that's for certain." Jo drummed her fingers on the table. "Is your cousin a lawman, too?"

"Nope. He owns a sawmill back East. My father was a doctor. I'm the only one who went West."

"I guess that explains your parents' deaths."

His heart stuttered and stalled. "Explains what?"

"You know, the smallpox. Doctors get exposed to all that kind of stuff all the time."

His blood gradually resumed pumping again, moving sluggishly through his frozen veins.

"Of course," he replied.

These people respected him, gave him their trust. What would they do if they knew of his past? A lawman, the son of a murderer. They'd run him out of town on a rail. If he and Cora settled here, he'd have to guard the secret with even greater care. He wasn't alone anymore.

Garrett braced his left palm on the table and his right one against his chest.

Jo leaned forward, a crease between her delicately arched brows. "Are you all right? You don't look so good."

"Fine."

Avoiding her penetrating gaze, he glanced instead at her fingers. They were long and tapered, the nails blunt and neatly rounded. A smudge of ink darkened the tip of her index finger.

He turned from the distraction. Cora scribbled away, her head bent in concentration. Noting his interest, she lifted her paper and proudly displayed her picture. Even with her rudimentary skills, Garrett recognized his sister and her husband on either side of Cora, their hands linked together.

Cora's lower lip trembled. "Look. I made my family."

His throat tight, Garrett knelt before her and pulled her into his embrace. She wrapped her arms around his neck and a single sob shook her delicate body.

"Oh, dear," the woman in burgundy exclaimed, half rising.

Jo gently waved the concerned woman aside. "She'll be all right. She's right where she needs to be."

Grateful for Jo's assistance, Garrett closed his eyes.

After Cora had calmed, he took his seat once more. Jo resumed the conversation as if there'd been no break, and her light chatter was a grateful distraction. As he watched her and Cora laugh, he let his mind wander. What would it be like, courting Jo? Actually courting her like a proper gentleman?

Garrett spread his work-roughened fingers over the stark white tablecloth. No use thinking the impossible. She deserved better. What if the evil that had snapped his father's soul lived within Garrett? He couldn't take the risk.

Jo rested her hand over his. "You don't have to be alone in this. I hope we can be friends."

"I'd like that."

Sour guilt swelled in his throat for even thinking about Jo romantically. She deserved someone who could love her with his whole heart, without reservations. Garrett wasn't that man.

That evening, Jo returned to her solitary room at the boardinghouse. She lit a single candle and perched on the edge of the bed. Without Cora for company, the room seemed unnaturally quiet.

Lately she'd begun to realize what a lonely place she'd carved out for herself. Rising at dawn each day, spending her shift at the telegraph office, home each evening. Every other weekend she helped her family on the farm. She kept herself busy, sure, but even that felt false.

Like at the mercantile, when Mr. Stuart ran low on supplies and spread out the remaining stock to make it look as if there were more goods available. That's how Jo felt lately, like she was spreading herself thin to make it appear there was more to her life. Covering up the empty places in her heart with bits of nonsense. Except she wasn't hiding them from other people, she was hiding from herself.

Always before, she'd known what she'd wanted, and she'd sought her goal with single-minded determination. Except she didn't know what she wanted anymore.

Jo stood and crossed the room, then pressed her forehead against the cool windowpane. She did know one thing—being with Cora and Garrett felt right.

Blowing out a warm breath, Jo fogged a circle on the glass. Garrett had accepted her offer of friendship. Together they'd look after Cora, ease her through the transition of losing her parents.

Simple as that.

The fog on the glass quickly dissipated. He hadn't shown signs of interest toward any of the single ladies in town earlier, now that he had Cora to look after... Her stomach pitched. A single man around these parts who needed a wife didn't stay single for long. There'd be no setting her cap for Marshal Cain. She'd never set herself up for that kind of demoralizing rejection again.

Jo glanced at the tips of her battered work boots. She knew what she wanted, all right: she wanted something that could never be.

## Chapter Three

A week after the marshal's return, Jo shaded her eyes with one hand and searched the horizon. A kick of dust indicated his timely arrival. Her ma had finally invited the marshal and Cora for dinner. By coincidence, this was Jo's weekend home.

A soft object thumped against the back of her head. She bent and retrieved a faded leather glove from the ground.

"Hey!" Frowning at her brother, Abraham, she waved the glove. "Did you throw this at me?"

"You weren't paying any attention." He tugged off his second glove. "Why all the daydreaming?"

"I wasn't daydreaming."

No matter what happened during the week, when Jo rounded the bend and caught sight of her childhood home on the horizon, her mood lightened. Lately, she needed the comforting sight more than ever. That strange yearning hadn't abated, and a restless need for something more in her life itched beneath her collar.

Abraham lifted an eyebrow. "It's like working with Caleb. Are you in love with Mary Louise Stuart, too?"

Jo winged the glove in Abraham's direction. He

ducked and easily avoided her revenge. At seventeen, he wasn't interested in courting just yet.

"I don't see what all the fuss is about Mary Louise," Jo grumbled. "What does anybody know about her other than she's pretty?"

"What else do you have to know?" Abraham shrugged.

"Be serious." Jo knelt before a hay bale and clipped the wire. "God gave her those looks. It's not like she had to work for anything."

"How do you think Mary Louise feels? She can't hardly step from behind the counter without causing a stampede."

"It's strange, you know, when you really think about it. Some people are rewarded for how they look, not who they are." Jo sat back on her heels. "While other people are paying the price for how they look, when none of it is their fault. And nobody's happy about it."

"You know what your problem is, Jo? You think too much." Abraham kicked the loose hay over the uneven ground of the muddy corral. "Looks like the marshal and his niece are here."

Her brother had a point. She *had* been thinking too much lately. Only the day before she'd offered to hold Mrs. Patterson's baby while the new mother shopped in the mercantile. When Jo had caught herself wondering how the marshal's coffee-colored eyes would look on a chubby little toddler, she'd promptly returned the baby and fled the store. That sort of behavior had to stop.

In desperation, she'd arrived at the farm earlier than normal and donned her comfortable trousers. She'd tackled her chores with vigor, hoping the physical exertion would ease her mental turmoil.

Her face damp with perspiration, Jo spread another

bale of hay while the wagon lumbered up the driveway, stopping only when her visitors halted before the barn.

She pinched off her gloves and met them on the drive.

"JoBeth!" Cora called.

The little girl leaned out of the wagon and wrapped her arms around Jo's neck. Marshal Cain met Jo's gaze over the girl's shoulder, and her breath strangled for a split second. There was something heady about having those dark eyes focused on her. She'd seen him every day this week, and his effect on her had grown rather than blunted. Each time she saw his face, her heart pounded, and her head spun as though she'd been twirling in a circle.

Attempting to break the mysterious spell, she squeezed Cora tight and pulled her from her perch, then set her gently on the ground.

Six-year-old Maxwell, Jo's youngest brother, bounded down the driveway, his knees pumping. "Jo-Beth, JoBeth!" he called. "Are they here yet?"

"Peas and carrots, Maxwell. Look with your own eyes. Can't you see? Slow down before you run us over."

Her brother skidded to a halt before them. He wore his usual uniform of a tan shirt and brown trousers with a pair of red suspenders. A crumpled hat covered his dark hair. "Who are you?" he demanded of Cora.

The little girl clutched her rag doll close. "I'm Cora."

"How old are you?" Maxwell asked.

"Five."

The front door swung open and Mrs. McCoy stepped onto the porch. "Who do we have here?" She descended the stairs, her fingers busy unknotting the apron wrapped around her waist. "Gracious, you must be the prettiest little girl this side of the Mississippi!"

"Our guests have arrived, Ma." Jo tucked Cora against her side. The McCoy clan could be overwhelming, and Jo didn't want the girl spooked.

Maxwell dashed up the stairs and tugged on his mother's skirts as she approached them. "That's Cora. She said she's five years old."

Edith McCoy smiled, her expression full of unspoken sympathy. "We're pleased to have you. Why don't you come on inside."

Edith labored up the walk, her gait stiff, and Jo sighed. Her ma's left hip sometimes acted up, but Edith McCoy never complained. Complaining wasn't ladylike. When Jo was younger, her ma had dressed her in frills and lace, but that hadn't lasted. Despite being a paragon of feminine qualities in an untamed land, Edith had never swayed her daughter into fripperies.

Her ma waved them toward the house. "Welcome to our home, Marshal Cain. I hope you like pot roast."

The marshal flashed a wry grin. "Just as long it's not fried chicken."

"I see you've taken the fried-chicken tour of all the single ladies in Cimarron Springs." Edith chuckled. "I figured I'd wait until the spring and let you enjoy a pot roast for a change."

Maxwell danced around them, his scuffed boots kicking up a whirl of dust. "Cora! Cora! The barn cat just had kittens. You wanna see them? Their eyes are open and everything."

The little girl tugged on Jo's hand. "Can I?"

Jo waited for Marshal Cain's nod of approval. "Of course you can."

Maxwell spun around, and Jo caught him by the cuff of his shirt. "Cora isn't from the country, so you be nice. No spiders, no frogs, no beetles…"

"Yeah, yeah, yeah." Maxwell rolled his eyes. "I know guest rules."

"Not just any guest. Cora is a special guest. I want you on your Sunday best."

"I'll be good."

Jo released Maxwell and planted her hands on her hips. "I bet Reverend Miller would have a thing or two to say about your Sunday best."

Her youngest brother scowled. "He boxed my ears last week."

"That's because he got to you before I did." Jo pointed a finger. "Now don't get Cora's pretty pink dress all dirty."

"I won't," Maxwell grumbled.

Edith McCoy sighed and shook her head. "I hope that's not her best dress, because dirt multiplies on this farm. And it doesn't wash out easy."

"Don't worry, Mrs. McCoy," the marshal replied, dusting his hands together. "She's got plenty more dresses where that one came from."

Jo and Marshal Cain followed Edith into the cozy farmhouse. The aromas of fresh-baked bread and pot roast drifted from the kitchen, sending Jo's mouth watering. Since the spring temperatures cooled after dark, a fire danced in the hearth.

"You two have a seat," Edith ordered. "I'm putting the finishing touches on dinner."

Marshal Cain pulled out a chair and paused. Jo glanced behind her. He waved his hand over the seat. "Ladies first."

A spoon clattered against the floor.

Her ma bent and retrieved the utensil. "Clumsy of me. I'll just rinse this off in the sink. If you don't mind my being forward, how are you getting along, Marshal?"

Jo snorted and flopped onto the proffered chair.

The marshal sat down across from her. "No need to apologize, Mrs. McCoy. I'm sure Jo has told you all about Cora."

"Not Jo, no. But gossip travels with the speed of boredom around here."

The marshal glanced around the tidy room, and Jo knew exactly what he was noticing. All of the spices above the stove were arranged alphabetically, the pots were hung by size, and even the glasses were arranged by height. When she was younger, her ma's habits had annoyed her, but as she grew older she realized that order made even the most cramped spaces cozy and welcoming.

Marshal Cain shook his head. "How do you manage to keep everything in place with children running underfoot?"

Mrs. McCoy wiped the spoon on a towel draped over the sink. "More help, I guess. I've got more people to make the mess, but I've also got more people to help with the chores."

"I don't think more children will solve my problems." The marshal rubbed a weary hand over his eyes. "I can't keep up. I feel like my whole jailhouse was hit with a pink bomb. That little girl must have come with a magic trunk, because when I opened it, the contents tripled in size."

Jo hid a grin. The marshal *did* look a bit disheveled. And she'd never heard him so talkative. As she pondered his uncharacteristic admissions, another thought darkened her mood. They'd seen each other in passing each day this week, and yet he'd never once confided his concerns with her.

The marshal pressed his thumb into the soft wax of the candle burning in the center of the table. "I hope nobody gets arrested, because Cora set up a tea party in the jail cell. I can't put a fugitive in there with a couple of rag dolls having tea. There's even a pink blanket on the cot."

Jo clapped her hands over her mouth.

Her ma lifted a lid from the roaster, sending a plume of steam drifting toward the ceiling. "I can see where that would be a problem," Edith replied, her voice ripe with amusement. "Sometimes I wish we had *more* pink in this house. We're full up on boys since Jo left, and she was never one for tea parties anyway."

Jo scowled, her amusement waning. Just because she didn't throw tea parties didn't mean she wasn't a girl. She was different, that's all. Why did everyone insist on bringing it up all the time?

"And it's not just her stuff." The marshal picked off a chunk of wax and rolled it into a ball between his thumb and forefinger. "Cora doesn't eat much in the morning. Should I be worried about that? And she never stops asking questions. Sometimes I don't know the answers. But if I tell her that I don't know the answer, she just asks the same question in another way. Is that normal?"

"That's a five-year-old child for you, all right. As curious as a kitten and just as precious." Edith placed a Mason jar filled with lemonade before the marshal. "You better drink something or you'll get parched."

A flush of color crept up the marshal's neck. "I guess I've been around Cora too much. I can't stop talking all of a sudden."

"Children don't come with instructions, that's for

certain." Her ma set out a loaf of bread and a pat of butter on wooden slab.

"I know." The marshal slathered his bread with the softened butter. "Like, how often should you wash them? What kind of soap should you use? I only have lye soap. Is that bad for girls?" A note of desperation crept into his voice. "I don't know what to do. What if I do the wrong thing?"

"The fact that you're worried makes you a better parent than most others." Edith dried her hands on the towel and crossed the room. "The bad folks aren't worried about what's right and wrong, you know?" She perched on a chair beside him and patted his hand. "You're doing fine."

The marshal raked his free hand through his hair. He paused for a moment, his Adam's apple working. "She cries at night."

"Of course she does," Jo exclaimed, her heart twisting at his words. "She's lost both of her parents. She's lost her home. That's enough to make anybody cry."

Something flickered in his eyes, but it passed quickly. Jo ached to reach out and comfort him, but she knew better. She never had words for times like these—soothing, comforting words. He'd said it himself over lunch last week. She was direct.

With grudging admiration, Jo studied her mother. While the rest of the McCoys were dark-haired with green eyes, Mrs. McCoy stood out with her pale blue eyes and dark blond hair. Even the streak of gray at her temple lent her an air of elegance.

Jo had never really valued cosseting before. Blunt truths were faster and more efficient. Now she realized there was a time and a place for coddling.

Marshal Cain pinched the bridge of his nose. "I don't know what to do," he repeated.

"Love her," Jo replied. "Just like you're doing."

"Jo is right." Edith smiled and patted his shoulder. "Love goes a long way."

The door swung open, and her brother Caleb stepped into the room surrounded by a noxious aroma. Jo waved a hand before her nose. "Gracious, did you take a swim in Pa's cologne?"

The tips of her brother's ears reddened. "Mind your own business, runt." He strutted across the room in his crisp blue shirt and navy trousers.

Caleb was the oldest of the boys at twenty-two, tall and slender with the distinctive McCoy coloring of dark brown hair and bright green eyes. They all took after their pa's looks in that regard, though Ely McCoy was short and stout. Jo was the only child who'd inherited his lack of height. Much to her chagrin, she was embarrassingly petite.

Being small with five younger—and much taller—brothers had taught her a thing or two about strategy. "I think someone is going into town. This must be your third trip to the mercantile this week."

"What's it to you?"

"Nothing." Jo studied the jagged tips of her blunt fingernails. "It's just that you're not the only one visiting the mercantile on a regular basis."

The owner's daughter was a pretty blonde with blue eyes and a ready smile, and since Mary Louise had turned eighteen and started working behind the counter, the store's revenue had leaped tenfold.

Caleb fisted his hands. "Who else have you been noticing?"

"There're too many to count. You better screw up your courage for courting or she's gonna slip away."

Her brother glanced around the room, caught sight of Marshal Cain and stopped short. "Evening, sir." Caleb straightened and tucked his shirttail into his pants before glaring at Jo. "It doesn't matter because I don't care. I'm going into town because Ma is out of sugar. Isn't that right?"

Edith smiled indulgently. "Of course."

"See?"

Caleb stomped out of the room, and her ma shot Jo a quelling glance. "Don't be too hard on the boy."

"What?" Jo drawled. "I'm just trying to help."

The marshal grinned. "Mary Louise better make up her mind soon or I'll be breaking up fights. There's nothing like a pretty girl to get a young man's blood boiling."

An uncharacteristic spark of jealousy pricked Jo. Apparently, Marshal Cain had noticed the pretty little blonde, too. She crossed her arms over her chest. "I bet her pa hopes she never decides on one suitor. He makes sure all those boys buy something while they're panting after Mary Louise. I heard he even ordered a new wagon from Wichita."

"No more gossiping, JoBeth," her ma scolded from her place by the stove. "And let up on that boy. Being in love is harder than it looks."

A huff of anger settled at the back of Jo's throat. They all acted as if she had no emotions. She couldn't recall one time when her ma had told the boys to let up on her.

Jo braced her arms against the table and locked her elbows. "How come you never tell them to go easy on me?"

"Because you're tougher than they are." Her mother

waved her wooden spoon for emphasis. "And smarter, too."

Jo caught the marshal studying her with those dark, intuitive eyes and decided it was time to change the subject. "How are the Elders?"

Her ma's face lit up. "I just got a letter. Watch the gravy while I fetch it."

Marshal Cain rested his hat on his knee, his enormous palm dwarfing the crown. "I think I've heard that name before."

"Probably." Jo stood and crossed to the stove. "The Elders used to live over the rise. They moved to Paris, Texas, going on ten years ago."

"Wasn't there something about an outlaw?"

"Mrs. Elder's first husband was a bank robber. He hid the loot in a cave by Hackberry Creek. The boys sell tours for a penny every summer."

"They do *what?*" The marshal set down the lemonade he'd raised to his lips. "Don't the new owners mind all those kids tramping across their property?"

"No one lives there." Jo shrugged. "The place has been empty for years"

Her pa stepped into the room. A great bear of a man, Ely McCoy vibrated the floorboards with his heavy steps. Jo dropped the gravy spoon and dashed toward him. "Pa!"

He enveloped her in a bone-crushing hug, lifting her feet from the floor. "There's my little girl. I heard you brought company."

Jo's heart soared. Her pa was the only person who treated her like a girl without making her feel weak. He was a stout man with a thick salt-and-pepper beard and a mop of unruly mahogany hair hanging over his twinkling green eyes.

"This is my pa, Ely McCoy."

Marshal Cain rose from his seat and held out his hand. "Nice to see you again, Mr. McCoy."

"Call me Ely."

Her pa slapped the marshal on the back, nearly launching him into the hearth. "Glad you're here, son. I need help balancing the pasture gate."

Jo grimaced. She loved her pa, but he was always putting the guests to work. "Why don't you get the boys to help you?"

"Because Caleb's cologne turns my stomach, and David has gone to Wichita to buy a horse."

"Glad to help," Marshal Cain replied easily.

Jo appreciated his calm acceptance of the request. She also liked how his chambray shirt stretched across his broad shoulders. He was quiet and thoughtful, never missing a detail. She liked watching as he sized up a room. He looked *at* people, not *through* them.

*What did he think of her?*

Did he see her as everyone else in town did—as an oddity? Somehow or other she didn't think so. He regarded her with the same deference he showed Cora and her ma. Maybe that's why he appealed to her—he treated everyone he encountered as though they were important, as though they were worthy of his time.

The marshal tossed a resigned grin over his shoulder and followed her pa out the door.

As the two men left together, Jo considered how different they were. Not just in size and shape, but in temperament. Her parents were opposites, too. Ely McCoy was a loud bear of a man whose bark was worse than his bite. Her ma was more refined, more reserved than her pa. Yet they worked well together, and no one expected either of them to change.

Jo had learned early on that boys expected *her* to change. At thirteen years old, a boy had told her flat out that if she wanted him to stop teasing her, she'd best let him win at marbles.

Jo had decided then and there that she'd rather win.

A scant few minutes later, a knock startled Jo from her vigil at the stove. She crossed the room and opened the door. The reverend stood on the doorstep, a dark shadow against the orange glow from the setting sun.

"Reverend Miller. What brings you here this time of the evening?"

He doffed his cap and smoothed his thinning hair. "A telegram arrived for the marshal. The clerk said the marshal should see it right away."

## Chapter Four

Garrett strained beneath the weight of the gate, a fine sheen of perspiration forming on his brow. The evening air was cool and a stiff breeze whipped the hair over his perspiring brow. The incessant, relentless gales dried up the earth and left every surface dusty and gritty. When a changing weather front blew in, Garrett stuffed rags around the windows and still awoke with grit on his tongue. He sometimes wondered why the whole prairie hadn't been swept away already.

Thankfully, as the evening stretched on, the breeze gentled, and the sun sank low on the horizon. Hills rolled toward Hackberry Creek, and a smattering of trees softened the view. Garrett didn't consider himself a sentimental man, but he appreciated the quiet beauty of nature settling into nightfall.

Ely broke the silence first, saying, "That little Cora sure is a cute one."

"That she is."

"Heard she's taken a shine to Jo."

"Word travels fast around these parts."

"That it does." Ely ratcheted the hinges tighter. "What are you planning on doing?"

Garrett gritted his teeth against the strain of the heavy metal gate. "Doing?"

"You gonna raise that little girl all on your own?"

"Not much other choice," Garrett bit out over his exertion.

At Ely's signal, Garrett released his hold and leaped back, scooting his boots free from a possible collapse. To his relief, the hinges held firm. He flexed his sore fingers. Ely must be twenty years his senior, but the older man didn't show any signs of strain. Mr. McCoy was a tough, portly man with a fierce scowl and a ready smile. Garrett recalled how Jo had launched herself at her pa earlier. Though Ely could snap a sturdy tree limb with one hand, his children didn't seem afraid of him.

The idea gave Garrett pause. What was it like for the McCoy children, not being afraid all the time?

Ely swung the bars back and forth, examining the smooth action with a satisfied expression. "When I look at your little girl, I wish I could go back in time."

Garrett glanced up in surprise. "Why?"

"Jo never had time to be a baby. To be a girl. By the time she was walking, we already had Caleb. Then David came along and Abraham and Michael. We had a little bit of time, but then Maxwell surprised us. With all those boys, well…let's just say she had to be tough."

Garrett couldn't help but wonder how Jo had survived with all those rough-and-tumble boys. She wasn't as tough as she pretended. He'd seen her vulnerability. Despite her confidence and bravado, she really was a tiny little thing. Those boys should be sheltering and protecting her, not the other way around. A half grin stretched across his face. Garrett had a feeling Jo would never stand for coddling.

Ely considered his dirt-stained hands. "The missus

used to dress her up. Jo wouldn't stand for it. It's funny, you know? The missus thinks they butt heads because they're too different. I think they're too much alike. You ever noticed that? It's the parts of ourselves we see in others that frustrate us most."

Ely's insight surprised Garrett. With all those children running underfoot, who had time for speculation?

The older man paused. "Probably why David and I argue like a couple of old-timers." He nodded. "We're too much alike."

A sense of helplessness chased away Garrett's earlier serenity. Ely's observations hit too close to the heart of the matter. That's what Garrett feared—being like his father. The blood of a murderer flowed through his veins like an unlit fuse.

The McCoys were unencumbered by the past. They didn't know the secret he bore like an albatross around his neck. They'd never been burdened with a scandal that had destroyed an entire family.

"Pa!" a voice called.

Garrett glanced up and saw the youngest McCoy dashing toward them.

Maxwell skidded to a halt and grasped his side, leaning over as he heaved in a noisy breath. "The reverend is here. He's got a telegram for Garrett. Says it's about Cora. And it's important. And it's bad news."

Even without the power of Ely's unexpected insight, Garrett had a sinking feeling this evening wasn't going to end well.

Jo watched as Marshal Cain paced before the fireplace, his hands on his hips, a fierce scowl darkening his handsome face. "I'll go back to St. Louis myself and fight this if I have to."

"No!" Jo exclaimed.

Her ma placed a gentle hand on her arm. "Let him be."

Reverend Miller worried the shallow brim of his black felt hat in his hands. "Perhaps it's better if the marshal's cousin and his wife raise the child. You're a single man with a dangerous job…"

"They don't want Cora," Garrett announced. "They want the money from my sister's estate. It says so right here. They want custody of Cora." He jabbed a finger at the telegram. "And the proceeds of the estate for her care and comfort." He crumpled the paper in his fist. "Care and comfort my foot. My sister's husband was an architect. Did well for himself."

The reverend hung his head, revealing the bald patch at his crown. "Still, we must consider what's best for the child."

The marshal braced his hands against the mantel and stared into the blazing fire. "That's not all. I heard a rumor that Edward's sawmill is failing. He doesn't want Cora, he wants an influx of cash for his business."

Mrs. McCoy stood and faced the group, her hands thrust out in a placating gesture. "I don't like this any better than the rest of you, but we don't know your cousin's motivations for certain. Right now it's only blind speculation."

Marshal Cain turned and shook his head. "Whatever his motivations, he's already got a judge on his side."

Ely fisted his hands beneath his biceps and propped his shoulder against the wall. "Let me get this straight. He told the judge that the little girl is in jeopardy because she has a marshal as a guardian?"

"Because I'm a single man. A single lawman. They think I can't care for her properly."

"Can you?" Edith bluntly demanded.

Four pairs of eyes turned in shock.

Jo glared at her ma, who returned the sharp glance and pursed her lips. "I don't mean because you're a man. But you voiced your own concerns rather eloquently earlier this evening. You can't have a little girl in the jailhouse with murderers and rapists."

"Edith!" Ely exclaimed. "Language."

Jo's ma directed an exasperated look at her husband. "It's the truth, whether we want to face it or not. You've got a sweet little girl living above a jail cell."

Marshal Cain adjusted the gun belt strapped around his narrow hips. "She's barely been here a week. I haven't sorted out all the details. If living in the jail is the problem, then we'll move." He faced the reverend. "What about the Elder place? The one just over the rise? I'll buy that."

"You can't," Reverend Miller declared. "Someone already owns it."

The room erupted into noisy chaos.

"Who?" Jo demanded.

"Why, Jack Elder's brother," the reverend declared. "I heard he was driving a herd of cattle from Texas."

Ely planted an elbow on the mantel. "When did this happen?"

"Last month or so. Haven't heard anything in a while."

"Longhorns, I suppose?" Ely ran a thumb and forefinger along his silver-streaked beard. "Huh. I guess there's good grazing land on the other side of the creek. He better move quick. There's talk of closing the borders farther east. Those longhorns bring Texas Fever."

"Does he have any kids?" Maxwell asked from the doorway.

The adults fell instantly silent at his sudden announcement. Not a one of them had noticed his arrival.

"Back outside." Edith broke the impasse and shooed the youngest McCoy toward the porch. "The adults are talking."

"Sounds like you're arguing."

"It's a heated discussion. You and Cora play with the kittens until I call you."

"I still say you're arguing," Max grumbled, but dutifully latched the door behind him.

Edith straightened the doormat with her heel. "It'll be nice having an Elder on the land again. We should check the roof before he gets here."

Ely grunted. "Enough. It doesn't matter right now who owns the old Elder farm. What matters is what's going to happen to Cora."

Visibly shaking off the distraction, Edith straightened her collar. "I don't think Marshal Cain has much of a choice. Keeping law in this town is unpredictable. If a judge looks at a husband and wife, also relatives, compared to a single man. A single *lawman*." She paused. "How can he think Marshal Cain is the best choice?"

"I am the best choice." The marshal punctuated each word with emotion. "I love her. I don't want her because she comes with a pile of money. I've been raising her for a week. We're struggling, sure. But I'm trying. I'll try harder."

Jo groaned as her ma set out the plates for supper. Heaven forbid Edith McCoy let a simple little thing like the ruin of a man's life disrupt a meal.

"What if you're called away?" Edith slid a plate across the table. "It took us almost a week to find you when we received the telegram about Cora."

The marshal made a sound of disgust.

Panic welled in Jo's throat. Didn't they see how much Marshal Cain and his niece needed each other? Her ma was more concerned with propriety than love.

Jo clenched her hands on the table. "I can help out if he's called away. Cora knows me."

"That's only one of his problems." Edith added flatware next to the plates with infuriating precision. "His job is dangerous. What if something happens? If he's wounded or worse. Who will take care of Cora then?"

Marshal Cain slapped his hat on his head. "I'm not giving up my girl." He gestured dismissively toward Reverend Miller. "If some judge in Missouri…." He glanced pointedly around the room. "Or anyone else tries to take my child, they'll have a fight on their hands."

His expression scornful, Marshal Cain strode toward the door.

The room erupted into noisy chatter once more as everyone began talking and gesturing in overlapping conversations.

"There's a perfectly obvious solution—" Edith began.

"Obvious to whom?" the reverend interrupted.

"You talk to him."

Ely touched his chest. "Me?"

Jo stomped her boot. "This is getting us nowhere."

Her pa's head swung between the competing conversations. The reverend flailed his arms at Ely while Edith pointed a finger at her husband.

Jo brushed past them and blocked the marshal's exit. "Let's get hitched."

"What?"

"You heard me." Jo declared. "Let's get married."

## Chapter Five

Shocked by her own words, Jo froze. Immediate silence descended on the room. Marshal Cain's jaw dropped. For several long moments nothing stirred the air except the steady *tick, tick, tick* of the clock on the mantel.

Jo felt her face flame. "That's the problem, isn't it? He doesn't have a wife. As Cora's uncle, he's a closer relative to her than a second cousin. What can the judge say if he's married?"

"Well, uh," the reverend sputtered. "You make a compelling argument."

Marshal Cain hadn't moved. He hadn't even blinked an eyelash. The more time stretched out without a response, the more frustrated Jo became. Why didn't he say something? *Yes, no, maybe, I'll think about it...*

If Mary Louise from the mercantile had asked, he probably would've jumped at the chance.

"Never mind," she declared.

"No." The marshal held up his hand. "Jo is right. If I have a wife, they've lost the balance of their case against me."

"JoBeth—" her ma placed a hand on her shoulder

"—think about what you're saying. This isn't a decision to take lightly."

Ely clutched his head. "You've lost me, Edith. Why were you dropping all those hints if you didn't want them to get married? Why put the idea in her head if you were just gonna talk her out of it?"

"I wasn't talking about Jo," Mrs. McCoy hissed through clenched teeth, her emphatic gaze encompassing their rapt audience. "I was talking about one of the ladies on the fried-chicken tour."

Jo whipped out of her mother's hold. "I might not have been featured on the *tour*, but I know what I'm doing."

She also knew she was acting like a child, but she didn't care right then.

"This is a disaster," Edith snapped.

Affronted, Jo challenged her ma. "How on earth does this qualify as a disaster?"

"Everybody out!" her pa shouted with a clap, startling both women into silence.

No one moved.

"I said everyone outside."

Spurred by the force of his booming command, Jo and Marshal Cain automatically turned toward the door.

"Not you two." Ely rolled his eyes. "The rest of us will leave."

He waved his wife and the reverend toward the door. Reverend Miller scooted out of the tense room as if his heels were on fire. Edith scowled and stubbornly bustled around the stove. "Let me turn down the fire on the gravy."

Ely grasped her elbow and coaxed her toward the door. "Come along, dear."

"But the table," her ma protested, dragging her feet. "The dinner..."

"The potatoes will be here in ten minutes. Those two need time alone more than they need a pot roast right now."

Her ma sputtered and resisted his gentle, persistent guidance. Ely McCoy remained adamant. The door closed resolutely on her muttered protest.

Jo gaped. It was a rare day indeed when her pa overrode her ma's wishes.

The scrape of boots as Garrett restlessly roamed about the cramped space yanked her attention back to the problem at hand. Alone with the marshal, Jo's courage faltered. She'd acted impulsively, backing herself into a corner once again.

He paced before the hearth, his expression intense. "This could work. Cora likes you."

*What about you?* The question balanced on the tip of her tongue.

"And you're not the romantic sort, are you?"

Jo studied her hands, the nicks and scars, the half-moon of dirt beneath her blunt fingernails. "Of course not."

His pacing halted. "There's no one else, is there? No one else you've set your cap for?"

Jo shook her head.

"You said it yourself. We're friends." The pacing resumed. "We get along okay, don't we?"

"Sure."

"And this wouldn't be a real marriage. More of a partnership."

Her legs trembled and Jo locked her knees. "A partnership."

"For Cora."

"For Cora," Jo repeated.

She set her jaw. What had she expected? That he'd fall to his knees with joy? She'd offered a solution, and he was, at the very least, considering her offer. This was a good idea. She'd have Cora. She'd have a family. Not a normal family like everybody else, but then again, when had she ever done anything the normal way? She'd have a child without childbirth. Perfect. Fabulous. Just what she'd always wanted.

And if no man ever looked at her the way her pa looked at her ma—as if she was the only candle in a world of darkness—then so be it.

Jo straightened her spine. She didn't need that sort of nonsense. She liked the marshal, and maybe someday he'd even come to like her, too. She might not be pretty like the other girls, but certainly he'd come to appreciate her other qualities.

Thus far, he hadn't laughed in her face or mocked her, and a friendship didn't risk her heart. She'd devised the perfect solution for both of them.

Marshal Cain rubbed the stubble on his chin, drawing Jo's eyes to his lips. He'd have to kiss her when they got married, wouldn't he? Tom had once bussed her with a slobbery peck on the cheek behind the livery and she hadn't been keen on repeating the experience. Marshal Cain was different, though, and she wouldn't mind trying again.

Jo pressed a hand against her quaking stomach.

Garrett stretched his arms nearer the dwindling fire and rubbed his hands together. "We've done great together this week, taking Cora back and forth. With the judge coming through town next week, we don't even need a ceremony. We could just sign the papers and call it good."

*No ceremony. No kiss.* Jo flipped a length of hair off her forehead. "Nope. No ceremony."

"I mean, we're both solitary people. Independent. And people have gotten married for worse reasons."

The marshal was only repeating her thoughts. Yet her heart wrenched at his words. She had a feeling she'd discovered the source of her strange yearnings. Lately the idea of having babies didn't seem so bad. Caroline from school had five children and she'd once fainted when Tom Walby broke his nose during a game of kick ball. If Caroline kept having children, there was hope for all of them.

But the marshal didn't want a real marriage.

No matter what happened, Jo wouldn't let the marshal see that occasionally, in her weaker moments, she wanted more. "Getting hitched solves all your problems."

*Yep, she was JoBeth McCoy, problem solver to the world.*

He circled the room and sank onto a chair before his empty dinner plate. "No. This is crazy." Elbows on the table, he cradled his head. "I'm sorry. I don't know what I was thinking. I'm not myself lately."

He was hiding something, she was certain. Jo rubbed the back of her neck. She had a feeling she knew the source of his reluctance.

No matter the personal cost, she'd pry the truth from him. "Would you say yes if someone else asked?" She fought the rough edge in her voice. "Because there are plenty of other ladies in town."

Marshal Cain bolted upright. "This is the rest of my life. You're the only one I'd even consider."

"Ooo…kay."

That was a decent response, right? He hadn't exactly

explained why he'd choose her over someone else, but Jo guessed that was about as good an answer as she was going to get. While she might have hoped for something more revealing, at least he was still considering her suggestion. He hadn't outright refused her yet.

Garrett unfurled a pink ribbon from his pocket and stretched it between his hands. "Cora loves you. You're all she talks about these days."

Jo's shoulders sagged. *Cora.* Of course, that's what he'd meant. He was thinking of his niece, not her.

She'd capitalize on his reluctant admission. Carefully formulating her response, Jo skirted the table. When she'd gathered her thoughts, she knelt before him and gently tugged the pink ribbon free. "We have to think of what's best for all of us."

A half smile lifted the corner of his lips, and her mouth went dry. She definitely wanted to try kissing again—just as a comparison. Gathering her wayward thoughts once more, she studied his hands, tanned and dwarfing her own. She didn't feel weak when he was near. She felt buoyant and powerful, as though his strength melded with hers. Despite her own certainty, she sensed his persistent doubt. If this marriage was going to happen, they both needed faith.

Jo swallowed around the lump in her throat. One thing she'd learned over time was never to predict the future. This might not be the ideal solution for Jo—she had an uneasy sense one of them had more at stake in the marriage than the other—but this was the best solution for Cora.

The marshal and his niece had been through so much, had lost so much. If Jo could hold their family together, she'd pay the personal price.

Perhaps in bringing peace to Cora and Garrett, she'd

find a measure for herself. "It's just like you said earlier. Neither of us is the romantic sort. We're not bothered by love. We'd be doing this for Cora. She needs a family, and, well, things are changing for me."

The marshal raised his head and met her steady gaze. "How do you mean?"

Stalling, Jo let her attention drift around the familiar room. "The boys will be marrying soon."

"How does that change things for you?"

"Caleb is a farmer, like Pa. He'll stay here and work the land. The house is already crowded as it is, and with another woman around…well, they won't need my help anymore."

Garrett flashed a wry grin. "Looks like Caleb will be spending a lot of time at the mercantile."

"I suppose." Jo resisted a smug rejoinder. Caleb definitely had it bad for Mary Louise. "And once he's married, David won't be far behind. Those boys have always followed each other."

"Even if your parents won't need as much of your help, you'll still have your job in town. At the telegraph office."

"I know. But I want more."

"What more could you possibly want?"

*What do you want?* His blunt question threw her off guard. No one else had thought to ask her what she wanted. She'd thought about what was best for her parents, for her brothers, for Cora and even for the marshal. But she'd never considered what was best for her.

Her ma had certainly given up on Jo ever marrying. While she loved her family, she wanted more. When her friends got married, it was as if they were automatically considered adults, but since Jo hadn't gotten hitched, they still treated her like a child. All a man had to do was turn eighteen and he was considered grown, but a woman wasn't given that luxury.

It was odd, really, since as far as she could tell, getting married didn't automatically endow you with more wisdom than anyone else. But everyone around her seemed to think so. Her married school friends would smile and give her a patronizing nod, as though they'd somehow been granted admission into a secret club and Jo wasn't invited.

Marrying the marshal bypassed all that courting and foolishness. And at least the marshal hadn't said he'd rather court his grandfather's mule.

Jo glanced away. "I love Cora. I can't explain how it happened, but when she stepped off that train, I felt a kinship. Mrs. Smith was pacing the platform and wailing about Indians, but Cora just stood there with those big, solemn eyes. She was lost and alone, but now she has us. We can make a family."

"I know what you mean about Cora." The marshal ran his hand along his chin. "When I saw her that day at church, peeking out from behind your skirts, I felt the same way."

Jo's heart soared at his reluctant admission. He was softening toward her idea, she could tell.

"This is a lifetime decision, Jo." His dark gaze ran the length of her and Jo suddenly realized she was still wearing trousers. "You're young. Someday you'll fall in love."

She pulled out the chair beside him and hitched her pant legs over her knees, then she sat facing him. If Garrett was disappointed in what he saw, that was his loss.

No matter what happened, she wouldn't change who she was—not on the inside, and certainly not on the outside. "Maybe this is God's way of bringing two people together who wouldn't normally marry otherwise."

"But what if you want children of your own someday?" he spoke, not quite meeting her eyes.

The memories of all the births she'd attended rippled through her. All the fragile bodies she and her ma had swaddled in christening blankets for untimely burials. Not every mother survived the process, and not every baby. Garrett might be a marshal, yet Jo was certain she'd seen more death than he had.

She pushed back a wash of sadness. "We'll cross that bridge when we get there. No one knows what the future will bring. But we do know what needs to be done right now."

She leaned forward and cradled his hands. They looked at each other for a long moment, and her breath grew shallow. His shoulders were broad, strong and capable. Sitting this close, the room bathed in lamplight, she noticed how his eyes were rimmed by a darker circle, making the color appear even deeper.

Could she do this? Could she spend the rest of her life as his friend without wanting more?

He rubbed the pad of his thumb over the back of her hand and her whole body pulsed with his touch.

Jo tightened her grip. What choice did she have? She could marry him and risk her heart, or risk never seeing him again. As much as she adored Cora, they were a package deal. She couldn't have one without the other.

He dragged his hands away, stood and turned his back. A sudden sense of emptiness overwhelmed Jo. In that moment, the room appeared lifeless, abandoned. Unfinished place settings covered the table, unfilled waterglasses sat near the sink, empty chairs remained strewn haphazardly around the room.

When he faced her again, his face had smoothed into an unreadable mask. "We can't rush into this."

A heavy weight settled on Jo's chest. She felt him moving away, physically and mentally, regretting his hasty words already. Her last, best chance for a family of her own was slipping away. Was she selfish for wanting him to agree?

Her stomach churned. "Please don't make any decisions without telling me first."

"I couldn't keep something from you even if I tried." He tossed her a knowing look. "Not with Cora around."

"You can't keep secrets with a child underfoot."

He chuckled, the sound more grim than amused. A flash of lightning sparked in the distance, brightening the room for an instant and illuminating his somber expression.

Garrett squinted out the window. "Looks like we might get some rain. That's bad timing with the creek rising fast from the melting up north."

"Not much use in worrying about something you can't control. My pa likes to say, 'Keep your faith in God, and one eye on the river.'"

"I like the sound of that."

The image of the raging creek resonated in Jo's head. It felt as though her beliefs about herself were slipping away, eroding beneath a deluge of new possibilities. Somehow, she'd always imagined things going on just the way they had. The boys growing and marrying. Her little room at the boardinghouse. Coming home for dinner on Sundays.

Then she'd found herself picturing her own family, having her own Sunday dinners.

Marshal Cain approached her and grasped her shoulders, his touch light. "You have to know something about me. I'm not good husband material. If you're looking for love, if you think this might grow into love someday, you'll be disappointed." He interrupted her murmured protest. "It's not that I don't like you, admire you, but I just can't."

*Can't or won't?* Once again the words balanced on the tip of her tongue, but her courage deserted her when she needed it most. Besides, what did it matter?

She must remain focused on the true problem. "We'll be friends. We'll both love Cora, and that will be enough love for all of us."

"I still need to think." He rubbed his forehead. "I'm not saying no, but I need to think this through. We can't make a rash decision. There are things about me you don't know."

He said the last words so quietly, she barely registered them.

"You said it yourself," Jo urged. "People have married for worse reasons. At least you and I have good intentions. How can things go wrong if we're making a decision based on what's best for Cora?"

"Things can go wrong." He tipped back on his heels, his voice somber. "Believe me, things can always go wrong."

Jo glanced at her scuffed boots. Once again she wondered if he'd make a rash decision if she looked like Mary Louise at the mercantile. Probably so. Men made rash decisions about pretty women every day. With tomboys, they made rational, thoughtful decisions based on logic.

Jo plucked at a loose thread on her trousers. Was she willing to change? For Marshal Cain? For a man?

*Never.*

*But what about Cora?*

Jo yanked the thread loose, exposing a tear in the fabric. Even if she could change, she didn't want to. She liked the person she was—*inside and out.* Marshal Cain either accepted her the way she was or not at all. As simple as that.

"Maybe," Marshal Cain spoke, his voice hesitant. "The answer is maybe. Let's leave it there for now."

Tears threatened, and Jo hastily blinked them away. This was no time for going soft. In life, *maybe* meant *no.* "Promise me you'll think about it."

"I promise."

"Can I still take Cora to the telegraph office with me tomorrow?" she added hopefully.

"Of course. This doesn't change anything."

"Of course."

With fisted hands, Jo rubbed her eyes in tight circles. Her hasty words had changed *everything.* Yet she didn't regret them, not for an instant. "Either way, we should think about finding you and Cora a new place to live. Outlaws and tea parties make strange bedfellows."

The marshal threw back his head and laughed, a rich hearty sound that vibrated in her chest and sent her blood thrumming through her veins.

"I can't argue with you in that regard." He swiped at his eyes. "Thank you. I needed a good laugh."

Feeling brazen, Jo grinned. "Can you imagine if word reached Wichita there was a pink afghan in the jailhouse?"

"Maybe crime would go down. It's hard to be a tough guy when there's a doll in your cell."

"This could be the best thing that happened to Cimarron Springs in a long while."

Garrett stared down at her, and Jo tipped back her

head. Their gazes collided and they stood frozen for a long moment.

He reached out and tucked a stray lock of hair behind her ear, his finger coasting along the sensitive skin of her neck. "I had a job in Colorado Springs before this. My deputy told me I was a fool for coming to Kansas. He was wrong. Coming here was the best decision I ever made."

"Even with all that's happening?"

"Especially now. You've been heaven-sent for Cora."

His admission awakened a sliver of hope. "I have next Monday off from work. Cora and I are picking mulberries down by the creek."

Garrett grasped her hand, caressing her blunt nails. "Come Monday afternoon, you'll have purple fingers."

"And purple lips."

His eyes widened and he made a strangled sound in his throat. "Uh, well," he muttered as he dropped her hand and stumbled back a step. "I'd best get Cora home. I don't want her out in the rain." He jerked one thumb over his shoulder. "The wagon and the rain and all."

Frowning, Jo touched her cheek as he made a hasty retreat. Why did he run off every time she thought they were making progress?

She crossed her arms over her chest. The fool man was running hot and cold and his indecision was driving her mad. Either way, he had to make up his mind on his own. She wasn't chasing down someone who didn't want her, no matter how stupid he was for rejecting her.

Even if she wasn't pretty on the outside like Mary Louise, she was worthy on the inside.

How did she convince Garrett of that truth?

# *Chapter Six*

Garrett plucked a stuffed bunny from his favorite chair and collapsed onto the seat. In five short days, Cora had stamped herself indelibly on the few rooms he occupied above the jailhouse. Before the little girl's arrival, he'd thought the space more than adequate. Now there simply wasn't enough room for all the fripperies that accompanied a little girl.

As he dug a pink ribbon from beneath the cushions, a soft whimper caught his attention. Garrett cocked his head and realized the gentle noise was coming from Cora's room. Worried, he heeled off his boots in a jack and crossed the distance in his stocking feet, then peered behind the partition. Cora rested on her side facing him, her rag doll clutched against her chest.

Tears streamed down her face.

A nauseating wave of sadness buckled Garrett's knees. He knelt beside Cora's bed and brushed the damp curls from her forehead. Her eyes remained closed, and Garrett realized she was crying in her sleep. Hesitant and uncertain, he murmured soothing nonsense words and gently rubbed her back until her sobs eased.

Surrounded again by silence, long-buried memories leaped into his head. He'd been strong for Deirdre after their parents had died, and he'd be strong for Cora, too. He gently tucked the blankets over Cora's thin shoulders.

Doubt chipped away at his resolve. Cora was younger, more innocent and vulnerable than Deirdre had ever been. He and his only sister had been old before their time. Their lives had been torn asunder by their father's frequent rages. A devastating back injury during the war had driven him into constant pain, and the alcohol he'd used to dull the agony turned him mean.

Garrett's father had been a physician, and his inability to heal himself had driven him mad. Garrett used to believe the whiskey bottle held madness, because with each drink, the bottle drained and the rage in his father grew.

When the alcohol had ceased working, he'd turned to laudanum. That's when the hallucinations had started. He'd see things. Hear things. He'd relive the war, shouting commands and calling for his dead comrades. His paranoia ruled the family. Then one day he'd mistaken his wife for an enemy soldier.

He'd shot her.

When he'd sobered and realized what he'd done, he couldn't live with the pain.

Garrett and Deidre had set out on their own for a short time before staying with his uncle. There had been no love lost on the siblings when they'd been thrust upon his aunt and uncle all those years ago. In desperation Garrett had fled, joining the army scouts at seventeen. He'd hoped they'd treat Deirdre more kindly without him around as a constant reminder of their father.

His sacrifice had been unnecessary—Deirdre had

soon married a fine man, an architect with good standing in the community.

No matter what happened, Garrett wouldn't let Edward raise Cora. His cousin had a pinch-faced wife with a perpetual expression of sour disappointment. They also had four more children on whom they doted. Garrett might as well send Cora to an orphanage.

Fifteen years had passed and the wound still ached. And now Garrett had another soul to protect. Cora was innocent of all the tragedy in the past. She deserved better than a set of rooms above the jailhouse.

Jo's solution tugged at his conscience.

His legs stiff from the awkward position, Garrett pushed himself upright. The town had been mercifully quiet, but what would happen if he was called out late at night? What happened if a prisoner had to stay downstairs in the jail overnight or longer? A jailhouse was no place for a little girl and he couldn't count on Jo every time he needed someone to watch Cora. He was already too beholden to her already.

Not to mention his other problem. Truth be told, he liked spending time with Jo and he didn't know what to make of his new affliction. Garrett absently rubbed his chest. She deserved someone without a past. She was too honorable for her own good. She'd sacrifice herself to make Cora happy. He couldn't let her.

What did Garrett know about making a woman happy? The only thing he'd ever seen in his life had been pain. Jo needed more. She deserved what she'd had growing up—love and warmth. The only love Garrett had known was hard love, and he was a hard man for it.

He paired up Cora's discarded boots and glanced at the farm-filthy dress hanging in the corner of the room. Mrs. McCoy hadn't lied—dirt sure had a way of finding you on the McCoy farm. When he'd arrived, even Jo had had a charming smudge on her check.

*Jo.*

He wasn't a fool. He recognized the signs of fear— heart pounding, palm sweating. But what was he afraid of?

*He was terrified Jo was someone he could love.*

The more time he spent around her the more time with her he craved. He wanted to protect her from bullies like Tom and Bert Walby. He wanted to hear her laugh. He wondered if she ever thought of him, too.

Only this morning the shaving lather had dried on his face while he pondered whether or not he looked better with a beard. He'd bought two new shirts and he didn't even really need new shirts. His old ones were fine except for a little wear around the seams. He couldn't recall when another person's opinion of him had carried such weight.

Garrett didn't know if he believed in a higher power, but he knew right then he was lost. Always before there had been a clear path in his head, a clear way out of trouble. Not anymore.

"Dear Lord," he pleaded. "Guide me. I've never asked for anything for myself, but Cora deserves better."

He'd done the right thing by Deirdre. He'd given his sister a fresh start by taking with him the reminders of their father. The reminders he carried with him every day—in his looks, in his mannerisms, in his very voice. Things he couldn't change or alter.

Since he hadn't refused Jo's proposal outright, he'd left her a sliver of hope. His weakness didn't serve either of them.

Garrett had thought leaving Deirdre behind was the greatest sacrifice he'd ever made. Little did he know, one day he'd meet an even greater challenge. Turned out facing a difficult choice was a whole lot more agonizing than running away.

# Chapter Seven

The following morning, Jo crossed the distance to the jailhouse fifteen minutes before her shift at the telegraph office began. This was her favorite time of day, watching and listening as the town sputtered awake. In the distance, the steady clang of the blacksmith's hammer beat out a comforting rhythm. The mercantile owner flipped his window sign reading Open and propped up a slate board declaring the daily specials meticulously spelled out in chalk.

A harnessed set of horses stomped and snorted between the buildings. Jo scooted into the street, giving them a wide birth. The cranky old swayback mare on the left nipped if you strayed too close. As Jo passed the butcher, the mouthwatering aroma of smoking bacon filled the air. She inhaled a deep breath.

Sometimes she loathed Cimarron Springs, feeling frustrated and trapped by the hackneyed town. But at times like this, the familiar sights and sounds soothed her like an old pair of boots—battered and worn, but comfortable for having been broken in.

Jo paused and took another deep breath before facing the marshal again. When she encountered him this morning, she'd act nonchalant. They'd go on as they had before, as though nothing had changed.

Jostled along with the bustling morning activity, she nodded greetings to familiar faces. A hesitant figure standing in the alcove between the saloon and mercantile caught her attention.

"Beatrice?" Jo stepped closer, and the figure emerged from the shadows.

The auburn-haired woman lived above the saloon and danced with the cowboys for a nickel a song. She was older than Jo in years and decades older in experience. Beatrice had traveled around the country and seen things Jo couldn't even imagine. Most of the townspeople spurned the saloon workers, but Jo understood a thing or two about being different, and she always made a point of exchanging conversation when they met. She and Beatrice had even become friends over the past year.

"Jo." Beatrice's cautious gaze darted over the crowd, searching for any sign of censure. "Are we still meeting tonight?"

"Same as always. I'll work up some examples this afternoon."

Beatrice wanted a job as a telegraph operator, but feared her boss would fire her if he discovered her plan. Since she still needed her place next to the saloon, Jo met with her after dinner three days a week. Beatrice's work didn't begin until after dark, which gave them plenty of time for their informal lessons.

"I just wondered." The auburn-haired woman's gaze turned mischievous. "Since things have changed and all."

"Nothing has changed," Jo assured her. "You'll be a

full-fledged operator in no time. Why would you think something was different?"

Beatrice winked. "I heard the marshal was having dinner at the McCoy place last night."

Jo hustled Beatrice deeper into the darkened passageway. "What else did you hear?"

"I didn't hear anything. It's just that's he's all any of the girls talk about these days." The older woman patted her auburn hair. "I might just want that handsome marshal to rescue me from outlaws."

She giggled like a schoolgirl, and Jo's eyes widened.

"Beatrice. You sly thing. You've got a crush on Marshal Cain."

"I may be older than you, but my eyes work just fine." Beatrice wiggled her index finger. "If I were five years younger, that man wouldn't know what hit him."

"There are other men more handsome," Jo teased. "He's a bit rough around the edges."

"He's got honest eyes."

Jo pictured the marshal's rugged face and warmth flooded through her. He *did* have honest eyes—compassionate and earnest. She'd only known two other men with eyes like that—Jack Elder and her pa. Mr. Elder had married Elizabeth, the woman whose late husband had robbed banks. Jack was a good man and a good father. As far as she could tell, he was a good husband, too. His wife, Elizabeth, certainly adored him.

Unbidden and unwelcome, elusive longings tugged at Jo's heart again. Everything had seemed so simple a few years ago, but Marshal Cain's presence had muddied the waters. It was easy staying single when there was no one who caught her fancy.

Glancing behind her, Jo searched the street. Satisfied

no one was paying attention, she faced Beatrice once more. "I asked the marshal to marry me."

"You did not!" Beatrice's eyes widened into twin saucers. "What did he say?"

"He said maybe." Jo huffed. "That's how people say no when they don't want to hurt your feelings."

The amusement on Beatrice's face instantly faded. "Well, it's his loss. That's what I say. Did he tell you why not?"

"Not really. Just some nonsense about things in his past that I wouldn't understand."

"That doesn't seem so bad." Beatrice tugged her lower lip between her teeth and studied Jo. "Maybe we just need to butter the biscuit a little."

"What on earth are you talking about?"

"You know." Beatrice touched Jo's sensible bowler hat. "Put a little sauce on the pudding. A little gravy over the turkey. Sweeten the pot a little."

Certain her friend had lost her senses, Jo stared blankly.

Beatrice rolled her eyes. "Fix yourself up. Buy a new dress and let me cut your hair. We'll have a wedding in no time."

"No." Jo huffed with dawning understanding. "Absolutely not. He likes me the way I am or not at all. I didn't let Percy win at marbles so he'd like me better, and I'm not changing for Marshal Garrett Cain. He likes me the way I am or not at all."

"I'm not saying you need to change. Just spruce up the package a bit."

"The package is just fine the way it is." Jo tapped her foot. "Now, I'd best go. I don't want to be late."

The older woman shook her head. "Suit yourself."

"My mind is made up." Jo adjusted her hat. "Besides, he's the one who needs me. Not the other way around."

Beatrice lifted an eyebrow. "Whatever you say."

Jo kept her silence.

"Ah, don't be sore," Beatrice pleaded. "I'm just trying to help."

"I'm not sore. I'm just—" Jo heaved a sigh "—confused."

"Men will do that." Beatrice yanked Jo into a quick embrace. "And thank you. For the lessons. A lot of people wouldn't go to the trouble for someone like me."

"And that's *their* loss. I'll see you at six," Jo replied with no hard feelings. "There should even be some apple cobbler left."

Beatrice flashed a relieved grin and set off in the opposite direction.

Jo caught sight of the marshal and Cora on the boardwalk outside the sheriff's office.

The cool morning air was burning off with the rising sun. The marshal had whitewashed the front of the sheriff's office, and the building appeared too cheerful for prisoners. They'd even etched the oval front window with his name. The marshal kept an open-door policy, and the shades were always raised.

"Good morning," Jo called, her voice a touch too loud.

"Mornin'."

His gaze didn't quite meet hers. He studied the tips of his boots. "Nice weather we're having."

"Seasonal."

"Could be worse."

"Yep."

The knotted muscles in Jo's neck tightened. This wasn't going quite as smoothly as she'd hoped.

He cleared his throat and focused his attention on his niece. The marshal hovered behind Cora, and Jo's pulse trembled. His dark hair hung low over his forehead, and his coffee-colored eyes flashed with worry. "Are you sure you're gonna be all right?"

The little girl leaped up and launched herself at Jo, gripping her around the waist. "You're here!"

Jo mocked an exaggerated stumble. "Easy there."

"I guess that answers my question," the marshal declared.

Cora glanced over her shoulder. "Jo is teaching me how to be a telegram operator today."

"Tele*graph* operator," Jo corrected.

Garrett crouched and handed her a pail. "This is Cora's lunch. If you need anything, I'll be at the lawyer's office. He's got some information from Missouri."

"We'll be fine."

"And after that I'll be in my office going over some paperwork. The judge is coming through town next week."

"Okay."

"I might have lunch at the hotel. If you can't find me at my office or with the lawyer, check over at the hotel."

Jo rolled her eyes. The man was circling like a mother hen. "Relax. I'm taking her to the telegraph office, not a wolf den. Cora and I have developed our own routine. Don't forget, we've already been doing this for a couple of days."

Remorse flitted across his bold features, and once again her conscience pricked. How come she never said the right thing?

Hooking his thumbs into his belt loops, Marshal Cain glanced down the street. "I reckon you're right. This business with my cousin, Edward, has me shook up. I'd best let you two get to work."

"Don't worry, I'll keep her safe."

"I know you will."

"I promise."

"Okay, then."

The marshal tipped his hat with a murmured "Ladies," and set off.

Jo and Cora watched his receding steps before strolling along the boardwalk. So much for all her previous resolutions. She'd blown it on their very first conversation after her staunch resolution only moments before. Her feet slowed.

Cora stared at her expectantly, and Jo plastered a smile on her face. "Ready?"

"Ready!" Cora declared.

Tapping her foot, Jo paused a moment. "I give him an hour before he comes and checks on you."

Cora giggled, and together they crossed the short distance, passing the depot and the platform.

Because telegraph lines followed train tracks, Jo's office sat near the station. Upon arriving, she unlocked the door and flipped over the sign reading Open. The office was little more than a lean-to jutting from the depot. The government had provided a single desk, swivel chair, a brass lamp with a bottle-green shade and a small table. A storeroom had been portioned off along the back. If someone left a package unclaimed at the station, Jo locked it up or delivered the parcel herself when she found time.

The space was cozy, but two windows on opposite sides gave her a cross breeze in the summer. A squat, potbellied stove provided heat in the winter.

She'd put Marshal Cain out of her mind and concen-

trate on her job. Work was the best balm and the ulti-
mate distraction.

Despite Jo's resolve, her thoughts wandered as she
spun around on her chair and arranged her supplies.
Outside, a train whistle blew.

She met Cora's frightened gaze. "That's the eight-
thirty from Wichita. She's half an hour early."

As was her routine, the little girl scooted beneath
the desk and stuck her fingers in her ears. The train
rumbled past, rattling the windowpanes and vibrating
the floorboards.

When silence descended once more, Jo ducked her
head beneath the desk. "That was a coal train. Those
trains are the longest, but they usually travel the fastest."

"They're loud."

"You get used to it. When I first moved to town, I
woke up with the five-fifteen every morning. Now I
don't even notice."

"Really?"

"Really."

Cora had arrived in Cimarron Springs ready for adventures—as long as that adventure didn't involve the
teeth-jarring clatter of a passing train.

A moment later Cora emerged from her hiding place
and returned to the makeshift play area Jo had set up
for the little girl. There was a square of slate board and
chalk, several rag dolls and a set of marbles.

An hour later, her busywork finished, Jo tipped back
in her chair and considered the child. Cora drew flowers, trees and stick figures on her slate board, but never
words. "You said you know your letters, didn't you?"

"Some."

Jo remembered being a child and how much she
loathed being forced into learning. Perhaps if she

couched the lesson in another way, Cora would show interest. "You want to see what I do?"

Cora danced on the balls of her feet. "Yes, yes, yes!"

Jo laughed. "Okay, pull your chair over here and I'll show you."

They settled side by side, and Jo dug out a sheet of paper.

The bell above the door jingled. Marshal Cain stuck his head in. "I just happened to be in the neighborhood."

Jo suppressed a grin. He'd gone a whole hour without checking on them, and it had obviously taxed him. "Of course you were."

"What are you ladies up to?"

Frowning, Jo studied his expression. That was the second time today he'd used the formal term. No one had ever referred to her as a "lady" and she wasn't sure if she was being mocked.

Then again, he'd never shown any other signs of mockery, and he'd had plenty of opportunity. Especially when she'd bluntly asked him to marry her.

Her cheeks heated at the memory.

"I was about to show Cora how Morse code works. What are you doing, other than checking up on us?"

The marshal glanced around, his gaze innocent of mischief. "Mr. Stuart at the mercantile said he's having problems with a group of boys. I have a bad feeling it's that bunch we saw the other day. One of them is Tom Walby's son. Thought they might have come this way."

Jo quirked a questioning eyebrow.

Marshal Cain set his hat back on his head and revealed an abashed grin. "Okay. I was checking on Cora. But as long as I'm here, I might as well brush up on my skills. It's been years since I've used Morse code. I used to know my letters. Can I look at your cipher sheet?"

Not many people in town understood her work, and Jo appreciated having someone she could talk with other than Beatrice. "You're a man of many talents."

He shrugged. "It's a good tool if you're in a pinch. I've heard of men signaling each other at night."

"How do they do that?" Cora asked.

"They use a lamp."

Jo tapped her pencil. "I've heard of blasting crews sending signals down the mountain with mirrors reflecting the sunlight. Doesn't seem too efficient to me."

"I guess you learn 'take cover' pretty well."

Jo giggled. She pinched the worn and ink-stained edges and slid her alphabet cipher sheet across the table. Cora and Marshal Cain flanked her, and Jo's heart did a curious ripple. She cleared her throat and scooted her chair tighter toward the desk, then pointed at the sheet, surprised by the tremble in her finger.

She fisted her hand a few times and pointed again. "Each letter has a corresponding set of dots and dashes. You put the dots and dashes together to form letters. For example, the letter *s* is three dots." Jo quickly tapped her finger three times on the desk. "And for an *o,* it's three dashes." She tapped her finger slower.

The telegraph machine whirred, and the twitter of an incoming message filled the room. "Here comes one now."

"Yeah!" Cora leaped off her chair and dashed across the room.

Using her heels, Jo twisted her chair and scooted across the floor. She needed distance between her and Marshal Cain. Talking with him left her as breathless as though she'd run the length of a field.

After setting out a pencil and paper, Jo acknowledged her station by typing in her call numbers. The telegraph operator on the other end of the line began transferring his message. Jo quickly jotted down the letters, transcribing a rapid-fire series of dots and dashes into words on a neat square of paper.

Cora danced around the table. "What does it say? What does it say?"

"I have a strict rule against gossip." Jo folded the paper with the words facing inside. "Luckily, I have a terrible memory. I couldn't tell you most of what came through yesterday, let alone last week."

Marshal Cain and Cora tipped their heads, their expressions twin mirrors of confusion.

"It's hard to explain… ah …" Jo stalled. "But I try to write things down without paying much attention. It's easier that way."

After only a short time on the job, Jo had trained herself until the Morse code she translated into words bypassed the part of her brain that remembered details. If she didn't, the tales rumbled through her memory and interrupted her sleep with dots and dashes clicking in her dreams. People sometimes forgot their words were read by others, and they wrote of deeply personal tribulations. Deaths and births, marriages and broken hearts, a deluge of human emotions filtered down into an economy of words.

Marshal Cain rubbed his chin. "That's amazing. I know a little bit of Morse code, but I only translated about three of those words. You're really good. And you just do that automatically?"

"Yep. I hear the dots and dashes like they're words. I remember when the rail line came through town, listening to the Chinese workers talking together, then switching back to English with the foremen. It's like that. It's like learning a foreign language."

"Except not many people have the gumption to learn another language," the marshal said, his voice flush with admiration.

Jo's chest expanded. Most folks took her skill for granted. Certainly no one had ever once asked if learning the process had been difficult.

The marshal glanced around the sparse office. "How did you learn?"

"I left the farm a couple of years ago."

Jo twisted her lips. Her ma had wanted her to take over the midwife duties, and Jo's refusal had driven a wedge between them.

Her ma saw every birth as a marvel of life while all Jo could think about were the potential dangers. The calls they made on laboring mothers filled her ma with anticipation, but Jo felt only dread.

Moving to town had been easier than arguing. "That was around the time the Western Union office arrived. They posted an ad on the building and I applied."

Western Union had specifically requested *female* operators. The men in town had scoffed, saying they wanted women so they could pay less. The company's motivation hadn't mattered. The job was perfect for Jo. Her boss only came through town every few weeks, and the telegrams kept her busy, but not too busy. If the office walls sometimes felt confining, she volunteered for delivery duty or helped out with the ticket counter.

And the job gave her independence. She wasn't beholden on a man to take care of her. She had freedom and security, two things most women could only dream about. Her life was perfect, *wasn't it?*

Cora touched the telegraph machine. "Is it hard to learn?"

"At first." Jo grimaced at the recollections. "For a

while, I was so frustrated I felt like screaming. All those
dots and dashes sounded like a bunch of gobbledygook.
Eventually, though, things started making sense. At
first I could pick out a few words, then sentences, then
everything just made sense all of a sudden. It's almost
like listening to people talk now."

Marshal Cain absently picked up an envelope. "But
you don't pay attention to what they say?"

"Everyone has secrets, and keeping them is a powerful responsibility. I don't dwell on the messages. It
doesn't seem right, you know?"

Marshal Cain kept his gaze focused on her, his brows
knit in a frown. Once again she had that same feeling
he was sizing her up, gauging her answers as though
he was cataloging her responses for future reference.

*Had she passed the test?* She couldn't tell by his expression. The longer he stared, the more self-conscious
she became. As the moments ticked by, Jo itched to
reach up and smooth her braid. Did she have pear blossoms in her hair again? Was he noticing the blueberry
stain on her lapel? A scuffle sounded from the train
platform, and she broke his gaze.

Marshal Cain straightened and peered out the window. "I sure do hate being right sometimes. It's the boys
again from the other day, stirring up trouble. They're
chasing something. Probably an animal. I better see
to it."

He set his hat on his head and tipped the brim. "Ladies."

Jo inclined her head as he turned and strode out the
door. Relieved his attention was no longer focused on
her, she released her pent-up breath. She'd never actually seen him at work, and she wondered how he'd deal
with the boys. You learned a lot about a person from

how they handled conflict, and for some reason, she wanted to know everything she could about the marshal.

She faced Cora and planted her hands on her hips. "You want to follow him?"

With a mischievous grin, the little girl nodded.

Jo threw back her shoulders. She'd survived one conversation without sticking her boot in her mouth. She was on a roll. What could possibly go wrong now?

## Chapter Eight

Marshal Cain rounded the edge of the building, and Jo and Cora angled closer until they could peer around. When he glanced over his shoulder, they scurried into the shadows, stifling nervous laughter.

The noonday sun had dried the rain from the previous days, and the streets were mud free for the first time in weeks. Cora appeared lighter, her face less shadowed with their silly antics. Seeing her happy was worth a little skulking around in the afternoon sunlight. They joined hands and followed the marshal from a safe distance.

Jo glanced up and down the deserted street, relieved there were no customers approaching. Observing the marshal sounded a lot more fun than typing out Mrs. Babcock's travel itinerary with the fewest possible letters while the frugal woman huffed and criticized Jo's every choice of word.

A crowd of boys greeted their curious stares. Jeering and jostling each other, the four young mischief makers flocked together. Two of the boys held sticks and poked at something from a jumpy distance. They kicked up dust motes with their boots, obscuring Jo's view of their target. Marshal Cain blew out a piercing whistle. The raucous horseplay ceased in a rolling wave as each boy in line caught sight of the marshal in turn and elbowed the next boy into attention.

From the corner of her eye, Jo caught one of the boys slinking along the wall, his gaze darting between the marshal and freedom. Not fooled for a minute, the marshal cleared his throat, halting the sly escape. Effectively snared, the boy innocently shrugged his shoulders and attempted another step away. The marshal crooked his finger, his expression brooking no refusal. Resigned, the boy dragged his feet into line with the others.

Adjusting his gun belt for emphasis, the marshal sauntered before the cowed group. "What's all the excitement?"

"We're not doing anything bad, sir," the youngest boy, a towheaded cherub with apple cheeks, replied.

Jo recognized the stout troublemaker as Phillip Ryan. Twin dimples appeared on those rosy cheeks as Phillip conjured up his most persuasive smile.

Jo grunted. *That figured.* His mother had practically gotten away with murder in school just by flashing her dimples and flipping her blond curls. Looked as if the apple cheeks hadn't fallen far from the tree.

Keeping hidden, Jo studied the marshal's reaction, relieved at his unbending stance. It was nice to find at least one person who wasn't fooled by a winsome smile and curly golden hair.

When the boy realized his feigned innocence and appealing grin weren't working on the marshal, his dimples retreated and an ugly scowl took their place. "It's just a snake."

The marshal's hands dropped to his sides, and he took a step back. "How big is it?"

"It's big, but we're gonna kill it good."

Jo clenched her jaw. She loathed unnecessary cruelty of any kind. Sure, she'd killed plenty of snakes, but only when necessary, and always humanely. Torturing a creature didn't sit well with her.

"It's huge," Phillip declared, his eyes wide. "And dangerous. We're doing the town a service by killin' it."

Bristling with annoyance, Jo jostled through the crowd until she reached the center.

Sure enough, a three-foot-long red, black and yellow snake lay coiled in the corner of the building. Jo glared at the boys. Hardly a giant at all. And certainly not dangerous. "There's no call for cruelty. A snake is one of God's creatures, too."

The Ryan boy scuffed the ground with his booted toe. "Not the good kind."

"I see." Jo crouched until she was eye to eye with the boy. "You can tell if something is good or bad just by looking at it?"

He shrugged.

Jo huffed as she turned her attention on the snake's brilliant red body, the color broken by bands of yellow flanked with narrow circles of black. She knelt before the terrified creature and murmured softly. Reaching out, she gently grasped the creature around the neck. The snake's tail coiled around her arm.

Jo stood and faced her stunned audience. "See. It's just scared."

Marshal Cain gaped at her, then his face paled.

Her heart thumped at his hard stare. "Did I do something wrong?"

Maybe he didn't like her interfering with his lawman's work.

"Put that down." Marshal Cain held out his hands in

a defensive gesture, his voice ominously low. "That's a venomous coral snake."

Relief flooded through her veins. He wasn't mad, he was just scared. "Nah. You can't tell from where you're standing. This here is just a milk snake. It's not poisonous. Come closer and you'll see." She extended her arm.

The marshal stumbled back another step.

Jo thoughtfully angled her hand. "It kinda looks like a coral snake from a distance, but you gotta check the color bands. Like my pa taught us, red to black is a friend to Jack. Red to yellow will kill a fellow. Or you can just remember that yellow next to red will kill you dead. Both kinds of snakes live in the same places, too, which confuses most folks. Except, you know, one'll kill you and the other won't."

"'Course, it's a milk snake," the marshal spoke, his voice husky. "I couldn't see it that well from over here. I musta had some dust in my face."

He poked one finger in his eye, and Jo lifted her face heavenward. "Don't rub 'em like that. You'll only make it worse."

She searched the gathering and found Cora frozen near the edge, her face as pale as the marshal's. Jo sidled closer. "Why do you suppose fur makes everything cuter? Have you ever noticed that? Take a rat—disgusting. Add some brown fur to its body and slap on a fluffy tail. You've got yourself a cute little squirrel. People would probably keep these critters as house pets if they were furry."

Cora giggled.

"I think snakes are misunderstood," Jo continued, her words low and soothing. "They keep mice and rats out of the grain bin. They help out with the grasshoppers, too. I'd rather have a snake in the barn than a furry raccoon anyday. And snakes are really quite beautiful if you take the time to look close."

"I think they're icky," Cora replied.

"I like the way they move. Like they're going sideways and forward at the same time."

The marshal grunted. Jo never understood why people liked pretty things even if they were useless, and shunned ugly things even if they served a valued purpose. "You want to touch him?"

Cora grimaced and clasped her palms together, twisting her hands back and forth. "Is it slimy?"

Despite her protest, Jo felt the little girl softening. "Nah. He's not slimy. He's actually pretty smooth."

As Jo crossed through the boys, the crowd stumbled out of her way, giving her a wide berth. She knelt before Cora and smiled. "It's okay. He won't hurt you."

Cora's seeking hand tentatively reached out. The snake tightened on Jo's arm and she kept her grip loose and friendly.

Cora stroked the brightly colored scales and sucked her lower lip between her teeth. As the seconds ticked away, her whisper-light touch gradually grew bolder. When the snake hissed, its tongue flicking the air, Cora yelped and jumped back.

The little girl skipped toward her uncle and tugged on his pant leg. "It's not slimy at all."

Marshal Cain patted her hair. "You sure are brave."

"And I'm dirty, too. Look at my boots! Jo says it's okay because if dirt makes flowers grow, it must make little children grow, too."

Jo grinned. Cora's hem revealed a fine layer of dust and her boots were scuffed. The prim and proper city girl was relaxing her rigid stance and learning to enjoy the country. She still had a long way to go, but she grew bolder every day.

"What about you boys?" Jo faced her rapt audience. "Would you like to touch the snake?"

Two of the boys shook their heads and took off running, their shirttails flapping in the breeze.

"Look at that, Cora." Jo chuckled. "You're tougher than a couple of boys."

The little girl puffed up. "I touched a snake and I didn't even scream or cry."

"What about the rest of you?" Jo continued. "Who's feeling brave today?"

One of the two remaining boys, Tom Walby's son, sneered. "My dad says you're a freak. You're just a stupid, ugly snake-lover!" He turned tail and dashed through alley.

Jo glared at the boy. Just like his father. When he felt threatened, he lashed out. The snake squirmed, and Jo realized she'd instinctively tightened her grip. Tom and his son were both just like the snake. Attacking when they were scared. She didn't think the Walbys would appreciate the comparison, but it was true.

"Hey!" Marshal Cain shouted after the boy.

Jo held up a restraining hand. "Don't mind him. He learned it from his pa. Tom Walby still hasn't forgiven me for making a fool of him when we were kids." She turned away and discreetly reached down her bodice, fishing out the snake's tail. "I tell you, if that man had half the fortitude for working as he does for holding grudges, his life would be a whole lot easier."

"Can't argue with that."

Marshal Cain rubbed his chin, and she noticed his gaze resting on the last remaining boy, a pale, sandy-haired six-year-old too scared to run. Again, Jo couldn't help but note the child's resemblance to his parents. Josh's dad had always gotten caught when they were growing up because he froze like a raccoon caught in a lamplight.

The marshal pulled a paper-wrapped peppermint from his pocket and knelt before the frightened boy. "You catch up with your friends and tell 'em to stay out of trouble for the rest of the day. Got it?"

The plump-cheeked boy snatched the candy, nodded and took off running.

Jo tsked. "That's the Smith boy. He's too good for hanging around with that bunch. I better have a talk with his ma." She faced Cora and gestured with her snake-wrapped arm. "You remember that. The people you run with can raise you up or bring you down. Isn't that right, Marshal?"

He gave a distracted nod. Come to think of it, seemed as if he hadn't looked at her direct since she picked up the snake.

Jo scratched her ear with her free hand. "You still look a little pale, Marshal. You okay?"

"Fine." He shook his head as though clearing his thoughts. "I better get back. To, uh. To work."

The marshal pivoted on one heel and strode away.

Jo tapped her boot, pondering his uncharacteristic behavior. The snake's tail wriggled up her sleeve and she considered another explanation for his abrupt departure. Could the marshal be afraid of snakes? When her pa found a snake in the feed bin, he'd fetch the barn cat and let nature take its course. For some reason, she found a lot of men were afraid of snakes.

Jo released the snake and watched it slither off, then stuck out her hand for Cora. "Are you ready to get back to work?"

"Yep."

"Jo," Cora began, her voice hesitant. "Are you afraid of anything?"

"Well, let's see. I used to think I was afraid of always staying the same, but now I'm not so certain."

A woman's life was fixed as train tracks. First stop marriage, second stop babies. Jo had jumped the tracks when she'd taken the position at the telegraph office. For a while the job had kept her distracted, and her restless spirit had bloomed with the challenge.

But lately things had gone stagnant.

Cora wrapped a blond curl around her finger. "I'm not afraid of snakes anymore. But I think Uncle Garrett is still afraid."

Jo glanced down the street and groaned. So much for all her good intentions. In a few short days Garrett had discovered how she'd socked Tom Walby in the eye and now he'd seen her with a snake wrapped around her arm.

No wonder he didn't see her as marriage material.

Jo sighed. "The trouble with change is figuring out which path is the correct path."

She glanced at the dusty, rickrack tracks the snake had left in the dust.

Even if there'd been a slim chance of the marshal seeing her as good material for a wife and mother, she'd gone and blown it.

## Chapter Nine

That evening Garrett dreamed he and his sister, Deirdre, were children again. They were living in Illinois, and he and Deirdre were sitting on the back of their pa's wagon, their legs swinging as they bumped along the deep rivets in the muddy road. Deirdre held her stuffed bunny over the street, then yanked it back against her chest. They played the game and giggled while their parents argued. Garrett sensed the tension even though neither of them raised their voices.

As the trip lengthened, and their mother's voice grew shrill, the game became more manic. Garrett snatched the bunny and held it over the road, pretending to drop it. Deirdre squealed in delight. Emboldened by her response, Garrett repeated the teasing bluff, only this time the wagon hit a deep rut and the heavy jolt knocked him sideways. He grasped the sideboard and steadied himself.

"My bunny!" Deirdre shouted.

Garrett glanced down in horror. One floppy ear and a single paw showed stark white against the boggy street.

"Stop!" he'd called. "We have to go back."

There was still time. If they stopped, Ma could clean up the bunny and make it new again.

His father whipped around, a black look twisting his face. "Serves you right. Maybe now you'll give me some peace and quiet."

Garrett caught Deirdre's stricken gaze. Her eyes welled with tears and she stuck her thumb in her mouth.

"Don't be a bab—" He stopped the words.

She was ten years old and too big for such a childish activity, but he sensed it made her feel better. He couldn't scold her.

He reached out a hand, and she pulled away. His heartbeat turned uneven and his blood grew thick like slow-moving molasses. He hadn't meant to lose her toy, it had been an accident—a bit of tomfoolery gone wrong. They'd both lost something that day, something they could never regain. *He'd lost her trust.*

"I'm sorry."

"It's not your fault," she'd replied solemnly.

But she blamed him, he knew she did. He saw the betrayal in her sorrowful eyes.

"I'm sorry," he called again, but the moment was lost in time. "I'm sorry."

Garrett shot upright in bed, his body soaked in sweat. Disoriented, he glanced around the room. A fierce pounding from the second-floor door had awakened him. Fearful of disturbing Cora, he shot out of bed, quickly tossing on a shirt as he padded barefoot across the room.

Without breaking stride, he snagged his holster from its hiding place atop the wardrobe and strapped his gun around one thigh, then angled himself near the exit. Keeping his body protected from the flimsy door, he yanked out his pistol and cocked the next round into the chamber. "Who is it?"

"It's me. JoBeth McCoy."

Sensing the urgency in her voice, Garrett quickly holstered his weapon. The stubborn dead bolt caught. After a sharp twist to the left, he forced open the lock. "What's wrong?"

Backlit by the moonlight, she huddled on the top stair, the alley a dark shadow below. A gust of wind sent tendrils of her hair sweeping across her forehead. She impatiently shoved it aside. "Trouble at the saloon."

"What kind of trouble?"

"I don't know. But it's keeping us awake at the boardinghouse."

Garrett waved her inside, hastily fastened his shirt and took a surreptitious look at Jo. She'd obviously dressed in haste, the buttons on her shirtwaist were mismatched with the third button skipped altogether. Her hair hung in one thick braid down her back as usual, but it was tousled and loose. Her eyes drooped, still heavy with sleep, and she flashed him a wan half smile.

His protective instincts roared to life. He wanted to wrap her in a blanket and keep her safe. Garrett steeled his focus.

He had other priorities right then. "Can you stay with Cora? I'll take a gander. Probably just the boys tying one on."

"I'll wait."

"The railroad workers got their paychecks today and they're spending it at the saloon. This shouldn't take long."

She hovered near the door while he donned his socks and boots, then snatched his hat. Drawn by something he didn't understand, he cast a last reassuring look over his shoulder before stepping outside. Once the cool evening air hit his face, he paused. He was still off kilter from his dream, his thoughts scattered back through the years. Cora's arrival had shaken his peaceful existence. He'd locked away Deirdre's memory, but Cora was too much like her mother. She wouldn't let him forget.

Garrett loped down the stairs. He'd been marking time in his life, keeping the past at bay, but he no longer had that luxury.

A shot rang out, halting his wayward thoughts.

Even a drunk could get off a lucky round, and he needed his mind clear.

Seconds later he crept along the boardwalk, his hearing focused on the raucous sounds. As he reached the double bat-wing doors, a drunken cowboy with a bedraggled beard stumbled outside and collapsed into a heap on the street.

Garrett knelt down and felt the man's neck, relieved at the strong pulse. Judging from the noxious whiskey fumes, Garrett assumed he'd passed out. The drunken man would keep until order was restored.

Drawing his gun, Garrett edged along the side of the building, when another shot rang out. He straightened his back and burst into the room. A deafening melee greeted his arrival.

At least two dozen men had paired up in fisticuffs throughout the room. Fists flew and splattered drinks covered the floor in a slick mess. Two of the enormous round tables had been tipped on their sides, scattering playing cards and betting chips over the sawdust-strewn floor.

An industrious cowboy scooted on his hands and knees between the overturned tables and scooped up discarded coins, shoving them into his bulging pockets. Garrett blew out a shrill whistle. Several startled heads turned in his direction.

"That's enough. Everybody outside."

A groan erupted from several of the fighting pairs as they realized the brawl was over. From the corner of his eye, Garrett caught a man cocking back his arm over another gambler.

Garrett spun around and pointed his gun. "I said, that's enough."

The aggressor dropped his arm with a grumble. Garrett plucked a cowboy from the floor and tossed him out the bat-wing doors. His arrival had dampened the crowd's enthusiasm, and he felt the mood of the room calm. The weary railroad workers reluctantly dispersed. He stalked between the tables, yanking people upright and setting them on chairs. A group of painted ladies huddled near the piano, their wilted feathers a sad sight against their elaborately coiffed hair.

Garrett didn't feel any censure toward the women, only sorrow. The West was hard, especially on women and children. "Why don't you ladies wait next door."

The neighboring space was taken with the rooms. This half, the part Tom liked to shoot at, featured a cavernous room with a crude two-story stage at the east end.

One of the women, a buxom brunette with rouged lips, stuck out a hip and giggled. "You're in the wrong place for ladies, Marshal."

"I'll be the judge of that." He felt his ears heat up beneath her amused regard. "I can't get my job done if I'm worrying about you."

"Well, ain't he just the cutest thing," one of them trilled.

With a bawdy look she sauntered away.

As they retreated through the side door, Garrett pivoted on one heel, surprised to find David McCoy stalking toward him.

Garrett crunched over broken glass toward the McCoy boy. "Did you see who started all this?"

"Mr. Stuart and Mr. Hodges were fighting about the new store."

"That figures."

Garrett wasn't surprised the two men had been arguing. Mr. Stuart had been running the only mercantile in town for over a decade until Mr. Hodges had arrived from St. Louis and bought up a storefront right across the street. Garrett figured the town had grown large enough for two thriving stores, but Mr. Stuart saw money slipping between his fingers.

David glanced around the demolished room. "A couple of cowboys took advantage of the commotion and that's when the bullets started flying."

"Where'd they go?"

The third-oldest McCoy was tall and dark-haired like his brothers, probably going on eighteen or nineteen, twenty at most.

David scanned the room. "Don't know."

Garrett adjusted his hat. He sometimes deputized the mercantile owner, Mr. Stuart, when he needed extra help. But since his occasional deputy had been knee deep in the brawl, he'd lost his backup.

Garrett studied David's sheepish expression. "We'll talk about what you're doing here later."

An uneasy silence descended around them. The room had mostly cleared upon his arrival, though one or two men remained, too drunk to flee. An overturned glass of beer dripped steadily onto a scattering of playing cards like sour rain. The mingled odors of alcohol and cigar smoke turned Garrett's stomach. He picked his way through the glass and approached the auburn-haired woman hovering near the door. She looked as if she wanted to say something, and he never turned away a witness.

Tipping his hat, Garrett offered a friendly greeting. "You're Beatrice, right? Did you see the men who started this? Or the shooter?"

"Probably Tom." She shook her head and the drooping purple feather in her hair fluttered. "The whole place went mad at once. There was a new group this evening. They came in from Wichita earlier in the day."

"How many?"

"Four, maybe five. I didn't pay much attention. They didn't seem interested in dancing."

A tingle of apprehension darted along Garrett's spine. "You notice anything else unusual?"

"I noticed one of the McCoy boys in here. That's unusual. He better hope his pa never finds out. Or his sister, for that matter."

Garrett flashed a wry grin. "I'll take care of David."

The woman winked at him and he started, then fixed his attention on the sawdust-strewn floor. He sure was getting winked at a lot these days. "Thank you, Miss Beatrice. You think of anything else, let me know."

"Oh, I'll let you know," she murmured suggestively.

"Don't you get sassy on me, Miss Beatrice."

"You're real cute when you blush." She twisted her waist from side to side, sending her fringed skirt fluttering. "She's cute, too, your niece." Beatrice fiddled with an auburn corkscrew curl resting on her shoulder. "Tell you what, because you called us ladies, I'll help you keep an eye on that David McCoy. I didn't see him drink or gamble, and he wasn't hanging around the girls. He seemed more interested in Mr. Stuart than anything else. Except Mr. Stuart was busy fighting with Mr. Hodges. Besides…"

She studied her tapered fingernails. "I owe JoBeth." Beatrice met his curious gaze. "She's been teaching me Morse code. I'm getting a job in Denver as a telegraph operator. A real job. Not dancing with cowboys for nickels."

"That's a fine goal," Garrett replied.

Another mark in Jo's favor. He'd been raised around people who wouldn't lift a finger for someone below their class, and that had never sat well with him. Seemed like the Bible was pretty clear on ministering to the poor as well as the poor in spirit.

Garrett touched his forehead in a brief salute. "When you and Jo finish your studies, you let me know if you need a reference."

This time Beatrice blushed, making her appear younger, almost girlish. "You're too soft for a marshal."

"And you're too smart for this place."

With that parting comment, Garrett turned. Behind him, the steady clip-clip of heels echoed through the open building as Beatrice walked through the adjoining door.

Garrett sighted David stationed near the door and motioned him over. "Let's straighten up."

Together with Schmitty the bartender, they set about clearing the room. Garrett righted a chair and reached for an overturned table. A pair of boots caught his attention. Another casualty of the brawl, no doubt.

Garrett nudged one of the boots. "Wake up, mister. Time to take it home."

The body remained ominously still. Garrett heaved the table upright, revealing Mr. Hodges. His blank eyes stared at the ceiling, glassy and unmoving. A darkening patch of red covered his white shirt and bled into his faded gray coat. Garrett flipped him onto one side, already knowing what he'd find. A bullet had passed clean through the man's body.

The bartender, a diminutive man with unnaturally dark, slicked-back hair, leaned over Garrett's shoulder. "He's dead. Someone musta shot him."

"I figured that much, Schmitty."

To Garrett's frustration, all of his witnesses had scattered. He'd recognized most of the faces, but there were still the cowboys passing through town he didn't know—the kind of men accustomed to the previous sheriff's corruption. Garrett pinched the bridge of his nose. Despite the lawless atmosphere of the town, there hadn't been a murder in Cimarron Springs for years.

"David." Garrett caught the younger man's stunned expression. "Let the doc know we've got a casualty here."

His Adam's apple working, David jerked his head in a nod and turned away from the gruesome sight. Garrett ticked off another point in the young man's favor. Though shaken, he hadn't shirked from his duties. Cimarron Springs might have a new deputy soon.

Garrett had a feeling he was going to need all the help he could get. He drummed his fingers on his bent knee. By morning, everyone in town would assume Mr. Stuart had shot Mr. Hodges over the new mercantile store. And for all Garrett knew, he might have.

Money and business had a way of forcing men into desperate measures. Yet Mr. Stuart struck him as the sort of man who was all talk and no action. The mercantile owner rarely ventured from his uneasy vigil behind the counter, and he doted on his daughter. Garrett couldn't see him risking a lynching.

Hushed whispers fell around him and he could almost feel the budding rumors flying through the air. If Mr. Stuart was innocent he'd have an uphill battle saving his reputation. Trying to squash gossip was like trying to put out a brushfire with a cup of tea.

The saloon doors slammed open and David burst into the room. "Come quick, Marshal. The jailhouse is on fire!"

# Chapter Ten

Jo settled her head against the back of the chair and lazily fanned herself with a paper. The space atop the jailhouse was long, narrow and airless. A bedroom had been cordoned off by a tall screen, but the only windows were in the kitchen area, where the hazy panes faced the darkened alley. After attempting to pry them open, Jo had discovered they were painted shut. Not that it mattered much since the front of the building was boarded over with a false facade, effectively blocking any chance of a crosswind.

An industrious tenant had cut holes into the floor and fitted the openings with iron grates to vent air from the first level. That meager improvement barely stirred a stale breeze. Jo figured the place must heat up something fierce in the summertime.

She unbuttoned her cuffs and rolled back her sleeves. A faint hint of Garrett's masculine scent lingered in the seat cushions and teased her senses. Cora remained asleep, wrapped in a pink blanket, her rag doll clutched against her chest. The heat lulled Jo, and she let her eyes drift shut.

Glass shattered and Jo bolted upright from her half

slumber. The sound had come from the first floor. She wobbled to her feet and glanced around. Two sets of stairs accessed the upper level, an outside set descending into the alley, and the inside set, which spilled into the open space below. She took a few steps and paused. Probably it was nothing, she might have dreamed up the whole thing, but she'd best check anyway.

As Jo descended the stairs, her raspy breathing stirred the eerily quiet building.

Growing uneasy at the unnatural quiet, she sidled nearer the wall. "Marshal Cain? Garrett?"

She cautiously made her way through Garrett's office, her eyes gradually adjusted to the dim light. Glass crunched beneath her feet and she realized one of the panes from the large double-hung windows had been shattered.

Lifting a shard, she angled the glass toward the light. Letters from the marshal's etched name remained partially visible. All that meticulous work, wasted. Kneeling down, she closed her fingers around a weighty brick. Voices called to each other from the street. She crouched and scooted forward until her fingers gripped the sill. When another moment passed without incident, she raised up on her knees and peered through the jagged hole created from the shattered glass.

Four riders galloped by, whooping and hollering. Jo groaned. Looked as if the marshal hadn't succeeded in busting up the fight. It also looked as if neither of them would get a wink of sleep tonight. She stifled a yawn. If those drunken cowboys kept this up much longer, she'd pay for her late evening during her double shift at the telegraph office the following day.

Glass burst above her head. Jarred from her sleepy contemplations, Jo dropped back into a crouch. Pointed shards rained overhead. A piercing sting slashed across her cheek. She threw one arm over her eyes and ducked her head. She cowered in a ball as a warm stream of blood slid beneath her chin.

Light arced through the window at her right. A bottle with a flaming rag stuffed in the neck hit the floor and clumsily rolled along the ridges in the rag rug. Her breath strangled in her throat.

*They were lighting the jail on fire.* Spurred by a fierce urgency, Jo crawled along the floor toward the flame, wincing as pain seared her palm. Before her horrified gaze, the rag-stuffed bottle ignited the braided rug. She snatched the trailing edge of a pink blanket draped over a chair and beat at the flames. Heat singed her face. The blaze chewed up the fire at an alarming rate. With growing alarm Jo realized her efforts were fruitless against the dry kindling.

Dismayed by the rapidly growing cloud of smoke, she stood and backed her way toward the stairs. Keeping her arms splayed for balance, her eyes on the merciless inferno, she stumbled over broken debris. The pungent scent of whiskey and smoke filled her nostrils. Before she reached the first riser, flickering embers were already lapping against the sheriff's desk.

From the second floor, Cora screamed. Wrenching her transfixed gaze from the growing fire, Jo dashed up the stairs and shoved the partition aside. The little girl sat up in the center of the bed, her hair in beribboned pigtails, her rag doll clutched against her eyelet night rail. Jo scooped her into her arms. The little girl wrapped her legs around Jo's waist and clung to her neck.

"What's happening?" Cora sobbed into her shoulder. "Where is Uncle Garrett?"

"He isn't here. There's a fire downstairs." Jo skirted through the hazy room. "We'll take the back stairs. He'll probably be waiting for us in the alley."

Jo wrapped her fingers around the knob and turned. The latch held firm. She twisted the lock. The brass knob refused to budge. Her arms full, she reared back and kicked. The frame opened an inch then smacked against the stubborn dead bolt. She stumbled back, braced herself and kicked at the base again. Searing pain shot up her leg and into her hip, but the door didn't budged.

After setting down Cora, Jo twisted the knob. As pungent fumes stung her nostrils and sent her eyes watering, her stomach clenched.

Cora hovered beside her, worrying her lower lip between her teeth. "Why won't the door open?"

"It's stuck." Jo gave the little girl a comforting squeeze. "We're going to have an adventure. How does that sound?"

Voices shouted in the distance. The townspeople had discovered the fire. With no windows facing the street and their exit blocked by flames, there was little chance of attracting attention. Jo chewed a thumbnail and glanced around. Would anyone think to circle around back and check on them? Only Marshal Cain knew they were up here and he had his hands full in the saloon.

Certainly he'd hear the commotion and check on them. Then again, what if they waited and no one came? Jo glanced at the terrified little girl and realized she couldn't risk Cora's safety.

She gently set Cora away from her and met her fearful gaze. "Don't worry, everything will be fine. I think we can get out the back door if we go downstairs. That's where the fire started, but it's mostly in the front. We'll get some fresh air first and hold our breaths for as long as we can."

She gave the frightened girl an encouraging smile. "It might get dark, but we'll stay low, below the smoke and everything will be fine."

"Okay," Cora replied, a tremble in her small voice.

"You're braver than all those boys, remember?"

"I remember."

Relieved she'd donned her trousers before fetching Marshal Cain, Jo slipped out of her skirts.

More muffled shouts and calls sounded outside and she hoped the local townsfolk were setting up a bucket brigade. If the building next door caught fire, the whole town would follow.

How long would it take before the marshal realized they were still trapped inside?

*What if he was injured?*

Sickening dread pounded in her head. She and Cora would have to assume they were on their own for now.

Centering her thoughts, Jo sucked in a deep breath. "Remember, I won't let go of you."

"Promise?"

"Promise."

With no time to waste, Jo crawled along the floor and felt for the legs of the washbasin. She grasped a dangling rag and wetted it in the bowl, then held it over her face. Encouraged by the improvement in the quality of the air, she snagged a second rag. There'd been a fire on the Elder farm years ago, and she'd seen Jack Elder block the smoke the same way.

She held out her rag for Cora. "Hold that over your nose and mouth and it will help keep the smoke out."

Tears pooled in the little girl's cornflower-blue eyes. "Are we going to die like my mommy and daddy?"

"We'll be fine," Jo lied, a cold knot of dread in her stomach.

She considered shouting for help again, but her throat was sore from smoke and her previous calls. With the crackle of the fire and the commotion out front, no one would hear her anyway.

"I'll keep you safe. I gave you my word and I never break a promise."

Jo clutched the back of Cora's head and pressed her face against her shoulder. They made it down half the flight before billowing smoke blackened the way. The suffocating cloud quickly enveloped them, and Jo worried they'd be hopelessly lost in moments if they moved forward. Her eyes and nose watered profusely, blurring the risers into a hazy obstacle.

Cora gasped and coughed, keeping a death grip on Jo's hand. "I can't breathe."

The racket of splitting wood sounded from outside as the bucket brigade worked to douse the flames. How could help be so close, yet so far away? If Jo couldn't even make it down the stairs, there was little chance of navigating the jail to reach the alley. While she knew the layout of the marshal's office, she'd never been in the lockup.

If only she *had* been a cattle thief, Jo thought wryly.

By the time she reached the last step, her lungs burned and her eyes watered. Smoke frothed near the ceiling, forcing her to kneel and feel her way along the wall. The flames had definitely abated, but the embers burned like black tar. Time slowed as she coughed and sputtered. Heat stung her cheeks and lapped at her heels.

With renewed purpose, Jo kept low. Freeing one arm, she inched along and felt…a sturdy chair leg. She pried open her eyes and saw nothing but gray smoke. Somehow, she'd gotten them turned around.

Panic welled in her throat and she reached out a hand, searching for anything familiar. Only a few feet separated her from help—a few feet and a wall of smoke and flames.

"Help!" she called fruitlessly.

She reached out her fingers and collided with a wall of hard muscle. A strong hand looped under her arm. Desperate for an escape, Jo clutched the lifeline, then recalled the drunken cowboys who'd started this whole mess. "Who's there?"

"It's me, Marshal Cain," a husky voice reassured her.

He plucked Cora from her weak arms and Jo sagged against his side. For a moment she gave up on being strong and let someone else guide her.

He wrapped his arm around her waist and half dragged, half carried her toward safety. "Stay low and I'll lead you out."

She stilled, instinctively responding to the gentle command in his voice. Her head swam, and she couldn't get enough air into her lungs. She felt as if she was suffocating, drowning in a black sea of smoke. Her legs gave way and she was floating. Heat crushed against her.

Wood splintered and suddenly cool air swept over her cheeks. She coughed and sputtered, her lungs burning. Tears streamed down her face, and her stomach lurched.

In stark contrast to the empty alley behind the building, Main Street bustled with activity. Three separate bucket brigades had formed—two lines protecting the buildings on either side of the jailhouse, and one, the largest, concentrating on the main fire.

Voices shouted and horses scuffled along the street as more people responded to the urgent clang of the church bell. Unsteady and desperate for oxygen, Jo paused in wonder.

Her thoughts cleared a notch and she frantically searched the growing crowd. "Cora?" she shouted over the din.

Garrett had been holding her and now his arms were empty.

"She's fine. You blacked out for a minute. The doc's checking her over. You're both fine."

"Here's water for her," a voice spoke.

A cup was pressed against her lips, and Jo greedily sucked down the soothing liquid.

"Not too fast," Marshal Cain cautioned. "Cora is fine, but you seem to have taken the worst of the smoke."

Her stomach churned, and she weakly shoved the water aside. "Enough," she croaked, her throat raw. Despite all the commotion surrounding her, she needed the marshal's attention. "I couldn't open the door."

Garrett muttered something beneath his breath. "It's the lock. It sticks sometimes. You twist it to the left. I never thought to tell you…"

"I'm sorry. I panicked."

"There's nothing to be sorry about. We'll talk about this later," Garrett replied, his voice soothing. "Did you see what started the fire?"

"Someone tossed a full whiskey bottle with a lit rag stuffed in the neck through the window."

"Who?" he asked sharply.

"I don't know. Some cowboys. They lobbed a brick first. I went downstairs to check on the noise."

"You should have stayed safe," he chastised, though his kind eyes blunted the rebuke.

The dirt-packed street waved like a mirage on a sultry summer day. Jo didn't know if it was the heat from the fire or her swimming head. "There were men and horses. Three of them. They ran down the street shouting and calling, then one of them threw the bottle."

"Three you say?"

The world kicked and bucked and Jo swallowed hard. "I think so. Maybe four. I don't remember."

Regret flickered in his gaze. "I shouldn't have left you alone."

"What else could you have done?" Jo questioned quietly.

He wearily rubbed his face. "I should have been there for you two."

"Don't blame yourself. It could have been anybody…" Her voice trailed off. Her thoughts scattered and her tongue grew thick and uncooperative.

She stared at the night sky, her gaze focused on the jagged edge of the half moon.

A gentle hand brushed the hair from her forehead. "Close your eyes. We can talk later. After you've rested."

"No." Jo struggled, unable to sit upright. "We should help."

The bucket brigade kept a steady stream of water traveling from the well, and the smoke had abated. The two lines keeping watch over the building on either side had broken apart and people milled around.

The mood of the crowd shifted, and Jo's ears buzzed. The townsfolk stared at her and the marshal. Hands cupped ears and Jo felt as if she was watching a game of secrets on the playground. One person whispering a phrase to another until the words ended up jumbled and unrecognizable from misquotes. A loud whisper caught her attention. *He pulled her and Cora from the jailhouse. Saw him rush in with my own eyes, then not a minute later, out they came.*

Jo moaned and clutched her head. What must people be thinking? What speculation was running rampant in the crowd? Tight knots of townspeople formed as the work of putting out the fire lessened. How in the name of little green apples was she going to talk her way out of this one? When her pa found out she'd been caught in the jailhouse after midnight, there'd be a reckoning. She might not live at home, but she was still a McCoy.

*And her brothers.*

"Jo—" Marshal Cain began.

He'd caught the crowd's droning. She could see it in his resigned gaze.

She held her hand over his mouth and silenced his denial. "I know what you're going to say, but you don't have to." The last thing she wanted was his sympathy. "We can explain this. I'll say I saw the fire and went in to help with Cora."

"Sure."

He didn't protest further, but she saw the emotions flashing in his eyes. By dawn, everyone in town would know she'd been in Marshal Cain's rooms.

*Alone.*

*After midnight.*

Her presence put the marshal in an impossible situation. If word got out that he'd left his niece alone, and Cora had nearly died in a fire, he'd be vilified. If he admitted Jo had been there, her reputation was ruined.

She'd fight her own battles, but she couldn't let the marshal take the blame for something over which he had no control. He'd do the honorable thing, she had no doubt of that. Too bad she already knew how he felt about marriage to her.

"Don't worry about the talk," she spoke over her tender throat, wishing the night would end soon. "No one sees me as a girl anyway," she added. "What they say won't matter."

He glanced around the crowded street. "I don't count myself a prideful man, but I do have my honor."

Her gut twisted. She feared he'd say that.

Then again, what did it matter about his reputation? If she refused his impending offer of marriage, the censure would remain with her. People were hypocritical that way. According to society, succumbing to temptation was a man's prerogative and a woman's shame.

For the first time in a very long time, she was stumped. Was Marshal Cain better off if they married, or better off if she spurned his proposal? If only her thoughts weren't as thick as day-old gravy.

He'd lost so much. Jo had her whole family. Marshal Cain was a solitary man who'd suffered more than his fair share of tragedy. All he had left was little Cora, his pride and the respect of his community. Garrett was too honorable for his own good, even though she admired him for his chivalrous ways.

"They'll blame me, not you." She grasped for an argument even as her strength sapped away. "You can go on as though nothing happened."

"Do I have any say in the matter?" he asked gently.

Jo knew where this was leading, and she desperately needed more time. "We don't have to make any decisions tonight."

"Not tonight, no," he replied, his voice low and his face turned away from the curious bystanders. "But morning will come soon, and if I'm not mistaken, so will your pa."

Jo's head throbbed. Her pa wasn't likely to listen to reason. "I'm a grown woman."

"Trust me, you'll always be his little girl."

Confusion swirled in her brain. She had asked him to marry her for practical reasons, and he'd balked. Now they were stuck in an absurd misunderstanding and she didn't trust her own motivations. Her pride still smarted from his rejection, and she couldn't let him see her weakness.

She'd give him an opening and gauge his reaction. If he wanted the marriage, she'd know by his answers. "I'm a strong woman, Garrett Cain, stronger than words and gossip."

She wanted to say more, had more reasons and arguments, but her stomach pitched. The events of the evening were catching up with her stamina, and she desperately wanted to close her eyes and rest.

They stared at each other for a long moment, cocooned in their own world. The townspeople bustled around them. She remained detached from the commotion. Their voices faded, as though she had cotton in her ears. Jo studied his somber expression, searching for answers.

"Believe me," she continued, keeping her voice as bright as her chafed throat permitted. "People's memories are short. They'll forget about tonight soon enough. We'll act as though nothing happened and eventually there'll be something else fit for gossip."

"I won't forget." Garrett jerked his chin over one shoulder. "And I will face your pa an honorable man."

"I hope he doesn't bring any of my brothers," she joked weakly.

They both smiled, though neither mustered a laugh. Even the slightest movement jarred her aching head, sending jolts of pain exploding through her skull.

Marshal Cain doffed and his hat and stared at her, his expression intense. "We suit each other. Circumstances have brought us together, and I think we could get along fine. You said it yourself—we both love Cora."

Weakly lifting her arm, Jo placed two fingers over his lips. If only she weren't so sluggish, she'd argue him out of his hasty decision. "Think about what you're doing."

He clasped her fingers and cradled her hand in his own against his chest. "JoBeth McCoy, will you marry me?"

She took a breath, and her vision blurred. Offering up a quick prayer for a reprieve, she worked her throat. She just had to hold on for another few seconds. "Maybe."

## Chapter Eleven

"Ouch." Jo yanked her hand away and shook her wrist.

Garrett tossed her a withering stare. "I have to change the dressing or this will get infected. Now stop fussing or you'll wake Cora."

They sat across from each other in the cozy boardinghouse parlor. Jo's mother, Edith, was upstairs sitting with Cora, and the sounds of breakfast clattered from the kitchen. They weren't quite alone but at least they had a modicum of privacy.

"I'm not fussing," Jo said, dutifully lowering her voice. "Where's the doc, anyway?"

"Busy." Garrett cradled her palm in his hands. "Now sit still."

Exhausted and grumpy, Jo slouched in her chair. Garrett bent over her hand, and she stared at the top of his head. An unexpected urge to run her fingers through his shiny hair gripped her, and she bolted upright. The color reminded her of a buttery-soft bolt of brown corduroy she'd seen in the mercantile.

"Sit still," Garrett gently scolded. "Or this will hurt even more."

Their gazes tangled, and Jo offered a hesitant nod.

He ducked his head. "Don't make me feel any worse than I already do."

"It wasn't your fault."

"I knew about the lock. I should have said something."

A pall fell over his expression, and her chest ached in sympathy. Today his hair curled around his ears, and she realized he needed a haircut. The stubble covering his chin had darkened from the previous evening and there were shadows beneath his eyes. He needed a shave.

He'd also take the blame for her injuries no matter what she said.

Jo stifled a grimace as he ministered to her hand. "Did you sleep at all last night?"

"Some."

His gaze flicked away.

"You're lying."

"Don't distract me," he ordered gruffly.

"If I sit still, will you have a rest this afternoon?"

"I'm an adult. I don't take naps."

Jo rolled her eyes.

Garrett cleared his throat. "You never answered my question."

"Which question?" She teased, knowing full well what he meant.

"Jo," he said in a tone indicating his patience was thin.

"Maybe nobody noticed me last night." She avoided answering directly. She wasn't sure which answer he'd prefer.

Her comment earned a dry chuckle. "Even you don't believe that."

"The answer is yes," Jo whispered.

His shoulder sagged and if Jo didn't know better, she'd say he was relieved. She reached out and tentatively touched the scar along his eyebrow.

She'd buy them some time and think of a way out later. "How did you get this?"

He touched his forehead, and their fingers brushed together. Something fierce and insistent vibrated in the air between them. Mesmerized by his coffee-colored eyes, the painful throbbing in her hand faded.

Garrett captured her wrist and turned her hand palm up. "That scar is from the time I fought a grizzly with nothing but a peashooter and my wits."

"You did not." Jo laughed. He peeled off the last layer of bandage and she squealed. "That hurt!"

"And now it's over."

He had secrets. Those secrets had carved lines of worry into his weathered face. "Tell me the real way you got that scar."

A cynical smile twisted his lips. "I got it because I was too young and too stupid to know better."

"I won't let you bandage this until you tell me the truth." Jo fisted her hand. "And I'm very stubborn."

"That's one of my favorite things about you."

He stared into the distance, as though gathering himself. A chill raised the hair on the nape of her neck.

She'd gone and done it again. Hammered him with the blunt end of her curiosity.

Before she could retract her demand, he spoke. "My parents died and there wasn't much money left after we paid off the mortgages he'd taken against the house. He was a physician, a decorated veteran of the War Between the States."

Garrett paused, collecting himself. "I found work on the docks. They always needed strong backs to unload cargo and they didn't care how old you were. One day I was hooking up a shipping crate and the chain snapped. It barely grazed me. Still split my face clean open."

Using her free hand, Jo rubbed the pad of her thumb over the scar. "That must have hurt."

"Like the dickens." He held still beneath her ministrations. "The foreman stitched me up right on the dock and I went back to work."

"I'm sorry," she said.

Garrett blinked. "For what?"

"All of my life I've had family around. If the boys at school teased me, my brothers rallied around. If I got hurt, my ma held my hand." Jo paused, fighting a rush of emotion. "I'm sorry you didn't have someone to take care of you."

His expression faltered for a moment before his easy grin returned. "I don't need taking care of. And we had some family. My uncle took us in after that. Deirdre stayed on after I went West."

"That's all?"

"That's all."

He'd effectively closed the subject, but she'd seen a glimpse of the real man and she hungered for more. "What were your parents like?"

"Just parents."

He lifted a shoulder and drew in a deep breath. She sensed he was gathering his courage, as though he wanted to say more. She let the silence stretch out, waiting. After a moment, her patience won out.

Garrett exhaled. "I look at Tom's boy and I hurt for him. I wish Tom knew how hard it was on his boy with all that arguing in the house."

Jo might not be as intuitive as her ma, but even she

realized he'd revealed something very personal about himself.

Her throat burned. "Tom's parents were the same way when he was growing up. That's all he knows." Jo winced as Garrett rubbed salve onto her cut. "Why do you suppose some people change and others don't?"

"Maybe they don't change. Maybe they just cover up who they really are."

"You don't think people can overcome their faults?"

"Doesn't seem likely."

Jo considered all the people in her life. How many bad habits were passed down from generation to generation without pause? Did she really know anyone who'd changed for good? She couldn't think of a single soul, yet she desperately wanted an example for Garrett.

She sensed the gravity of his statement, and the weight of her next words. "People can change if they want to. I think that's the difference. Tom doesn't see anything wrong with what he's doing, which means he's not likely to do anything different."

"Name one person you know who actually succeeded in changing."

Jo searched her memory and snapped her fingers. "Jack Elder."

"That the fellow who married the widow?"

"Yep. Jack changed. He didn't want a family, he didn't want to settle down. But once he met Elizabeth and her baby, he changed. He fell in love."

She expected Garrett to laugh, or at least make a joke at her example. Her brothers certainly would have mocked her. Instead, he remained silent as he unraveled a length of bandage and knotted the fabric around her hand.

He tucked his knuckles beneath her chin and angled

her face toward the light, studying the wound on her cheek. "The doc says you shouldn't have a scar."

To her disappointment, he didn't appear swayed by her example. "Would you mind very much if I had a scar?" Jo dredged up a smile, attempting to lighten the somber mood. "Would you be upset if I was ugly?"

Garrett lifted a dark eyebrow. "You could never be ugly."

"I could never be pretty."

"That's because pretty is for debutantes and silly girls. You're beautiful."

Resentment welled in her chest. "I'm not. And I'll sock you for teasing me."

"Don't you call me a liar, Miss JoBeth McCoy." Garrett cupped the side of her face with his warm hand and studied her bandaged cheek. "Do you know why Tom is so mean to you?"

"Because I made him look like a fool in front of his friends."

"Nope." Garrett removed the comfort of his touch. "Because you broke his heart."

"I think you musta hit your head last night."

"Don't forget, I was a young man once, too. I know the signs."

"I sure wasn't Tom's first anything."

"Did he ever try and kiss you?" Garrett asked with a knowing grin.

"Once. I stomped on his toe."

"That's your proof. A man will forgive being made a fool of, but he never forgets his first love."

Jo scoffed. "If he had a crush on me, wouldn't he be nice?"

"Boys aren't always good at knowing what to do with their feelings."

Her head spun with his words and she latched on to his earlier comment. "Who was your first love?"

"I never had one."

"Then you don't really know for certain. And you're wrong about Tom. He's told me I'm ugly a thousand times."

"I'm right," Garrett declared. "And someday I'll prove it to you. Just like I'll finally make you realize how beautiful you are."

"Quit foolin' with me."

"For a smart woman, you're awfully dumb about some things." Garrett coasted the backs of his knuckles along her bruised cheek. "The doc stitched this up nicely. Does it hurt very much?"

"Nope."

Her gaze dipped to his lips, and Jo tilted her head. The last time she'd been kissed had left her singularly unimpressed, and she wanted a comparison.

Before she could talk herself out of the impulsive gesture, she leaned forward and pressed her lips against Garrett's. Aching for more, but fearful of being rejected, she pulled away. A gentle touch on her shoulder stilled her retreat. Garrett angled his head, deepening the kiss, and Jo gasped softly.

She threaded her fingers through his hair, astonished at the soft texture. Her heart fluttered in anticipation, and a curious longing surged through her veins. Jo slid her hands behind his head and tugged him closer.

He cradled the back of her neck and he stroked her jaw with his thumb. The sweet awareness growing inside her heightened. His gentle touch felt good and right and she didn't want the wondrous feelings to end.

With a soft sound of regret, he pulled away. Jo

pressed two fingers against her swollen lips, mourning the loss of her startling discovery.

Garrett hastily stood. "You're healing really well. I don't think you'll have any problems."

The shadows were back in his eyes. He strode out of the room, and Jo stomped her foot. The one time she'd finally decided she liked kissing, and her partner had fled.

She crossed her arms over her chest and narrowed her gaze. He felt something for her, but she sensed he was frightened and she didn't know why.

No matter what the personal cost, she was going to pry his secrets loose.

## Chapter Twelve

*This was going to hurt.*

Garrett sat on a low stool in the livery while Mr. McCoy paced before him. The sky was clear and cloudless, a faded indigo bleached by the sun. After taking one look at Ely's face, Mr. Lynch, the livery owner, had fled. Garrett wished he could have followed.

The red-faced man crossed back and forth and back and forth again, muttering all the while. This odd ritual had been repeated for fifteen minutes, and Garrett was growing restless. He had an appointment with the lawyer that afternoon. When Mr. McCoy reached the far end of the enclosure, Garrett discreetly fished out his pocketwatch.

"I'm sorry," Mr. McCoy boomed. "Am I taking up your precious time?"

Garrett hastily stowed the watch. "Well, no, but…"

"I had other plans for this morning," the incensed man continued. "And they didn't include that busybody, Mrs. Fletcher, stopping me on the street at first light."

"I'm—"

"I'd like to know how my daughter ended up in your rooms in the middle of the night."

"She—"

"I know she was sitting with Cora while you broke up the fight at the saloon, but that doesn't explain how the two of you wound up lying on the street together."

"We—"

"You rescued her from the fire. Sure." Mr. McCoy raked his fingers through his thick mop of hair. "Jo has always been headstrong, but you're a lawman. You should know better." He paused and glared. "I blame you."

"I blame myself, sir."

"That's, well…" Mr. McCoy sputtered. "Good."

Garrett opened his mouth for a response. Mr. McCoy's fierce scowl silenced his defense.

"I don't know what you two were thinking," Ely continued. "But the missus isn't happy. She's not happy at all. And if she's not happy, I'm not happy. You get my point?"

*Not really.* "Uh…"

"Jo is special. Not a lot of people realize that, but I think you do. That's why I'm not going to kill you."

"I apprec—"

"You're gonna do the right thing, ain't ya?" Ely glared.

"I already have. Looks like she'll have me after all."

"Oh, she'll have you. Her ma will see to that. But if I hear one bad thing, if you hurt her in any way, I'm gonna, well, I'm gonna…I'm gonna pin your ears back."

Garrett had a feeling Mr. McCoy wanted to expand on his threat or at the very least increase the stakes, but the older man suddenly seemed at a loss for words.

Keeping his head down, Garrett replied, "Yes, sir."

Mr. McCoy stuck out his hand. Garrett jerked back, then flailed as the stool tipped.

The older man grabbed his hand, hauled him forward and slapped him on the back. "Call me Ely."

"Pa," a youthful voice called.

The two men faced the youngest McCoy, Maxwell, who'd been patiently waiting during the past twenty minutes of pacing and muttering. The boy had braced his toes on the lowest railing of the corral fence and draped his body over the top railing. His hands dangled and his hat rested brim up beneath his bent head.

Max raised his eyes. "Pa, does this mean you're not gonna shoot Marshal Cain like you said earlier?"

"Of course not, son. We're family after the wedding. I can't very well shoot my own son-in-law."

The boy screwed up his face as he weighed the answer. A flash of disappointment crossed his expression before he lifted his shoulders in an upside-down, resigned shrug. "Can I drive the wagon?"

"Maybe next year."

Max scrambled over the fence and retrieved his hat, then scuffed at the dirt with his toe. "I thought this day was gonna be fun. But you're not gonna shoot anyone and I can't even drive the wagon."

As Garrett absently rubbed his chest, he pondered the boy's answer. Which part was more disappointing? Not being able to drive the wagon or missing the opportunity to see a man shot? He decided not to ask.

Ely fisted his hands beneath his biceps and Garrett thanked his lucky stars once more that he hadn't had to fight the man.

The McCoy patriarch thoughtfully scratched his chin. "This town hasn't had a wedding in a month of Sundays. This'll be quite a shindig."

"About that." Garrett shifted on his feet. "I think

we'll go before the judge when he comes through town in a few weeks. There's no need for anything fancy."

Ely threw back his head and guffawed. "You got a lot to learn about women, son. A lot to learn." The older man chaffed his hands together. "This is going to be fun."

"Jo and I agreed on this." Garrett bristled beneath Ely's amused regard.

"It ain't Jo you gotta worry about." Ely motioned for his son. "Come along, Max. I need a salt lick for the south pasture and a word with Caleb. I believe we'll find both things at the mercantile."

Abandoning Garrett in confused silence, Ely pivoted on his heel, his merry whistle floating behind him on the breeze.

Garrett scratched the back of his neck. Who would protest if he and Jo went before the judge?

Max threw one last disappointed look over his shoulder, then shrugged in resignation. "You bringing Jo for dinner next Sunday?"

"Maybe."

"Can I shoot your gun?"

"No."

"Peas and carrots. I never get to do anything fun."

The boy flapped his arm in a dismissive gesture and Garrett sketched a hesitant wave in return. That hadn't gone so badly, had it? He'd been dreading the encounter with Ely all morning, but it seemed like Jo's pa wasn't opposed to the marriage. The conversation had been disjointed, but not overly violent. Except for that last cryptic remark.

*He had a lot to learn.* Garrett slapped his hat against his pant leg before replacing it. He couldn't argue with that.

Either way, Jo wasn't the sort of woman who wanted a big fancy wedding. Thank heaven. The thought of standing before a congregation of people in his Sunday best sent shivers down his spine. Outside of his job, he loathed being the center of attention. Nothing attracted more attention than standing at the altar. That wasn't even the worst part. Afterward, he'd have to sip punch and make small talk.

Memories of his youth drifted through his exhausted brain. A long-dormant sadness suffocated his emotions. In better days, his family had been part of the St. Louis social elite, and his parents had thrown parties nearly every weekend during the summer. He hadn't realized it as a child, but his mother had been putting on a show. Dressing them up and making the world believe they were one big, happy family. Good thing no one had seen behind closed doors.

Garrett didn't want to repeat the same pattern. Plastering on fake smiles and pretending things were one way, when in reality, they were living an entirely different truth.

He shrugged and faced his horse, a bay gelding with a white strip down its nose. "Don't worry, old Blue." Garrett patted the horse's muzzle. "I've only known JoBeth a few months, but I know enough. We've got nothing to worry about."

"JoBeth McCoy," her ma admonished. "You'll have a church wedding and that's the last I'll say on the matter."

"I agreed to the marriage." Jo sulked. "Isn't that enough?"

Edith's pacing stilled in a huff.

Jo drummed her fingers on the arm of her chintz armrest.

Her ma perched on the edge of a wingback chair. Jo had expected her parents to voice an opinion, but not this soon.

Her ma carefully arranged her blue calico skirts over her bent knees. "I was against this marriage in the beginning, but my thoughts on the matter have changed. Marshal Cain has proved himself to be an honorable man, and I respect that."

Jo bit off a groan. Her ma was correct. She'd seen it in Garrett's eyes. He'd do the honorable thing even if it meant shackling himself to her for the rest of his life.

The traits she admired about him were the very things that would make this marriage such a disaster. Would his honor hold up through the years, or would he grow to resent her? She feared the outcome of their hasty union if the marshal felt as if he'd been coerced into the marriage.

Jo dug her heels into the carpet and lifted her toes. "Garrett and I are getting married, but we're going before the judge. Not some fancy church wedding."

"And that's how you want to begin your married life together?" Her ma lifted an eyebrow at the familiar use of the marshal's name. "Alone. Before a judge?"

"I'm agreeing with you and you're still criticizing me?" Jo stalled with a throat-soothing gulp of cool water. "I agreed to the marriage. What else matters?" she repeated.

"You're my only girl, JoBeth." Her ma fiddled with the crocheted lace at her collar. "When the boys get married, their wives will arrange the wedding."

Jo shrugged. It didn't matter who planned the wedding. "I'm making things easier on you this way."

"Don't you start with me, JoBeth. Nothing about this is easy. In fact, the whole thing is a disaster. Everyone in town already thinks the worst." Edith stood and crossed before the cold hearth once more. "If you and the marshal sneak off before a judge, you'll only give the gossips more fodder."

"There's going to be talk anyway," Jo pointed out helpfully. "The last exciting thing that happened in town occurred when the sheriff got himself arrested and replaced by a county marshal. This will blow over as soon as Tom Walby goes on another bender or Mrs. Fletcher's goat gets into another garden. I'll simply stay low until the next gossip-worthy event. Once someone else slips up, the marshal and I will be old news."

Agnes, her landlady, appeared in the arched doorway from the kitchen. She held a tray with a red-rose-enameled teapot and two cups. A lace napkin fluttered over the edges. Agnes took one look at Edith's stiff back, spun around and retreated.

Her ma cut her hands through the air. "It matters because people's impressions are difficult to change. You're not a goat or a drunk. This sort of gossip sticks. Elizabeth and Jack have been gone for ten years, and their courtship is still legendary around these parts."

"I'll give you that one." For some reason, gossip about a romance had more staying power than other news. "People should have better things to do than talk."

"Of course they should, but that's not the point. You and Marshal Cain have made a real mess of this. Don't make it any worse."

Jo felt herself losing ground. "Don't you see? Having a church wedding would be a disaster. I'm not like Mary Louise. I'll look like a fool all decked out like a sugar cake, and everyone will laugh at me." Jo slapped her glass onto the table, sloshing water over her sleeve. "I'd rather be known as a fallen woman than a laughingstock."

A fine sheen of tears appeared in Ma's eyes, and her mouth crumpled along the edges. "I've never asked you to be anything but who you are, JoBeth. I never forced you into skirts or made you put up your hair. Maybe I should have, but even when I was tempted, your pa wouldn't let me." Edith swiped at her eyes. "But I'm asking you for this. Let your pa and I give you a nice wedding."

Jo sopped up the spilled water with her sleeve. Sheer desperation kept her arguing. "You have five other children. Why are you picking on me?"

Her ma gasped. "How on earth is planning a lovely wedding, even though I don't agree with the circumstances, picking on you?"

"We don't need a ceremony." Jo sagged in her chair and threw her arms over the sides. "How many times do I have to tell you that? The judge is coming through town in a few weeks, and we'll sign the papers."

"You are making a covenant before God." Her ma planted her hands on her hips and loomed over Jo. "And even if the two of you don't take that seriously, I do."

Rising, Jo imitated her mother's implacable stance. "It's not your wedding. I'm an adult and I can make my own decisions."

"As an adult, you have responsibilities."

"I already have plenty of responsibilities. I take care of myself. I have my own place and my own job."

"You're being selfish."

Jo's jaw dropped. "I'm not selfish."

"Your actions reflect on the people around you." Her mother's voice caught on the last word, and Jo's chest tightened. Guilt finally won out over the thought of being ostracized in front of the entire town. Though she dreaded the idea of Mary Louise and the others snickering over her, she couldn't refuse her ma's plea.

Edith McCoy had never made a demand on Jo. Even when they'd argued over Jo's midwife duties, her ma had backed down. Obviously, this meant more to her than Jo understood. "If it means that much to you, then fine."

"Fine."

"Fine."

Her ma's face lit up at Jo's grudging reply and she felt like a first-rate heel for putting up such a fuss in the first place. Who cared what Tom Walby or Mary Louise thought of her? No one mattered but her family—and Garrett. She wouldn't embarrass him.

Her ma pulled her into a hug. "You've always been so independent. Let this be our gift to you."

How could Jo refuse? Her ma may have wanted her in frilly dresses with crimped hair, but she'd never forced the issue. When Jo wore trousers around the farm, her ma rolled her eyes but never insisted she wear skirts.

There was someone else they must take into consideration. "I'm not sure how Garrett will feel about all this. We kinda agreed on going before a judge."

"If he knows what's best for him, he'll agree in a lick."

"I suppose."

Jo didn't know much about men, but if she explained about her ma, surely Garrett would agree. She sure hoped so, otherwise she had another tangle to unravel.

"JoBeth, you're taking on an awful lot. I hope you know what you're doing."

For a brief moment Jo considered confiding in her ma, then changed her mind just as quickly.

How did she explain that somewhere along the line she'd gotten lost? That she'd felt a yearning for something she couldn't name, and marrying Marshal Cain felt like a step in the right direction. How could she explain that she was terrified of childbirth, and lately her fear had warred with her loneliness? That she was tired of being treated like a second-class citizen because she wasn't married and raising a family, and she was annoyed with herself for the vulnerability?

How could she explain that she liked how she felt when she was with Marshal Cain.

She and her ma were vastly different people, and sometimes Jo felt as if they were talking to each other in a foreign language. Each of them going through the motions, saying the right things, saying the wrong things, but never really hearing each other. Jo was different from other people, and she'd reveled in her uniqueness. She'd never wanted to be like anybody else. Lately, though, those differences had left her feeling isolated and alone. More and more she wondered if she'd merely been pushing people away.

She and Garrett were solitary people. But they had each other, and that would be enough. They were making their own future.

Edith straightened Jo's collar and flicked a disapproving glare at the hole in the fabric Jo had never bothered darning. "Bring this by when you come for dinner and I'll mend the tear."

"It's fine." Jo wriggled away. "No one cares but you."

"When you marry the marshal, your appearance will reflect on him. He has a certain standing in the community. As does his family."

Jo considered how her mother always looked impeccable. How she pressed her clothes and put up her hair, even if she wasn't going into town that day. "How come you always look just as nice at home as you do when you're going into town?"

"Because my family is the most important thing in the world to me," Edith replied easily. "Why wouldn't I want to look nice for them?"

Jo pondered the unexpected answer. Somehow, she'd always associated her mother's quirk with vanity. She'd assumed people primped because they liked showing off their looks, but her ma's reply had shattered that assumption.

Humbled, Jo hung her head. "Thank you for helping me with the wedding."

Edith cupped her cheek. "Someday you'll thank me for this."

Jo lifted her eyes heavenward. Getting married meant dressing up like a girl, something she knew nothing about.

How many times had the Walby brothers teased her about her clothes and hair? She touched her serviceable brown skirts. She didn't look as if she dressed in a barn, did she? Cold fear pitted in her stomach.

Jo crossed her arms. "A church wedding and dress. But that's all."

Maybe then her ma would finally understand that she couldn't change Jo into the daughter she wanted. By the time all this wedding nonsense had run its course, she hoped Edith McCoy finally accepted the daughter God had given her.

## Chapter Thirteen

Garrett plunged his face into the rain barrel and shook off the excess water. He'd passed the first test, talking with Jo's pa. He wasn't quite sure he'd passed the second test. Kissing Jo had been a revelation and a wonder. Because of his past, he'd learned to shut out physical needs and ignore loneliness. He'd thought he could bury his attraction to Jo, as well. He hadn't counted on the emotional connection. The more time they spent together, the more familiarity developed.

He didn't regret asking her to marry him, but he was terrified of the feeling stirring in his chest. Emotions leaked through the barriers he'd erected, spilling into his heart. How could a lifetime of steeling himself against affection crumble in one fell landslide?

He liked Jo, he admired her, but he couldn't love her. He couldn't let the madness take hold of him as it had his father. He owed that much to Jo.

To Jo *and* Cora, he reminded himself.

Garrett combed his fingers through his damp hair. He could do this. He was an honorable man.

Drawing in a steadying breath, he replaced his hat and straightened the brim. There'd been a murder, and he couldn't let his personal troubles distract him from his job.

He had one witness in particular he needed to question, and he let the short walk along the boardwalk focus his scattered thoughts. As he swung open the mercantile door, the room stilled.

His head bent, David McCoy lounged against a display of leather belts while the mercantile owner's pretty daughter, Mary Louise, held up a supple mahogany length for his approval. Garrett narrowed his gaze. A certain hitch in the boy's posture indicated he was interested in more than belts.

Garrett sensed trouble brewing like a spring squall. Caleb had already made it clear he was interested in Mary Louise. If both brothers courted the same girl, a heap of trouble followed. Garrett didn't need a blood feud on top of everything else—*especially* between Jo's brothers.

The bell above the door chimed, and David smiled a greeting at someone hidden from Garrett's view. "Hey, runt."

Garrett followed the boy's gaze and his pulse quickened. "JoBeth! What are you doing here? You're supposed to be resting."

She limped into the room looking like an old-timer returning from war with the bandage over her cheek and another knotted over her hand. Why on earth was she up and about? The doctor had declared her fit, but she needed quiet.

His new fiancée tossed him a withering glare. "I can't stay cooped up all day. I need supplies."

Guilt gnawed at his chest. If he hadn't asked her to stay with Cora, she'd be fine. Had the assault on the jail been an attempt to distract attention from the murder?

Or were the two incidents separate? He couldn't discount any possibilities just yet.

"Jo." Garrett kept his voice low, conscious of the tightening crowd. "The doctor said you should be resting."

"Then he should have brought me coffee," she snapped.

Garrett hovered uncertainly near her elbow. Why hadn't he thought to ask her if she needed anything that morning?

Because her enchanting kiss, a sweet combination of boldness and innocence, had distracted him. "Sit. I'll get your supplies."

"I'm perfectly capable of fetching a tin of coffee."

"But…" Garrett started, then thought better. This didn't seem like the best time to point out her surly behavior.

No doubt her wounds pained her. Garrett spied a sturdy wooden chair near the door and scraped the legs across the floor. He set it out of the path to the counter so she wouldn't be bumped or jostled.

"Cora is with Ma." Jo answered his unspoken question and took a hesitant step. "She woke and ate breakfast, but she went right back to sleep."

"She's bound to be tired. That was quite a ruckus last night."

Garrett touched Jo's elbow and guided her toward the waiting chair. Despite her exasperation, she leaned heavily on his arm. He threaded their fingers together, and she rested her cheek against his shoulder. He tilted his head a notch and caught the scent of her hair— feminine and fresh. Not flowery, but more like a field of cypress trees.

Garrett guided her around a pickle barrel and maneuvered her between two waist-high stacks of twenty-pound flour bags. They closed the distance to the chair entirely too quickly for his liking. With harnessed regret he released her hand and assisted her as she lowered herself onto the seat.

Rubbing the spot where her cheek had rested against his shoulder, he spoke. "You should be relaxing, not running around town. Tell me what you need, and I'll get it."

"Hey." David blocked his path. "You're getting awfully friendly with my sister."

"My *fiancée*." Garrett emphasized the word for the growing crowd hanging on every nuance of their exchange.

"She is not." David appeared horrified by the suggestion. "Jo's never getting married."

The source of their argument crossed her arms and huffed. "He's telling the truth."

She'd bit out the words like gristle.

"I might remind you," Garrett began, a ball of anxiety knotting in his belly, "you asked me first."

Their curious gawkers tittered. There had been a handful of people in the store when Garrett had arrived. Now that Jo had joined them, the whole town would have their faces pressed against the glass before long.

Twin spots of color appeared on Jo's cheeks. "I didn't come here to debate the facts."

David swung his gaze between them, his expression incredulous. "When did you two start liking each other? When did you get engaged?"

Garrett cut a sidelong glance at Jo's disgruntled expression. "Last night."

"You're his fiancée?" David threw back his head and chortled. "That's the funniest thing I ever heard."

His sister socked him in the gut. "Who's laughing now, huh?"

"That hurt." Scowling, David rubbed his belly. "You're awful cranky for a bride."

"And don't you forget it."

Garrett stepped between them before their good-natured ribbing escalated. "We can celebrate later. Right now we need to get Jo back home."

David sputtered. "I'll be keeping my eye on you two from now on. No funny business before you're married."

Heat crept up Garrett's neck. They'd kissed that morning, nothing more. And David wasn't a mind reader—he didn't know. "Show some respect for your sister, boy." He faced Jo. "Do you have a list?"

"No, I don't have a list. And I don't need your help, either. I'm perfectly capable—" A fit of coughing silenced her outraged reply.

Garrett immediately dropped on one knee beside her chair. He rubbed her back until the coughing stilled, then felt her forehead with the back of his hand, relieved she didn't have a fever. "You inhaled a lot of smoke last night. The doc said you'll probably have a cough for a week or two." He shook his head. "The least you can do is let me help."

"Let *us* help," David chimed in.

"Fine." JoBeth huffed. "I need three candles, a tin of matches, a sliver of soap and a pound of coffee."

In a flurry of arms and legs accompanied by the scuffle of boots, Garrett and David scrambled in opposite directions. Garrett scanned the shelves for soap and came up empty. David scooted past him, arrogantly displaying his haul of soap and candles.

The younger man had the advantage. He'd lived near

the town his whole life and obviously knew the store like the back of his hand. By the time they both approached the counter, out of breath and huffing in unison, all Garrett had acquired was the pound of coffee.

They set their supplies on the counter, and Garrett reached in his pocket. He might not have found the items, but he was sure as shooting going to pay for them. David slapped a handful of coins onto the counter first. Garrett shoved them aside. David shoved them back. The mercantile owner cleared his throat.

The two competitors glared at each other.

Garrett set his jaw. "I'll pay the bill. She's my fiancée."

"I'll pay the bill. She's my sister."

The bell above the door chimed, and Garrett lifted his eyes heavenward. That's just what they needed, more witnesses. They already had a rapt crowd following their every move. Good thing the town didn't have a regular newspaper, or they'd be front-page news tomorrow. As Garrett surveyed the entrance, he realized Jo's chair sat empty in the middle of the room.

David frowned. "Did she leave?"

"I think she left."

"Why'd she do that?"

"I dunno." Garrett shot the younger man a disgruntled glare. "It was probably something *you* said."

While they'd argued, Jo had limped home alone. Garrett dashed for the door and searched the boardwalk, but she'd already disappeared. David joined him outside while a press of noses jostled against the windows behind them.

*Great.*

They might not be front-page news, but they'd definitely dominate the dinner conversation around Cimarron Springs tonight.

"Something I said?" David innocently rested his hand over his heart. "I was just trying to help. You're the one acting like a bull in spring."

The barb struck home. Garrett tightened his lips as the door behind them swung open once more. Covering his embarrassment, he faced Mr. Stuart. "How much do I owe you?"

"Miss McCoy already paid. She has an account."

The three men stepped back inside, and the dozen or so people who'd crowded the store during the unexpected entertainment slowly dispersed. Still annoyed with the younger man's interference, Garrett pointed a finger at David. "This is your fault. I'm her fiancé. I should pay."

"I'm her brother." David threw back his shoulders. "I should pay."

Mr. Stuart tugged on his black-elastic arm garters. "If you fellows don't mind me saying so, looks like the lady is doing fine taking care of herself."

Garrett and David exchanged a guilty look. Feeling sheepish, Garrett nodded. "Has she always been so stubborn?"

David flashed an abashed grin. "That's JoBeth for you."

"Say, is there anything else your sister likes? You know, if you were buying her a gift?"

David grinned from ear to ear and bobbed his head. "Rosewater. She loves rosewater. Practically bathes in the stuff at home."

"That's odd," Garrett replied slowly. "I've never noticed that particular scent around her before."

David avoided his gaze and hung his head forlornly.

"Probably can't afford it since she lives in town. Too bad really."

The younger man glanced up, his eyes wide and deceptively innocent.

Barely covering his grin, David fisted one hand near his mouth and cleared his throat. "We'd best get over to the jailhouse. Check out the damage from the fire."

Their curious onlookers had dispersed, leaving them isolated. Garrett studied a display of tinned peaches. "Does Caleb know about you and Mary Louise?"

David gaped at the blunt question. "No."

"Don't let a woman come between you. If she's playing the two of you against each other, she's not worth it."

The tips of the younger man's ears reddened, and his hands curled at his sides, but he kept his expression neutral. "She knows who she wants."

"That's why you were at the saloon, isn't it? You were approaching her pa?"

"She gave me permission to court her, but I needed her pa's, too."

Garrett stared through the front window at the row of shops across the way. They were all connected, each sharing a wall, supporting the other. He sure hoped Mary Louise didn't drive a wedge between the brothers, but he was afraid it was already too late. "Fair enough. Why don't you go on ahead of me. I'll catch up to you at the jailhouse in a minute."

Garrett had felt the mercantile owner's glare boring into his back during their talk, and decided he'd better give the man another chance to speak. After the door closed behind David, Garrett crossed the room and braced his hands on either side of the spot Mr. Stuart had been rubbing for the past ten minutes.

"You're gonna wear a hole in the marble. Must be quite a stain you keep cleaning."

A telling muscle ticked along Mr. Stuart's jaw. He stuffed the rag into the belted tie of his apron. "I didn't shoot Mr. Hodges. I didn't like him. But I didn't kill him."

"You threatened to kill him. On more than one occasion, as I recall."

"He threatened me enough plenty of times, too, you know. I've also threatened to shoot that McCoy boy, Caleb, if he doesn't stop sniffing around my daughter. And he ain't dead yet."

"Let's keep it that way," Garrett drawled. "Or things won't look too good for you, will they? Besides, the McCoys are a good family."

"Mary Louise has better choices."

"Like who?"

"Like someone from St. Louis, or Omaha or Chicago. She's deserves better than the fellows around here."

"She'll make a fine choice, I'm sure," Garrett replied evasively.

No matter what happened, the courting of Mary Louise Stuart was going to end badly, that much he knew for certain.

Mr. Stuart rested his knuckles on the counter and tilted his head. "You really gonna marry that McCoy girl?"

Garrett's hackles rose at the obvious disbelief in the man's voice. "Why do you ask?"

"Just wondering. She didn't seem like the sort who'd marry."

"Guess I changed her mind." Garrett raised an eyebrow, challenging the man to dispute his answer. Clearly realizing he'd overstepped his boundaries, Mr. Stuart wisely remained silent.

Garrett tamped down his fuming anger. He didn't like the folks around town and their malicious gossip. And he especially didn't like people questioning Jo's suitability for marriage. He sometimes felt that her very strength was an affront to some weaker folks. She put up a good wall, pretending she didn't have any feelings on the matter, but Garrett suspected otherwise.

Mr. Stuart leaned in with a whisper, "Say, don't listen to David when it comes to his sister. He's pulling your leg. If you really want to buy her a present, she's had her eye on this."

He reached beneath the counter and retrieved a boy's leather hat.

Garrett accepted the offering and circled the sturdy brim in his hands. The brown leather was supple enough for comfort yet sturdy enough for practicality. The stitching was close and even and thick for long wear. A perfect gift for his new fiancée.

"I'll take it." Garrett glanced around the shop and spied the pretty yellow bonnet he'd noticed earlier. "And that one, too."

Cora would like the flashy piece. She seemed drawn to brightly colored things with an abundance of frills and lace. Once again he was struck by the difference between the two females and their obvious connection. "If you think of anything else, you let me know."

Mr. Stuart nodded but kept his gaze averted. Garrett took one last look around the mercantile and caught Mary Louise staring at him. She hastily ducked behind a tower of tinned beans when he caught her gaze. Garrett ran his hands down his face. This town was full of undercurrents, and if he wasn't careful, one of those undercurrents was bound to pull him under.

## Chapter Fourteen

Two days following the fire, Jo paced before the jail-house in anxious vigil. They'd boarded up the front window, and she missed the etched glass. When Garrett appeared, she gingerly waved her arm to catch his attention. "Marshal Cain," she called. "Garrett."

He faced her, and for a brief moment her resolve wavered. As the marshal approached, she surreptitiously pleated her new moss-green calico skirts. Today he wore his hat low over his forehead and his dark hair touched his collar. He really did need a haircut, but she hoped he put it off. His shaggy locks lent him an enigmatic air of danger that sent her heartbeat racing.

His work and the separate living arrangements from Cora during the repairs on the jailhouse meant they'd only seen each other in passing. While he'd visited his niece twice, Cora had been sleeping both times. He hadn't lingered. They were both painfully aware of the watchful eyes of others. Neither wanted to stir up any-more gossip.

Jo touched the bandage on her cheek. Gracious, the man just kept getting better looking. Each time he was near, she found herself wanting to touch him, brush her hand against his. When they were apart, her thoughts strayed to the dimple in his left cheek that appeared when he smiled. He was a part of her day now, a part of her worries.

And now the two of them had a problem.

Garrett paused before her, his gaze intense. "What's wrong?"

Jo tilted back her head but couldn't get a clear look at his eyes since they were shaded by the brim of his hat. "It's Cora. I'm worried." She glanced around the boardwalk. There weren't many people stirring yet, but it only took one person to spread a rumor.

They'd caused enough talk already. "Let's go back to the boardinghouse."

Jo led him into the familiar boardinghouse parlor, gestured toward the pink-chintz chairs before the hearth and sat down across from him. Her ma had volunteered to sit with Cora while she and Garrett discussed her recovery. Jo's memory drifted to the last time they'd sat across from each other here. When they'd kissed.

The marshal doffed his hat. "Cora has been awfully quiet, but the doc says she's not hurt."

"Not physically, no." Jo paused and carefully measured her next words. "At first I thought she was just tired and I let her sleep as much as she wanted. My ma came by, and well, a lot has happened."

At her words, Garrett shifted in his chair and tugged on his collar as though it was strangling him. "I forgot to tell you, I talked with your pa."

"Oh, dear." Jo almost wished she'd witnessed the encounter. "You don't appear any the worse for wear. I guess that's a good sign."

The marshal chuckled. "He was looking out for his daughter. I'd expect no less."

"That's Pa for you." She braced the heels of her hands against her knees and locked her elbows. "I don't exactly know how to say this, but Cora has barely spoken since the fire."

Garrett narrowed his gaze. "Are you certain? Maybe her throat hurts from the smoke."

"I'm certain."

"She's seen a lot for one so young."

"I know. And this probably brought back all sorts of memories from the night her folks died. What happened, anyway?"

Garrett rested his elbows on his knees and clutched the brim of his hat with both hands. "I sent for the newspapers, but there wasn't much information available. The fire started in the kitchen and spread fast. Looked like a faulty stovepipe. Cora's pa got her outside and went back for Deirdre. They didn't make it."

"I can't imagine what it must have been like for her."

His expression closed, Garrett pinched the bridge of his nose. "I should have been there for her."

"We can't change the past. You did the best you could..." Jo let her voice trail off. She doubted he wanted her comfort. "I guess I shouldn't lecture you on not feeling guilty. I'm blaming myself, too." She curled her hands into fists. "When the fire started and the door was stuck, I didn't think fast enough. I panicked."

The marshal tipped forward out his chair and knelt before her, then grasped her clenched hands. "It's not your fault. Don't ever think that."

Drawn toward his comfort, Jo wrapped her arms around his strong shoulders and buried her face in his neck. "I didn't know what to do," she spoke, her voice muffled against his starched shirt.

Garrett kneaded her tense muscles, rubbing his

thumb in circles. "It's not your fault. We'll talk with the doc about Cora. He might have an idea."

He hadn't shaved, and the day's growth of beard along his jaw abraded her cheek. His warm breath caressed her ear with each word.

Her thoughts scattered. "I didn't even think of the doc. I don't know what's wrong with me lately."

"There's nothing wrong with you. It's been an exhausting forty-eight hours. Your body needs time to heal."

Jo relaxed into the luxury of his comforting embrace. The marshal was solid and sure, and it felt good to rest her head on his capable shoulder. Her tightly cinched emotions eased for a moment. Despite her various aches and pains and a throat raw from smoke, a curious serenity possessed her. She angled her head to one side and rested her chin deeper in the hollow of Garrett's neck.

The floor creaked. Jo glanced up and caught sight of Agnes in the arched doorway. The landlady held her tea tray with its red-rose enameled pot and cups. Her gaze slid over their embrace and she puffed a breath, fluttering the gray corkscrew curls resting on her forehead. With a mutter, she spun around and retreated.

Jo and Garrett sprang apart. Jo pressed one hand against her cheek, capturing the comfort of Garrett's touch. Gathering her wits about her, she turned and found her ma descending the stairs.

Edith twisted a lace handkerchief in her hands. "It's no use. She's awake, but she hasn't said a word."

Jo and Garrett exchanged a worried glance.

Edith paused on the landing, one hand holding the banister. "Maybe you two should talk with her, together. Show her that she's safe now."

Garrett stood and held out his hand for Jo. "Your ma is right. I think it's best if we go as a pair."

Numb with worry, Jo pushed off from her chair and stood.

Garrett touched her sleeve. "No sad faces. This isn't a funeral, after all."

Jo mustered a weak smile.

"That will have to do."

Together they ascended the stairs, and Garrett pressed open the door. Cora perched on the edge of the bed clutching her rag doll, her blond curls a shiny halo around her solemn face. They eased into the room, and Garrett and Jo settled on either side. Jo took in her surroundings. What must Garrett think of her small room? There were no samplers or chintz pillows.

Just the necessities.

"Cora," Jo began, "I hear you don't feel like talking."

The little girl's enormous cornflower-blue eyes blinked slowly as she shook her head from side to side.

"That's okay. You can talk when you feel like it." Jo offered a hesitant smile. "Uncle Garrett and I have a surprise for you. We're getting married. To each other."

Garrett made a strangled sound at her odd declaration.

A wide grin spread across Cora's face.

Encouraged, Jo continued, "Would you like that?"

The little girl nodded.

"Do you want a new dress for the wedding?"

Another hesitant nod.

"I understand you're scared, but don't forget how much we love you. When you're ready to talk, your uncle and I will be here, okay? Just remember, you're safe with us."

A small hand reached out and touched Jo's knee.

Garrett covered the tiny fingers and Jo felt his gentle pressure.

"I'll tell you a secret," he spoke in a conspiratorial whisper. "I'm afraid of snakes. When I saw Jo holding that ten-foot-long monster, I nearly fainted. Why, it was as big around as my leg."

Cora giggled.

"And the fangs." Garrett crooked two fingers like a hook in front of his upper lip. "They could put out a man's eye. But while all the boys were shaking in their boots, you braved that monster like it was a tiny little worm."

Jo couldn't tear her gaze away from the marshal's face. His voice wrapped around her like an afghan. The security of his hand felt comforting and right. They might have gone about it the wrong way, but marrying Garrett was the right thing to do. The three of them together supported each other, giving each other strength.

As long as they were focused on their family, only good could come from their union. Garrett had an affinity for children that surprised her. Cora's expression had lightened beneath his genuine confession.

While Cora still hadn't spoken, Jo was encouraged. "Tomorrow we'll spend the day together. Just the three of us."

Garrett snapped his fingers. "I almost forgot. I bought you something."

He reached into his coat pocket and retrieved a wrapped package.

Cora's eyes lit up. "For me?"

"Of course for you."

She ripped open the package and pulled out a yellow lace bonnet. "It's just like the one at the store!"

Jo smiled at his thoughtfulness.

Cora rubbed the lace edge of the bonnet between her fingers. "Will we still have to live over the jail?"

Jo and Garrett exchanged a glance over her head. Jo grasped for an answer. "I don't know where we'll live. I guess we haven't thought much about that yet, have we?"

Garrett considered each of them in turn. "There's the Miller place on the edge of town. It's big. Too big for the three of us, really. But it'll do in a pinch. We haven't much other choice."

A tinge of apprehension skipped down her spine. Her impending marriage had been at the forefront of her mind, but she hadn't considered their living arrangements. Of course, they'd need a new place. Garrett couldn't stay at the boardinghouse, and the jail was no place for a family. Despite the obvious conclusion, she'd imagined them all staying put.

*Living with Garrett.*

Jo mentally shrugged. It would be like living at the farm again, tripping over her brothers' discarded shoes and fighting over whose turn it was to fetch the water.

Garrett flashed an encouraging smile, and her skin tingled with nerves. This was what her ma had tried to warn her about. She wasn't just becoming a mother to Cora, she was becoming Garrett's wife.

Only her living arrangements would change. Her life needn't change with their marriage.

Three days later, Garrett walked Jo and Cora to the telegraph office. He would have preferred they rest another few days, but both of them were chafing at the confinement. Jo craved a return to her regular routine, and Cora's boundless energy had returned tenfold.

They'd promised him a shortened workday and he'd

accepted the compromise. An overwhelming list of tasks loomed ahead of him.

He tightened his grip on the package he held, the leather hat he'd bought for Jo. He'd thought of giving it to her a dozen times, but the moment had never been quite right. What if she didn't like the gift? Garrett blew out a hard breath. Maybe he'd find the courage tomorrow.

Upon reaching the jailhouse, he paused. The door hung open. Cautiously stepping inside, his eyebrows lifted at the sight of six McCoys lined up before the wall by height—Caleb, David, Abraham, Michael and Maxwell, with Ely rounding out the group.

He couldn't tell from their impassive expressions whether or not this was a friendly visit.

Garrett widened his stance and propped his hands on his hips. "What brings you folks around this early?"

Perhaps Mr. McCoy hadn't been as accepting of the situation as Garrett had supposed.

Ely stepped forward. "This place isn't livable. David gave us a list of the repairs. The office will need to be taken down to the studs and rebuilt before it's fit for work. We'll get your stuff out and finish boarding up the windows this afternoon. You know where you're staying in the meantime?"

"I thought I'd take a look at the old Miller place."

"Good choice. The boys and I will get started on the jail."

"I appreciate the help, but I can manage on my own."

"We're family now," Ely replied matter-of-factly, as though that explained everything.

Garrett wasn't adept at family life, and the McCoys would find that out soon enough. He swiped a hand across his forehead. "I'd be much obliged for the assistance."

"You're coming to dinner on Sunday, right?" Ely inquired in a voice that indicated an order rather than a question.

Usually Garrett spent his day off alone, but it sounded as if the McCoys had a ritual, and he didn't want Jo disappointed. "I'll be there."

"Good."

Uncomfortable with all the attention, Garrett glanced around. "I'll box up what's left upstairs, then I'll visit the lawyer's office about the deed."

David braced a hand against the soot-darkened wall. "I'd rather be busting down walls than sitting in a lawyer's office anyday."

Garrett grunted. "You and me both."

He'd been spending the majority of time in the law offices these days. Unsure what else to say, Garrett stood in silence while the McCoys filed past him. As each of them crossed his path, they chucked him on the arm. By the time it was Maxwell's turn, Garrett figured his arm was black and blue. The McCoys didn't seem to know their own strength.

The littlest McCoy stared up at him. "Are you going to be my new brother?"

"Um, yes."

Garrett hadn't considered the full significance of his decision. He wasn't just marrying Jo, he was marrying into her family. The feeling was odd, but not entirely unpleasant. The McCoys had seemingly accepted him without question.

Maxwell tugged a slingshot from his back pocket and extended his hand. "I made this. For you."

Garrett accepted the gift and made a point of studying the rudimentary craftsmanship. "This is a fine piece. I'm proud to have it."

"Jo is the best shot, but I've been practicing."

"That's good."

"I have a target range behind the barn."

"Um, that's nice."

"You can practice with me."

Garrett figured shooting *with* Max was better than being shot at *by* Max. "It's a deal."

The boy trailed behind his family and sketched a wave over his shoulder. Pondering the unexpected encounter, Garrett replaced his hat and adjusted the brim. He tested the stairs and gripped the banister, his hand coming away darkened with soot. He unfurled his bandanna and rubbed the black from his palm before continuing upstairs.

A fine layer of powdery gray dust had settled on every surface, and the pungent smell of burnt wood stung his nostrils. Even after a good cleaning and repainting, Garrett figured they'd be fighting a lingering stench.

They'd removed Cora's belongings first, washing and airing everything. The lingering scent of fire brought back too many disturbing memories. With the McCoys' help, he'd erase the evidence of the fire in no time.

They'd put their trust in him. Would they be as welcoming if they knew his past? Garrett shook his head. He'd kept his secrets this long—there was no reason he couldn't keep them forever.

## Chapter Fifteen

Two weeks later, Jo stood on a dais in the backroom of the mercantile wearing a perfectly ridiculous concoction of heavy ivory satin. The lace collar choked her throat and stretched so it tickled her earlobes.

"Stand still!" Mrs. Hankins ordered, the seamstress's words muffled around a mouthful of pins. "I can't properly measure the hem if you don't stop wiggling." The aggravated woman sat back on her heels. "Are these the shoes you'll wear?"

"Yes," Jo replied curtly.

Her ma clutched her chest. "While I'm afraid of the answer, I have to ask. What are you wearing?"

Jo hiked her skirts. "The usual."

"Oh, good gracious." Edith slapped one hand over her mouth. "You're wearing a drover's boot."

"Nope." Jo bent at the waist. "It's called a cowboy boot. Mr. Stuart says they're all the rage in Texas. Check out the stitching on the side." She tipped her stacked heel and admired the elaborate craftsmanship.

"I don't care what you call it. That shoe is positively hideous. You cannot wear those."

"No one will see them."

"*I'll* know you're wearing work boots during the ceremony. That is absolutely unacceptable."

"If no one can see them, why does it matter?"

"It matters."

Jo glowered. "That doesn't make any sense!"

Cora shifted in her perch on a chair in the corner and Jo immediately regretted her outburst. *Good heavens,* she was behaving like a child and frightening Cora in the process. Jo straightened and turned toward the little girl.

"It's all right," she called with a reassuring smile. "We're just agreeing on a dress." Pressing down a mountain of itchy ruffles with one hand, Jo grimaced. "What do you think of this one?"

Cora wrinkled her nose and shook her head.

Jo tossed a withering glare over one shoulder. "See, Ma? I told you I looked ridiculous."

"That's not the only dress in town." Edith raised her eyebrows. "If this wasn't such a rush, if we had more time, I could sew something nice for you."

"You're the one who insisted on setting a date for the wedding."

"And you're the one who's been avoiding me."

"I don't like to dress shop."

"Hiding from the task isn't going to change anything."

"Either way, I need a break from all this girl stuff." Jo scurried behind the screen. As she yanked the suffocating yards of satin and lace over her head, the bell above the mercantile door chimed.

Footsteps sounded and Mary Louise called out, "Marshal Cain is here. He wants to know if he can talk with you."

Jo's heart lodged in her throat. She hadn't seen him in days, and it felt like an eternity. "Be right out."

At least his timely arrival offered her a much-needed reprieve from wedding shopping. After licking her palms, she smoothed her hair and pinched her cheeks.

When Jo emerged from behind the screen, her mother stood before her, her arms crossed over her chest.

"Almost a reprieve," Jo muttered beneath her breath.

"I'd like a word with you."

*Uh-oh.*

"I can see you don't want my help." Edith ducked her head and tugged on the lapels of her jacket. "You wear whatever you think is appropriate for the occasion. Just promise you won't embarrass me in front of the whole town."

The comment prickled. Jo opened and closed her mouth. Anything she said was bound to drive the conversation in circles.

She glanced around the room and realized Cora was studying a rainbow display of ribbons. The little girl needed all the love and attention they could provide. "Maybe you could see about a dress for my most special attendant?"

Cora smiled and played with the other children in town, but she'd still suffered a trauma, and they were all hypervigilant to signs of difficulty.

"Would you like that?" Jo directed her question toward Cora. "Since Garrett and I are getting married, this is your grandma."

Her ma gasped and covered her heart with one hand. "A granddaughter. Why, I didn't even think… Well, what do you know…everything happened so quickly. What a perfectly wonderful thing." She cupped her hands over her mouth and stood for a moment in stunned silence.

When the realization finally registered, Edith grasped Cora's hand. "We'll buy you a new dress and some ribbons. You've got the most wonderful curls. We won't even have to put your hair up in rags. Would you like that?"

Cora stared up at the older woman in awe, but didn't seem to mind being hustled deeper into the store. Jo's heart warmed at their easy chatter. Why hadn't she thought of encouraging their relationship earlier? Cora was the perfect distraction against her mother's meddling. Not to mention the little girl could use a bit of fussing over.

Jo was still smiling when Garrett stepped into the room, his hat in his hands. Her smile faltered as she took in the serious look on his face. "What's wrong?"

"Nothing is wrong."

"You look like someone peppered your porridge this morning."

He attempted a halfhearted grin and pulled a folded square of paper from his breast pocket. "I bought the Miller place for us. I hope you don't mind."

Jo lifted one shoulder. "Why would I mind?"

"Because I realized that you haven't even seen the inside yet. It's been empty for almost a year. It needs a fresh coat of paint and some repairs, but I think it's worth the elbow grease."

"Whatever you think."

"You're sure you don't mind?" he asked, his voice rising in a question. "We'll have a lot of work ahead of us. What if you don't like the house?"

"It's a roof over our heads." Jo snorted. "Don't forget. I'm not like other ladies. I'm not afraid of getting dirty and it sure doesn't take much to make me happy."

Garrett flashed another half grin, then he tucked his chin to his chest and circled the brim of his hat in a now-familiar gesture. "That's one of my favorite things about you."

A giddy sense of joy filled her heart. For once she believed him. She truly believed he appreciated the qualities that made her different.

A perfectly brilliant idea sprang into her head. She couldn't believe she hadn't thought of it before.

Her old neighbor, Elizabeth Elder, had given Jo a dress for courting when she'd left for Texas. Jo had taken out the dress once before, but it was too fancy for Cimarron Springs. Maybe if she removed some of the trim and a yard or two of material from the skirts it might suit. She loathed sewing, but there was someone in town who owed her a favor—Beatrice.

Jo snapped her fingers. She'd stumbled upon the perfect solution. She'd have Beatrice fix her dress and arrange her hair, and keep her ma distracted with her new grandchild.

Garrett tilted his head. "What are you thinking about?"

Filled with a renewed sense of purpose, Jo pivoted on her heel. "I realized I own a dress I can wear for the ceremony. A dress that will even meet my ma's approval."

She made it to the door before realizing Garrett remained frozen where she'd left him.

He backed into a display of creamware and the whole shelf clattered ominously. "You're sure you're not upset about any of this?"

"Nah." She hesitated. "Actually, you've saved me a lot of trouble. Why are you so worried?"

"I'm used to doing things on my own. I keep forgetting I need to think of someone else."

"I guess it depends on the kind of things you're doing, right?" Jo nibbled on her jagged thumbnail. "You don't think it's bad, do you? That I don't care."

Garrett shook his head from side to side. "Nope. I don't think it's bad at all."

"There's something else I should warn you about. I know my ma said the wedding will be small, but I have a feeling the whole town is going to be there."

"Okay."

"Are you sure you don't mind? I know you wanted to go before the judge. Just the two of us."

"I don't mind." He cleared his throat. "Actually, I I'm glad we're having a church wedding."

They stood in awkward silence for a moment before Jo finally broke the impasse. "It never bothered me what other people thought when I was younger. But as I got older, something changed. I started worrying about what I *should* be doing and what I *should* be saying. Which only made things worse. I'll make you a deal. We'll both forget about everyone else and do what feels right instead."

"That's a deal."

Garrett studied an array of brightly colored sewing thread. Framed examples of samplers decorated the wall above the display. Cross-stitched alphabets as well as Bible verses and flowers.

He touched the edge of a wooden frame. "My mother once asked me to memorize a Bible verse. 'For we are his workmanship, created in Christ Jesus unto good works, which God hath before ordained that we should walk in them.'" He straightened a row of blue-speckled enamelware coffeepots. "I memorized the words but I never thought about why they were important to her."

"I suppose she wanted you to remember that we are created in God's image to do good things." Jo joined him before the display. "I believe in His word."

Clearing his throat, Garrett glanced away. "I don't know what I believe anymore. Seems like there's an awful lot of pain out there considering He has plans for us to grow and prosper and all that."

Once again Jo sensed a deep sorrow behind his words. Garrett had lost his parents and his sister. He had a right to be bitter, to question his faith. Other people had been shaken by lesser tragedies. Yet there was a profound agony behind his troubled spirit. Jo had a suspicion there was a dark place hidden in his soul. Despite her fears, her instincts urged her not to push him. He'd reveal his secrets when the time was right for him, and not a moment before.

The impulsive side of her nature chafed against the restraint. What if her instincts were wrong? Would his shadowed past prevent them from having a future together?

She offered the only wisdom she had. "You know how the rocks on the bank of a stream are jagged and sharp, but the rocks in the water are smooth and almost soft? I think that's how God sees our hardships, like water rushing over us and smoothing the hard edges, polishing us up for Heaven."

"Well, I must shine like a new penny." Garrett laughed humorlessly as he replaced his hat. "How about tomorrow we stop by the Miller place after we visit with the reverend?"

Jo nodded. "Let's bring Cora along, too."

"If we keep on agreeing all the time, we'll have the quietest marriage in history."

"Sure."

Jo shivered despite the heat. If they didn't have strong feelings now, would they ever? She considered Tom Walby and some of the other fellows she'd known over the years. Garrett wasn't likely to shoot up a saloon because of her, but did she really want that?

The marshal touched her shoulder, halting her exit. "I almost forgot, I need you to send a telegram."

Jo tilted her head to one side. "Mrs. Schlautman is working today. She'd be happy to help."

Garrett's expression grew somber. "It's about Cora. About the marriage. I'd like you to send it. I'm tired of people gossiping about us."

Jo nodded.

His trust with the correspondence was minor, but it was a start. Maybe someday he'd trust her with the secret corroding his soul.

They exited the shop and walked the length of the boardwalk beneath the curious stares and knowing smiles of several townspeople. They'd definitely become a source of entertainment for the townsfolk.

After arriving at the telegraph office, Jo sent out a missive addressed to a solicitor named Flynn O'Neills concerning an accounting of the estate of Cora's parents. Garrett directed the solicitor to put the little girl's inheritance into trust.

Jo printed out the final words and pulled her lower lip between her teeth. "You're a good man. She'll have a secure future."

"I'm not."

The despair in his voice startled her. "There's nothing you can say that will change my mind about you."

"You don't know that." He held her fingers, his grip bordering on painful. "You don't know that."

"Tell me then," she declared boldly. "Tell me one thing that will change my mind about you."

He held her gaze, his coffee-colored eyes dark with pain and indecision. She kept her eyes steadfast, unyielding, willing him to trust her with his pain.

They stayed like that for what seemed an eternity while an odd battle of wills played out between them.

Garrett released his hold first. "It's not too late—"

"I'm not calling off this marriage unless you give me a good reason."

She felt the indecision raging within him, a palpable thing. At last he spoke, "Thank you for helping with the telegram."

Jo sighed. "You're welcome."

He folded the notes she'd taken for his telegram and slid the paper into his breast pocket.

A lawman always had secrets. It was part of the job. She'd have to trust that he'd eventually confide his worries to her, because she had a feeling Marshal Garrett Cain knew a lot more about keeping secrets than most men.

## Chapter Sixteen

Almost three weeks after Garrett had purchased the Miller house, he squinted his left eye and leveled his hands.

"Shoot already," Maxwell ordered.

Tossing a quelling glare over one shoulder, Garrett aimed the slingshot once more. He released the elastic and the rock sprang free. A split second later, his tin-can target ricocheted off its perch.

"Peas and carrots." Maxwell stomped. "You beat me again."

"I haven't beaten you yet. If you make the next shot, it's a tie."

The young boy snatched another pebble from the mound at his feet. He bit his lip and took aim, his single front tooth showing white against his lower lip. He'd lost the other front tooth the previous evening and the story of how he'd wiggled it loose had been repeated with epic drama.

Maxwell squinted and released his fingers. His shot glanced off the edge of the second can and for an ago-nizing moment his target teetered before tumbling triumphantly off the stump. Maxwell waved his fists in the air, giddy at having matched an adult shot for shot.

Garrett swiped the back of his hand across his damp brow. "That's a tie."

He had a feeling they'd be here all night if Max had lost the round.

Jo smiled indulgently from her seat atop the corral fence. The sun flamed behind her, and he couldn't tear his gaze from the sharp relief of her profile. As was her custom, she wore her trousers for chores around her parents' farm. Today she'd donned a striped vest over a crisp white shirt. The combination should have been masculine. He'd never seen a more feminine sight in his life.

The buttoned vest accentuated the curve of her tiny waist. The collar of her shirt revealed the delicate hollow of her neck. She'd tucked her pants into the tops of her knee boots, and he couldn't help but notice her delightfully proportioned legs.

In town she carried an edge about her. In the country she relaxed. Steady, easy chatter rang between her and her brothers. They teased and taunted each other, always with underlying respect and restraint. She was akin to the hills rolling into the distance—quietly beautiful and deceptively fierce.

Not for the first time it struck him how constrained a woman's life must be. They toiled from sundown till sunset. They bore children and cared for elderly parents while their husbands worked the fields. The only weakness he'd ever observed amongst their fiery lot was men. Look at his mother. She'd remained married to a madman. A man who cared more about drink than his own family.

A man who'd murdered her and left his children orphans.

A hearty gust of balmy June wind whipped a lock of Jo's hair across her forehead, and she hastily shoved it aside. He'd never seen a more curious mix of temperaments in one person. She had a spine of forged steel and a heart of pure light. Even as he watched, she turned toward the house with a smile of dazzling joy. Distanced from the event, he felt his heart open as she threw back her head and laughed. He couldn't see the source of her amusement. He didn't care.

He clung to the moment. Time crystallized as she caught his transfixed gaze.

Her green eyes flashed with amusement, and they shared a brief moment of united thought. Though no words were spoken, he imagined they were connected, linked in a mutual appreciation of the beauty and joy surrounding them.

His feet drew him inexorably forward. He needed to touch her, ensure she was real. How, in such a short time, had she stitched her way into the very fabric of his existence? When they were apart, she remained at the forefront of his thoughts. When they were together, his senses remained attuned to her unique scent, that curious mixture of sunlight and evergreens. He felt her emotions as though they were his own. Her joy resonated in his chest and her sorrow wrapped around his heart like a vise. He didn't understand what was happening to him, and for once he didn't care.

He held out his hand to assist her down from her perch. "I think your brothers are warming to me."

"They must be. You're still alive, aren't you?"

Garrett laughed, and she clasped his fingers. As she

leaped off the top rung, her vest caught on a splinter. She stumbled into him.

He lassoed her around the waist. "Be careful. You're still healing."

"I'm fine. The fire was ages ago."

His heart thumped against his ribs as he gently touched the fading pink wound on her cheek. She captured his wrist and turned her face into his palm. His whole body quivered with awareness.

Jo lifted her head, her alluring eyes flashing with mischief. "Sometimes I think you're afraid of me. Like right now, you're trembling."

He glanced behind him and realized they were alone. A rare thing around the McCoy farm. "I'm terrified of you, JoBeth McCoy. You can outgun me, outscrap me and outsmart me. You're so beautiful you take my breath away."

"I've never seen you like this." Her voice caressed his palm. "I don't know whether you're teasing me or not."

"Funny, I was just thinking the same thing about you. Except I'd never tease a woman who can shoot a tin can from a hundred yards."

"Be serious." Her expression grew somber. "You really don't mind that I'm not like Mary Louise Stuart?"

Garrett held her at arm's length and made a point of studying her features as a delicate flush crept up her neck.

This was a side of Jo she kept hidden, her insecurities and worries. Yet she'd confided in him, trusted him. Her faith renewed his tattered soul. "The world is full of girls like Mary Louise, but there's only one JoBeth McCoy."

If anything good came of their marriage other than creating a family for Cora, he'd make Jo see that she was beautiful and desirable. "You have enough confidence for ten men in everything but your own appeal."

He felt as though he'd been given a precious gift. God had saved one perfect bloom. A treasure hidden in plain sight for him and no one else. She didn't know about his past, and there was no reason she'd ever discover his secrets. Maybe it was possible for people to change. The more time he spent with Jo, the stronger he felt. As though he could move mountains with his bare hands. He'd take on a grizzly with Maxwell's slingshot.

She ran the tip of her tongue along her full lower lip, and he couldn't resist the invitation. He leaned in, and she tilted her chin. The moment their lips touched, a sense of peace overwhelmed him. For the first time since the tragedy, he felt whole again, like his soul had finally begun to heal.

The dinner bell rang, startling them apart. Maxwell rounded the corner, his face flush with excitement. "Someone has come to call!"

Chafing at the interruption, Garrett glanced around the clearing. He'd been so distracted, an army of soldiers could have marched by and he wouldn't have noticed. Jo appeared dazed, her face adorably flushed and her lips parted.

Maxwell yanked on her vest. "Jo, did you hear me? There's a fancy gentleman here come for dinner."

Garrett threaded his fingers with Jo's, exchanging an indulgent grin before following the boy. They rounded the corner and Garrett froze.

"Garrett Cane!" Flynn O'Neills shouted. "As I live and breathe. I heard you were sheriff of some Podunk town, and here you are."

His father's solicitor, a man Garrett hadn't seen in over fifteen years, crossed the distance between them before Garrett could catch his breath. As Flynn embraced him, Garrett stiffened. He kept his hand firmly anchored in Jo's comforting grasp. The McCoys gathered around.

The whole family was home for Sunday dinner. Caleb and David stood together, Abraham hung back, Michael and Maxwell appeared in the door of the barn. Visitors were rare, and unexpected visitors even more so.

Flynn spread his arms in an encompassing gesture to the curious family. "I haven't seen Garrett here since he was a strapping lad full of fight like his old da."

Mr. and Mrs. McCoy, alerted by the commotion, emerged from the house.

The solicitor's hair was grayer and his face and chest softer, but other than that, he hadn't changed much over the years. Flynn was just as Garrett remembered him—larger than life and as slick as a moss-covered rock. He was stout and well groomed, his jowls and nose pink from years of drink. And he still had that same air of easy charm about him.

If he noticed Garrett's odd response, nothing showed on his face. His gray hair was greased back against his head, and his suit was impeccably cut. A heavy gold chain ran between his watch pockets.

The group exchanged a noisy round of greetings, and Flynn made a great show of repeating back the names of each McCoy in turn.

The past came rushing back, and Garrett struggled for breath.

Jo squeezed his hand. "Are you all right? You're whiter than a sheet on bluing day."

"Fine, I'm just surprised. That's all." Garrett shook his head, clearing the memories. "Flynn, what are you doing here? I didn't think Cimarron Springs was your sort of town."

The solicitor lifted his gold-tipped cane. "I got your telegram, of course."

Sensing the underlying current of tension, Edith McCoy gathered her family. "Let's set the table for dinner and give these gentlemen a chance to catch up."

While Flynn offered a few charming words, Mrs. McCoy blushed coyly, Jo loosened her grip.

She smiled at their unexpected guest. "I hope you'll join us for dinner, Mr. O'Neills. Especially after you've traveled all this way."

"Much obliged."

Garrett clung to her fingers for another long moment. He caught her gaze and saw the confusion in her eyes.

The solicitor sauntered over, his watch chain flashing in the brilliant sunlight, and made a point of sizing up Jo. "And who is this lovely young lady?"

His gaze dipped pointedly at their linked fingers.

Garrett released his hold. His feelings were too raw and new for sharing. "This is my fiancée, JoBeth McCoy. Flynn was my father's solicitor."

"More than that, surely," Flynn boomed. "I've been a close friend of the family for many, many years."

Jo and Flynn linked hands in a greeting, and apprehension snaked down Garrett's spine. What would Flynn say? Would he let something slip?

Garrett's hackles rose and he instinctively felt the need to protect her. "I'll meet you inside, Jo."

She hesitated, her curious gaze shifting between the two men, then dutifully retreated into the house.

Flynn slapped him on the back as the door closed behind her. "You always could pick a winner. That's a diamond in the rough you've discovered. I wouldn't have thought it possible in this wilderness."

Garrett clenched his jaw. "You're a long way from home."

"I'm on my way to Denver." Flynn tugged his leather gloves over his unnaturally pale wrists. "I couldn't pass up the opportunity to see an old friend of the family. Especially after you'd contacted me personally."

"Did you discover anything?"

"It's just as you suspected. Edward hasn't turned a profit since your uncle died. He isn't the businessman his dad was. Your sister, on the other hand, left a tidy sum."

"You think Edward is after Cora for the money?"

"It's a fair guess. He's been making a lot of noise around town. Bringing up the past."

Garrett felt the blood drain from his face. "Do you think that will hold sway with the judge?"

"Not if you're married. They can't hold your father's actions against you. And you've proven yourself an honorable man over the years."

Garrett's uneasiness grew with each word. He'd kept his life sequestered. He'd left St. Louis behind and started over. For fifteen years he'd kept his secrets hidden, safely tucked away in another time. With Flynn here, his past and future collided.

"Don't worry," Flynn spoke. "Edward hasn't the stamina for a fight. He'll drop the case once he realizes you won't give up Cora. He's a coward at heart."

Staring sightlessly into the distance, Garrett struggled with his growing dread. "My dad was a decorated hero during the war. Look what that got him."

Flynn braced both hands on his walking stick. "They don't know about your parents, do they?"

"They don't."

"You can't hide forever."

"I have to." Garrett paused. "For Cora's sake, don't say anything."

"I won't, but you should. A foundation of lies is a poor way to build a life. They're good people. Give them a chance."

"I'm a lawman, too. I have a family to support now. It's not just me, it's Cora's future I'm risking."

Garrett had already set the wheels in motion, and there was no halting the marriage. He'd compromised Jo in the eyes of the town, and he'd do the right thing by her. This time he'd stick to the original plan. He'd pull away and put some distance between them—physically and mentally.

A voice called and Garrett turned.

Jo motioned from the porch. "Supper is ready."

As for the kisses they'd shared, Garrett would lock away the precious memories. They'd go back to being friends, back to the way things were before the fire.

Jo rested her forehead on the door. "I don't want to interrupt, but if we don't sit down quick, the boys are going to gnaw into the wooden table."

Despair tightened in his chest. How could a person gain and lose everything in a single day?

The wagon tipped along a deep rut, throwing Jo into Garrett. She savored the contact until he steadied her with one hand, keeping his other fisted around the leather reins.

"Tell me about Flynn?" she asked.

He glanced at her, his face inscrutable in the twilight. "There isn't much to say."

"I thought you'd be happy seeing someone from your past."

"A lot of years have gone by," he replied, his tone clipped.

Jo recalled the inquiry she'd sent to the solicitor. "Did he have the information you were searching for?"

"Yep."

His curt tone raised her hackles. There'd been a ridge of tension around Garrett since his old friend's arrival. The camaraderie they'd shared was gone.

A dozing Cora stirred against Jo's side as Garrett halted the team and wrestled the brake into position.

He slanted a glance at his slumbering niece. "My cousin is in financial trouble, just as I suspected. Edward doesn't want custody to protect Cora from me. He needs her inheritance to save his business."

Jo titled her head. "Is something else wrong?"

"I wanted a minute to talk with you." Shadows played across his face. "While Cora is sleeping."

"Okay."

"I'm sorry. About earlier today. At the corral."

Jo grasped his arm. "I'm not."

"We agreed to get married for Cora's sake, to give her a family. I forgot myself, and I apologize for that. We agreed this was a partnership, a friendship, and I didn't hold up my end of the bargain."

"Does this have something to do with Flynn's visit?" Her voice cracked. "You've been different since he came along."

"I've just been thinking, that's all. Do you really want to get married?"

He was doing it again, running hot and cold. She should be used to his changing attitude by now, but she wasn't. "Are you sore at me?"

"No, of course not." He swiveled on the bench seat and grasped her shoulders. "I care about you, Jo. And I want what's best for you. We've been treating this whole thing like we don't have any other choice. But there's always a choice. If I leave, the gossip will die down soon enough."

His sudden change of heart wasn't about the two of them—this was about Flynn. The solicitor had said something that spooked him. "Did Flynn threaten you?"

"Of course not. This has…this has nothing to do with him. Maybe we were taking the easy way out. We can say we fought. I can say you called off the marriage. I'll take the blame."

He had secrets, but he was a good man. Jo knew it in her heart. Whatever Flynn held over him, she didn't care. Nothing could change her mind about the man she'd agreed to marry. "What do *you* want?"

The agonizing question stretched out between them while crickets chirped in an early-summer chorus. Jo clutched her hands together and waited. She'd thought they were growing closer. They talked together, they laughed together, he'd held her close and kissed her until she was breathless.

Another thought brought her up short. Unless he hadn't enjoyed their time together. Perhaps his indecision had nothing to do with Flynn's arrival, and everything to do with the kisses they'd shared.

Garrett shifted. "I want to do the right thing, but I don't know which choice is right."

"What's the best choice for Cora?"

"You are," he answered immediately, "You're the best thing for her. She loves you, and I don't want her to lose any more than she already has."

Jo's ma had accused her of being selfish. Was she?

After all, she'd moved into town rather than take over the midwife's duties.

She wasn't the kind of girl men courted—she'd known that from the beginning. He'd wanted a partnership; she was the one who'd wanted more. If he wanted a friend, she'd be a friend. They'd go back to the way things were.

Jo studied the purple-tinted twilight sky and gathered her nerve.

She touched his leather-clad hand, heartened by the almost imperceptible tremble she felt in his fingers. "Then let's do what's right for Cora, and never mind about anything else."

"Okay." Garrett spoke so quietly she wasn't even certain she'd heard him correctly.

Each tentative step she'd taken forward had been met with resistance. He'd called her beautiful, and then he'd pulled away. She feared this power he held over her. His embrace left her feeling exuberant and capable, his rejection shook her faith.

Jo squared her shoulders. She'd pull away, too, just as Garrett had. She refused to let him hurt her anymore.

# Chapter Seventeen

The house stood a half mile from the edge of town, a two-story white clapboard with a gabled roof and whitewashed picket fence. According to local gossip, the home had been empty for over a year since the Millers had moved to Denver.

Garrett yanked at the overgrown weeds until he found the gate hook. The fence had collapsed in two places and several of the boards were rotted through. He surveyed the sparse lawn and unlocked the front door with the rusted key he'd acquired from the lawyer, then pried open the stiff hinges. The dank, moldy smell of disuse triggered an unexpected jolt of melancholy.

How quickly abandonment turned to disrepair. Houses were meant to be lived in. A spindly chair rested on its side, and Garrett lifted it upright. Lulled by the quiet, he meandered around the sprawling floor plan, weaving his way through the sitting room, parlor, dining room and finally the kitchen.

He took the back steps to the second floor and discovered three good-size bedrooms devoid of furniture. The floorboards creaked as he crossed the spacious hallway and glanced out the window toward the rolling hills. Someone had planted a brace of poplar trees, and they'd grown as high as the second-floor eaves. An excellent windbreak.

Garrett rested his hands on the dusty sill. He wanted to ensure the house was sound before Jo arrived. Despite his good intentions, he'd hurt her last evening. She didn't understand and he couldn't offer an explanation without dredging up the past.

A train whistle sounded, and Garrett caught sight of the 3:15 from Wichita on the horizon. Everything was going according to plan, yet he couldn't shake his unease. *Nothing good ever lasted long.*

Garrett shook off the odd feeling. The train posed no danger. It was just another passenger train, just another group of weary travelers stopping for lunch on the way to someplace else. Families seeking a better life, soldiers transferring West, adventurers itching for their next exploit. Flynn's arrival had shaken him, that's all. And for good reason.

The country was shrinking. Each new set of rail tracks brought the coasts closer together. Once the Union and the Central Pacific rail lines had joined, there was no going back. The moment two merging railroads had driven in the golden stake at Promontory Summit, they'd forged the destiny of a nation.

A man couldn't hide anymore.

Garrett turned away from the window, but the sense of unease followed him. He'd run out of places to hide. How long before his past caught up with him?

Jo rested her chin on the rounded tip of the broom handle. She'd steeled herself against her attraction, and so far it had worked.

She and Garrett were getting along well, pretending nothing had sparked between them. "This isn't so bad."

Garrett sat back on his heels and wiped the perspiration from his forehead with the back of his hand. "Could be worse."

They'd been working since dawn, scrubbing floors and walls and trim. Beneath a year and a half of neglect they'd uncovered a relatively sound house. "If we paint tomorrow, I can oil the floors on Thursday."

"I'll help." Garrett ran the back of his hand over his forehead.

"Can you take that much time away from the town?"

He rose and dusted his hands together. "About that. What do you think of David as a permanent deputy?"

Scratching beneath the red bandanna she'd knotted over her hair, Jo considered his announcement. "I never thought about it. I figured he'd move to Wichita. He spends enough time there."

"He needs work. He's not a farmer like Caleb."

Jo lifted the broom and dusted the cobwebs hanging in the corner of the spacious dining room. "I still think he'll opt for Wichita."

"He'll stay."

"How can you be so certain?"

Garrett cleared his throat.

Stifling a sneeze, Jo dropped the broom and caught his guilty expression before he quickly turned away. "You're keeping a secret. What are you hiding?"

"Nothing."

"You're lying. I can tell." Brandishing her broom, she pointed the bristles at his chest. "Tell me or I'll cover you in cobwebs."

Garrett held up his hands. "He's been spending more time at the mercantile than Caleb."

Her hands went slack and the bristles hit the floor, stirring a plume of dust. "No."

"Yes."

"Well, what are you going to do?"

"Nothing." Garrett dropped his arms. "What am I supposed to do?"

"I don't know, talk to them. Mary Louise isn't worth fighting over."

"It's none of our business. But I suspect she's got a shine for David."

Jo groaned. "Then someone should talk with Mary Louise."

"Leave it alone. Anything you or I say will only make things worse. This has to play out on its own."

"Fine. But don't you think he's awfully young for all that responsibility?"

"You lost me." Garrett frowned. "Did we change subjects?"

"Don't avoid the question."

"David is young, but he'll learn. I was an army scout at seventeen."

She tried to imagine Garrett as a young man. Wide-eyed and innocent. The picture didn't form. "What was that like?"

"Hot in the summer, cold in the winter and hungry year-round."

"A dockworker at fifteen, an army scout at seventeen. You've led a full life, Garrett Cain."

A call from the second floor interrupted her next question. Jo dashed toward the stairs. "Cora?"

The little girl appeared at the head of the stairs. "I found another mice nest."

Propping her broom against the wall, Jo grimaced.

"I'll come and take a look. That'll be the fourth one we've found so far."

She took the stairs two at a time and followed Cora into the smallest of the upstairs rooms. The house was a basic foursquare, with a master suite, two good-size bedrooms and a utility space all grouped around an open landing.

Cora knelt before a cupboard and pointed. Sure enough, a soft nest of wool, leaves and a bright length of orange yarn nestled in the corner.

Garrett's footsteps sounded behind her. "More mice?"

Glancing over her shoulder, Jo nodded. "I think we should consider taking one of Maxwell's kittens."

"I don't like animals in the house." Garrett knelt beside her. "But I guess I'd rather have a cat than mice."

"The cat can stay in the house while we finish cleaning up. She can stay in the barn after that."

As he leaned in for a closer look, their shoulders brushed together. Garrett reached around her, and Jo leaned into his arm. He scooted back and she leaned the opposite direction, crowding him, forcing the contact. He wasn't immune to her, she knew it, felt it in her bones. Yet each time she initiated even the lightest touch, he pulled away.

It was wrong, it was dangerous, and she couldn't help herself.

Her reluctant fiancé sat back on his heels. "Sounds like a good compromise to me."

Though they didn't touch, he remained only a breath away. Warmth rushed through her veins, and her pulse quickened. The memory of their last kiss sent a shiver down her spine. She recalled the feel of his shoulders, the corded muscles against her fingertips.

Cora danced on the balls of her feet. "Can I pick the kitten? Please?"

Garrett rubbed his chin. "I suppose."

The little girl glanced around the tiny space with its single bank of whitewashed cupboards. "What's this room?"

"A nursery," Garrett replied.

Jo's legs quaked. If this were a real marriage, she'd have added curtains, and her mother would have passed on the hand-carved bassinet from her grandmother.

The realization sank through her body like a stone, dragging down her spirits. Emotions flickered across Garrett's face, and she wondered if he felt the same loss, the same disappointment.

Suddenly chilled, she wrapped her arms around her body. "This would make a better playroom for you than a nursery."

Garrett flinched and turned away.

Cora stepped between them, jerking Jo's thoughts back to the present.

"Which room is mine?" the little girl asked.

"You can pick," Garrett replied, his voice hoarse. "I guess Jo gets the biggest room."

"It doesn't matter." Jo ran her finger along the window sash. There'd be no need for curtains at all, not for a playroom. "You can have the larger room."

"I couldn't."

"Fine then." She turned, but couldn't bring herself to look him in the face. "I'll take the room at the head of the stairs."

Anything to end this painful conversation.

"How come you're not sharing?" Cora asked. "My mommy and daddy shared a room."

Jo sputtered, and Garrett coughed.

"Well." She cringed. "There are so many rooms, there's no need for any of us to share."

Jo snatched the bandanna from her head and rubbed the perspiration from the back of her neck. "You can pick the kitten. We can go next weekend."

"Today." Garrett spoke a notch too loudly. "We could leave right now."

Jo giggled at the absurdity of it all. The tension in the room eased at her outburst, and she and Garrett backed away from each other, putting space between them. Separating them from the swirl of emotions permeating the cramped room.

Garrett caught her amused expression, and a smile spread across his face. "Maybe it's time for a break."

"That's a good idea."

Jo remained in the room long after they'd both returned downstairs. There was no going back now. Even if she refused the marriage, where did that leave her? Back to her room at the boardinghouse, back to her job each morning, back to Sunday dinners at home.

The boys would bring home their new brides, and soon the babies would follow.

A baby.

It was like a revelation, this sudden driving need. Worse yet, it had appeared out of the thin blue sky with no warning. She'd long ago given up the thought of a family of her own. Standing with Garrett, imagining the nursery decorated as it was intended, she'd been rocked with a need stronger than anything she'd ever known.

Alone, her future was certain. Married, there was always a glimmer of hope. Perhaps through the years he'd come to see her as more than a tomboy. More than a companion.

She'd thought marrying someone out of friendship was the easy solution.

Turned out there were no shortcuts in life.

# Chapter Eighteen

Stunned, Jo focused on her image in the looking glass. "Is that really me?"

Beatrice fluffed her veil and let the lace settle around her shoulders like a gossamer mantle. "You're lovely."

A gasp sounded from the far side of the room and Jo turned. Her mother stood in the doorway, one hand clutching Cora's and the other covering her mouth.

"Oh, my goodness," Edith said, her voice watery with emotion. "How? When?"

Jo pleated her ivory skirts with two fingers. "This is the dress Elizabeth left for me. Beatrice took the lace off the collar and we left the pin tucks."

"But what about the dress from the mercantile?" Her ma took a hesitant step forward, her arm outstretched. "And your hair."

"Beatrice arranged it for me this morning." Jo touched the elaborate knot at the base of her neck. "How do I look?"

"Lovely. Absolutely lovely."

For once, Edith McCoy didn't look pressed and polished. Her ma had obviously dressed quickly that morning and a loose end of her shirttail hung limply beneath the bodice of her best Sunday dress. Her hair had been whipped into a serviceable braid and wrapped around her head, but one loose end trailed down her shoulder. She appeared more frazzled than Jo could ever recall seeing her.

"Ma, why don't you have a seat." Jo hooked her arm beneath the dazed woman's elbow. "You were up all night with Mrs. Hendrick's newborn. Didn't the doc's wife come by? She said she was going to help when the time came."

"She was dear," Edith replied with a distracted nod. "She trained as a nurse back East, you know."

"Pa said everything went all right."

"I couldn't leave the poor thing alone. Her husband had his hands full with the two little ones and she was frightened something would happen to the new baby. She's still terrified since the last one was stillborn."

"That's why we let you sleep." Jo pressed her finger against a poking hairpin near her ear.

Beatrice slapped away her hand. "You've got ten more minutes. Stop wiggling."

"But it hurts."

With an air of long suffering, Beatrice adjusted the pin. "That better?"

"Yes." Jo scratched at the sore spot. "Beauty is painful."

"And your veil," her ma added breathlessly. "Is that your grandmother's veil?"

"Don't you remember? You sent it over yesterday."

"I know, but I thought…I thought *I'd* help you get ready." A fine sheen of tears formed in her ma's eyes.

Unsure of the cause of Edith's distress, Jo awkwardly patted her hand. "I did just fine on my own."

Her ma choked out a sob.

"Uh…" Jo hesitated. Everything she said made the situation worse.

Beatrice clucked and steered the distressed woman before the looking glass. "You look a bit windblown from the ride. Why don't I fix your braid and give those cheeks a pinch of color."

"My cake didn't turn out," her ma moaned as Beatrice fussed around her, smoothing her hair and brushing the dust from her jacket. "It's too hot and the frosting melted. It looks like one of Maxwell's mud pies."

"I'm sure it tastes fine," Jo chimed in helpfully.

"And I didn't fix the lemonade," Edith continued without pause. "Now we'll be stuck with Mrs. Stuart's lemonade and she never puts in enough sugar."

"I'll have the boys sneak in an extra cup."

Edith remained limp beneath Beatrice's ministrations. "I wanted today to be special for you."

"It is special." Jo stood behind her ma and met her gaze in the mirror. "Now, stop worrying."

Her ma whirled and squeezed Jo until the tiny pearl buttons bit into her back. "I love you."

"I love you, too."

Jo groaned, and her ma loosened her hold and held her at a distance. "You look beautiful. You look just like your grandmother."

Jo grimaced at the dim memory she held of her paternal grandmother, a squat woman with dark, bushy eyebrows. "I guess I didn't know Grandma McCoy when she was young."

"Not her!" Edith lightly swatted Jo's shoulder. "*My* mother. She was quite a beauty in her time. Gracious, the stories they used to tell about her. Your grandfather followed her from England. He said he would have followed her around the world and back again."

A pang of emotion fluttered in Jo's chest. She resolutely tamped it down. This wasn't a dime novel, this was her life, and she was facing the truth of her situation head-on. They were doing this for Cora, and the sacrifice was well worth any personal doubts. Cora was opening up, smiling and talking. She still didn't speak of her parents or her loss. They took each good day as a blessing and each painful day as a cobblestone on the path toward healing.

A gentle knock sounded, and Mary Louise peered in. "Are you ready? Looks like the whole town turned out. They're getting restless."

"I'm ready." Jo glanced down as Cora lifted a basket for her inspection. "They look like pear blossoms, don't they?"

Cora nodded.

"I love you." Jo grinned, then knelt and embraced the little girl in a warm hug. "Do you know you get the seat of honor during the wedding? Right between Grandma and Grandpa."

The little girl's cornflower-blue eyes widened, and Edith sniffled. "Come along. We'd best claim our seats."

As Beatrice, Cora and her ma hustled from the room, Ely McCoy appeared in the doorway. He wore his finest navy suit, pressed and cleaned for the occasion. He'd even trimmed his mustache and shaved his beard for the occasion. When she'd seen him early that morning, he'd been as bristly as a bear.

Jo gaped. "You look so…so young! Did you go to the barber?"

Ely rubbed his hand down his face, dislodging a bit of cloth covering a nick from his close shave. "Couldn't walk my little girl down the aisle looking like a fur trapper."

Tears prickled in Jo's eyes as her pa pulled her into his comforting embrace.

He stepped back and held her at arm's length. "I don't want to muss you up now. You look as pretty as a princess."

"Thank you."

"You're sure this is what you want?"

"I'm sure," Jo lied with newly practiced ease. "More certain than I've ever been about anything in my life."

Her reply wasn't the whole truth—there were parts of her future she feared. No one need know of her unease.

"Because I've got the wagon hitched outside." He jerked his thumb over one shoulder. "We could high-tail it outta here."

"Pa," Jo warned. "Garrett Cain is a good man."

"I know. But I'm losing my little girl. Give your old man a chance to hang on a little longer."

"You'll never lose me, Pa."

"I will lose a part of you, but that's how it's meant to be. You grow and go your own way. It doesn't mean it's easy, though. I remember the first time I held you in my arms. You fit right in my hand." He held out his arm, palm up, as though reliving the memory. "I still you see you that way."

Jo pressed a hand against her quivering stomach. "I'm all grown up now."

"I want you to know what a blessing you've been in my life. You're the spring in my step each morning. I know you and Garrett will make a fine family together. Despite my teasing, I have a good feeling about you two. A real good feeling."

"I don't think Ma is too happy. She hasn't said anything outright, but whenever the subject comes up, she pinches her lips together and inhales through her nose."

"It's never good for any of us when your mother gets to looking like she ate a lemon. I do know one thing—your ma wants what's best for you."

"*This* is what's best for me."

"Then you'll have to show her, won't you? She'll come around."

They linked elbows, and her pa covered her hand with his and gave her fingers a squeeze. "You know in your heart if what you're doing is right."

"I know, Pa." If she said the words enough, maybe they'd come true. "I know for certain."

Cora needed her, and Garrett needed them both.

Ely searched her face. Appearing satisfied with what he saw, he asked, "Did you get the present I left you?"

Jo lifted the hem of her skirts, revealing her brand-new cowboy boots of butterscotch-colored leather with cream floral stitching. "They're perfect."

"I had 'em sent down on the train from Wichita special."

"Aren't you afraid of what Ma's going to do when she finds out?"

"Why should I be?" Her pa toed open the door. "She picked them out herself."

Garrett paced a tight circle in the tiny church vestibule, fidgeting with the red rose in his lapel. Had it only been a few short weeks since he'd sat before the reverend, absorbing the news of Deirdre's death?

Little Maxwell tugged on his pant leg. "Do you know why bees buzz?"

"Uh, no."

"Because they can't whistle."

Garrett chuckled. "That's a good one."

The little guy had attached himself to Garrett earlier

in the day and didn't show any signs of disappearing. "Shouldn't you be with your family?"

"Nah. I'm okay with you. Caleb said if you were nervous I should tell you jokes. Are you nervous?"

"A little bit."

"How come?"

"Because I want to do the right thing, and I'm not certain what that is anymore."

Garrett considered Flynn's advice. He should have told Jo the truth. He'd started telling her a thousand times and then stopped himself short. He craved her respect. She liked him, even trusted him. Exposing his past risked their untried friendship. Was he betraying Jo for his own peace of mind?

"I have another joke," Maxwell announced.

Garrett nodded. "I'm listening."

"How do you get a rooster to stop crowing on Sunday?"

"I dunno, how?"

"Eat him on Saturday."

Garrett chuckled again. "That's a good one, too."

"My ma says that she hopes Jo knows what's she's doing, or you two are going to be miserable."

"Your ma's right." Garrett thought of the one thing that had given him courage over the past weeks. "Have you ever known a time when Jo didn't know her own mind?"

The littlest McCoy screwed up his face in concentration. "Nope."

"Me neither."

"Can I come play with Cora when you and Jo are married?"

"Certainly."

A knot of townsfolk filed through the vestibule. Ely

McCoy approached the opposite door, and Garrett spun around. He didn't want to see JoBeth before the ceremony. Not that he counted himself a superstitious man, but he wanted to wait.

"Do you have a ring?" Maxwell asked.

"Yep." Garrett fished in his vest pocket and revealed a circlet of flat ruby stones set in gold. "What do you think? It's been in my family for generations."

Deirdre had insisted he keep the ring, and he was glad for once he'd listened.

"Wow." The young boy's eyes widened. "That's fancy."

Garrett ruffled Maxwell's dark hair, then turned at the press of a hand against his shoulder.

Reverend Miller motioned. "It's time."

Sucking in a deep breath, Garrett nodded. "Max, I reckon we're the two best-looking fellows in Cimarron Springs."

"I reckon we are."

The two joined hands and set off down the aisle. Garrett kept his attention focused on the altar. The church was packed with townspeople, and he felt their curious gazes following his progress. Voices rippled like waves with each of his steps.

Doubts crowded his thoughts. If his past was a lie, did he deserve a better future? As his steps slowed, he caught sight of the back of Cora's head, her coronet of flowers and the yellow ribbons trailing down her back. He shook his head, clearing the cobwebs. Cora deserved the best he could offer. Jo was a gift to each of them. He'd do right by her.

Sunlight streamed through the stained-glass window and cast angled rainbow patterns over the wooden floor. He'd pretend his past was the blank slate he'd created in his mind. The doubts would return; they'd worm their way into his heart and soul once more, but for now he held them at bay.

For today, he'd pretend nothing chained his soul.

He caught sight of Jo at the end of the aisle, and his heart tripped. She glided toward him, hand in hand with her father, an aged lace veil draped over her thick, dark hair. From beneath the fluttering edge, he caught the elegant curve of her neck. She wore an ivory gown—simple, elegant. His heart ached at the missing braid she usually wore tossed over one shoulder.

The barest glimpse of the nape of her neck warmed his blood. His gaze swept down the length of her, taking in the graceful sweep of her dress. The bodice had a modest V neck lined with delicate pin tucking, nipped in at an impossibly slim waist. She clutched a posy of wild red roses in her hand.

Her father flipped her veil over her hair, then kissed the bloom of each cheek. Garrett's palms dampened, and his mouth went dry.

She paused before him, and he found himself mesmerized by her rose-colored lips. The sound of someone clearing his throat sent the congregation tittering, and Garrett jerked his gaze away from Jo. Ely McCoy stared at him, one bushy eyebrow raised in censure.

Garrett flashed an abashed grin. "Sir."

Grasping his hand, Ely leaned in and whispered, "You take care of her or you'll answer to me."

Garrett nodded. The older man pumped his hand in a bone-crushing grip and took his seat in the first pew with Cora and his wife. The little girl remained solemn, but she appeared brighter than she had since the fire, and Garrett took that as a sign of encouragement.

The rest of the ceremony passed in a blur. The resonant words of the cleric echoed off the timber ceiling in solemn declaration. Garrett repeated his lines on cue and slipped the ring on Jo's finger when the moment arrived. She glanced at the rubies and back up at him. Garrett held his breath and waited for her reaction. When she smiled her approval, the tension drained from his shoulders. He hadn't even realized he was nervous until she'd flashed her assent.

The relief remained when Reverend Miller closed his Bible and cleared his throat. "You may now kiss the bride."

Garrett blinked.

Jo tipped back her head.

The church and all the congregants faded into the background. In that moment, only he and Jo existed. He slipped one hand around her waist, his callused fingers catching on the satin-wrapped buttons at her back. The arm clutching her bouquet lifted, and the scent of wild roses drifted through the air. For the rest of his life, he knew he'd always associate the scent with this moment.

The moment their lips touched, Jo sighed. Her hands crept up his neck, lifting her bouquet as a floral shield against their rapt audience. She clung to him with a fervor that matched his own before they broke apart and stared at each other in breathless silence.

The room erupted into noisy applause, and he and Jo faced the congregation. They trusted him, and he was more determined than ever to keep that trust.

# *Chapter Nineteen*

The next few hours passed in a blur for Jo. Seemed like everyone within a fifty-mile radius of Cimarron Springs had come. Her ma's cozy wedding had turned into a bustling crowd, and Jo's feet ached in her new boots. The party had been too large for the confines of the church and spilled into the sunny afternoon.

Checkered cloths covered the tables and children crowded hip to hip along the benches. They eagerly jostled forward, loading their plates with cakes and pies. Abraham emerged from around the corner of the church, a pitcher of lemonade in his hands, the contents sloshing from side to side.

He winked at her. "Sweet enough even for Ma."

Edith McCoy stood in a clutch of women holding their ribboned bonnets against the afternoon breeze. Once the ceremony had passed, her ma had finally relaxed.

Jo snagged a glass of lemonade and ducked behind the shed. Her solitude was short lived. Tom and his wife circled around the opposite side, their voices raised in harsh, arguing whispers. Jo gulped her lemonade and slipped around the other side. She didn't want Tom ruining her day with any of his rude comments.

Unaccustomed to being the center of attention, she plastered a stiff smile upon her face and called cheerful greetings in response to the many well-wishers.

Catching sight of her sagging against a doorjamb, Garrett grasped her hand and pulled her away from the crowd.

Jo groaned and patted her face. "My cheeks are going to crack if I smile anymore."

"Mine, too."

"Do you think we can sneak out of here?" she muttered. "Cora is staying with my family tonight, remember? Maxwell promised her a slingshot lesson in the morning."

Garrett rubbed his forehead. "I'll have two women who can outshoot me in the family now."

"Then you'd better behave yourself."

"Come along." Garrett clasped her hand. "If we cut behind the buildings, we can make it home in no time."

"It's a half mile down the road from town."

"A good stretch of the legs."

Jo groaned. Her feet ached, but she wanted an escape more than she wanted to rest.

They'd spent the past week painting and cleaning the house, and Jo had delivered her belongings that morning. Working beside Garrett had finally made their impending marriage real. After spending days scrubbing every dusty corner of the house, she'd grown no more accustomed to the idea of living with Garrett.

Together they tiptoed behind the livery, giggling and shushing each other. As they slunk around the corner, Garrett flung his arm around her waist and pressed a finger against his lips. Jo stilled. He cupped one hand against his ear and Jo leaned forward.

She caught the low hum of her brothers' voices from inside the livery.

She heard David's voice first.

"Are you sure you saw them leave?" he asked.

"They're sneaking back home, I know it," Caleb replied.

"We can throw the marshal in the horse tank."

"Nah," Caleb muttered. "This is better."

"Okay," David agreed. "I've got the lard for the doorknobs and pots and pans."

Jo gasped, and the marshal pressed a hand over her mouth, then scooted her away from the boys' hushed conversation.

"It's a shivaree!" she exclaimed in a harsh whisper.

"What's that?"

"A horrible country custom," Jo declared. "They'll run through the house making noise and causing pranks."

"Then let's not go home."

"What do you mean?" Torn between duty and propriety, Jo hesitated. "Where will we go?"

Garrett flashed a mischievous smile. "Do you trust me?"

"Yes," Jo answered, feeling as addled as when he'd kissed her at the altar.

"Then let's go for a ride."

Garrett grasped her hand and tugged her into a dash. Joy rushed through her, and the pain in her feet faded into the background. They rounded the corner of the livery, and Garrett peered in the door. He held a finger to his lips, compelling her to silence, and disappeared inside. A moment later he returned, grasping the reins of his horse.

Jo glanced behind her, relieved her brothers were distracted by their plotting. Garrett leaped onto the horse and held out his arm. She clambered onto the mounting block and perched sidesaddle before him, one knee looped around the saddle horn.

A voice called, and Jo craned her neck. Beatrice chased after them, waving her arms.

"Wait," she called breathlessly. "Don't ruin your grandmother's lace."

Jo reached up and touched her head. She still wore the heirloom veil. She quickly released the pins and shook off the decoration. "How did you find us?"

Gasping, Beatrice leaned heavily on Jo's leg and pressed a hand against her side. "I came to warn you. Your brothers are planning a shivaree."

"We caught them in the livery. They're getting lard for the doorknobs." Jo scowled. "And after I spent the whole week cleaning."

"Don't you worry. I'll let your pa know they're up to something. He'll keep them in line."

"You'll be saving their hides from me." Jo leaned down and shared an awkward embrace from her high perch. "Thank you for remembering my veil."

Beatrice sketched another wave and backed away from the prancing horse. Jo heaved a sigh of relief. Between her parents and Beatrice, the boys couldn't cause too much mischief.

Garrett fiddled with the saddlebag at her knee and pulled out the hat Jo had been eyeing at the mercantile weeks ago. A leather drover's hat.

"How did you know?" She gaped.

Garrett winked at her. "Can't a groom give his wife a wedding gift?"

She lifted her gift and felt the supple brown leather.

Garrett reached for the hat, and she pulled it away

"You don't have to wear it now," he said. "I didn't think about your hair."

Touching the pins poking her tender skull, Jo grimaced. "I think I can let it down now. I've suffered enough."

She loosened the pins and shook her hair free of all Beatrice's careful ministrations. For a blissful moment she ran her fingers over her sore scalp, groaning with relief. "That's better." Jo caught his pained expression. "Oh, dear, I didn't get you anything. I'm sorry."

"Yes, you did."

Jo searched his expression. "What?"

"I'll tell you later. Now hang on."

She slapped the hat on her head and smiled. It fit perfect. Not too loose and not too snug.

She sneaked a peek at his relaxed expression. He obviously wasn't holding a grudge over her oversight. "Let's go."

Kicking his horse into a gallop, Garrett let out a holler. Unused to the awkward position, Jo clutched the corded muscle of the arm anchored around her waist.

He was strong and solid. He'd never let her fall.

She clutched her hat with one hand and glanced over her shoulder. "Where are we going?"

"It's a surprise."

As the horse galloped, the wind tugged on her hair like a thousand fingers, ripping loose the carefully created curls at the nape of her neck Beatrice had worked on only hours before. With the wedding done, and the ground rushing by, Jo was herself again.

Garrett kept his right hand looped in the reins, his left arm protectively around her waist. "You okay?"

"Yes," Jo shouted over the whistling wind. She was more than okay. "I want to holler," she called.

"Then do it."

Jo whooped, her voice lost on the breeze. She released one hand and raised her palm to the sky.

The horse's gait slowed as they rounded a corner out of town, out of sight of any curious eyes that might have seen their escape.

Jo adjusted her hat and glanced around at the familiar surroundings. "Say, we're going back to the house."

"Not quite."

Garrett reined in the horse and cut across the field toward Hackberry Creek. Tall grass brushed at her knees, and Jo tucked her skirts tighter to her body as they crossed into the tree line.

When the underbrush became too impassable for the horse, Garrett halted. "We'll walk from here."

Growing more curious by the moment, Jo slid down first, and Garrett followed. He looped the reins around a low-hanging tree branch and fished in his saddlebags.

After a moment he turned and shook out a long duster. "Put this over your dress so you don't get too dirty."

He wrapped the enveloping coat around her shoulders, and Jo sank into its warmth. The sun was setting, cooling the evening air. Garrett clasped her hand and led her deeper into the wooded area surrounding the creek. The smell of damp earth teased her nostrils. Her feet sank into the soft earth, and branches tugged at her skirts. It would take a load of elbow grease to remove the stains, but she didn't mind. She was ready for an adventure, and nothing was going to hold her back.

Garrett halted and pointed toward the towering branches. "I found this when I was walking the property line."

Jo tilted back her head and shaded her eyes. "It's a tree house."

A great pin oak towered above the timberline, and someone had built a crude structure in the sheltering cradle of its branches. Jo circled the enormous trunk, her fingers trailing along the rough bark. "I bet if we held our hands together, we couldn't circle that trunk."

"This tree must be fifty years old."

"Can you imagine? Think what this tree has seen. There wasn't even a town around here fifty years ago."

Boards had been nailed into the sturdy trunk and Garrett grasped one. "They're solid. I climbed up myself two days ago. There's a break in the trees, and you can see all the way to the road."

Jo gauged the distance. "Let's climb up."

"Are you certain? You'll ruin your dress."

"I don't care."

His expression remained dubious. "Can you climb in skirts?"

Jo flashed a mischievous grin. "All my life."

She grasped the bottom rung and hoisted herself up. Her boot caught on her hem and Garrett tugged the material loose. She looped her skirts over one arm and easily climbed the rest of the way. The wood was rough with age, but she barely noticed with her work-roughened hands. A trapdoor had been cut into the floor, and she hoisted herself over the edge.

As Jo studied the tiny house, Garrett clambered inside. Someone had built a perfect little structure, complete with a roof and open-air windows. The enormous trunk burst right through the middle of the floor and the branches stuck out through the center of the shingled roof. Every surface was dusty, and Garrett's previous footprints showed in the dirt.

He pushed off with a hand on one knee and stood, his back hunched against the low ceiling, then reached for her. "C'mon, I'll show you the best part."

Curious, she let him guide her to the opposite edge. A window cut in the side offered a view all the way to the road, and the roof of their new house showed in the distance.

Clouds gathered on the horizon, blocking the setting sun. "Looks like we might get a storm."

Garrett shrugged out of his coat and laid it over the floor. He helped her down and sat beside her. "We can wait here for a while until your brothers lose interest."

"Or until the rain comes." Jo glanced up at the spotty ceiling. "There's not much shelter."

Jo shivered, and Garrett wrapped an arm around her shoulders. "Are you too cold? We don't have to stay."

"No," Jo protested quickly. She liked it here. She liked being alone for once. Since Cora's arrival, her life had been full of people and activity. Not that she minded, but having an hour to themselves felt like decadent luxury.

Jo studied her hands. "I saw you talking with Mr. Stuart."

"Yep."

"Are you any closer to finding out who shot Mr. Hodges?"

"Some."

His clipped response soured her jubilant mood. At times she thought she'd gained ground, earned his trust. Then she realized he remained rigid and unyielding, closed off from her behind his monosyllabic answers.

Garrett pressed his cheek against the top of her hair. "I'd rather talk about something more cheerful."

"Fair enough," Jo replied.

They sat in companionable silence as darkness fell. She yawned, and Garrett soon followed with a yawn of his own. "Why don't you close your eyes and rest a moment," he said. "I'll wake you when it's time."

A curious lethargy stole over Jo. She hadn't slept well the evening before, worrying about the wedding. She'd risen earlier than normal to get ready. "You don't mind?"

"Nope."

She closed her eyes and rested her head on his shoulder. Cottonwood leaves rustled overhead and crickets chirped around her, lulling her into sleep. She dozed off and on, comforted by the warmth of Garrett's embrace. At one point she heard voices in the distance, and figured the boys were up to their mischief.

"Garrett," she said around another yawn. "Thank you for a perfect day."

Garrett woke with a start. Disoriented, he glanced around and realized he and Jo had fallen asleep in the tree house. He rubbed his eyes with the heels of his hands and stretched. Dew dampened his hair and face, and he shivered in the purple light of dawn.

He hadn't won any awards for romance, that's for certain. Jo curled against his side for warmth, and he cradled her against his chest, savoring the moment. Rarely did he have the chance to study her, and, suddenly, it seemed important he take this rare opportunity. Her face was serene in repose, innocent. Surrendering his rigid self-control, he remained still until she stirred against his side.

He reluctantly broke the contact, determined to keep the promise he'd made to himself. To Jo.

The sun hadn't yet banked the horizon, and only a faint hint of Jo's ivory dress glowed in the darkness. Lightning sparked in the distance, briefly illuminating the canopy of leaves above his head. As much as he wanted to linger, he feared the gathering storm.

He felt around the floor for the lamp he'd left there earlier. Upon discovering the tree house, he'd made plans to show Jo the charming structure. Not on their wedding night, of course, he thought with a wry chuckle, but he was grateful they'd avoided the shivaree.

Careful not to jostle his sleeping bride, he lit the wick and adjusted the light. Jo grumbled beside him, then stretched and yawned. His heart thumped against his ribs. She'd been breathtakingly lovely in church, but he preferred her this way—wild and untamed. Her hair, shaken free from its pins, hung over her shoulders in loose waves beneath her leather hat.

Even as he watched, her eyes fluttered open. A delicate frown appeared between her brows. She stared at him for a long beat, her pale face sleepy and vulnerable. He'd give every possession he owned to kiss her awake, but he held himself rigidly in check. Since Flynn's arrival he'd kept his distance. Yesterday had been a dream, but it was after midnight and yesterday was gone. Their brief peck in the church had shaken his resolve, but he hadn't faltered.

Another flash of lightning startled her upright, and he immediately felt the loss of her comforting warmth.

Jo hugged his slicker around her shoulders and trembled. "Looks like we'll get more rain this evening."

Reluctant to abandon the precious cocoon of the evening, Garrett nodded. "We'd best get back."

He descended the crude ladder first and reached for the lantern. Jo handed down the light and scaled the ladder, her movements quick and agile.

"Do you know your way in the dark?" she asked.

"Mostly. Let me fetch my horse. Take my hand, there's a lot of underbrush."

Her fingers were cold, and he tucked them into the crook of his elbow. She tightened her grip and leaned into his support. Holding the lantern ahead of them, he lit their way through the darkness. Jo made a soft sound, and he halted. She plowed into his back.

"Is something wrong?" he asked.

"Nope," she replied, but he sensed the strain in her voice. "Actually, it's my feet. I'm breaking in a new pair of boots."

She revealed a pair of pointed-toe butterscotch-colored boots with cream stitching.

Garrett blew out a low whistle. "That's some fancy footwear."

"They're called cowboy boots. A fellow up in Wichita makes them. The stitching helps the leather keep its shape. My folks ordered them special."

"You sure are one of a kind."

Garrett let out another, louder whistle and his horse, Blue, nickered in response. The underbrush crackled as they neared the horse, and trees rustled overhead in the increasing wind.

He reached out one hand. "You can ride and I'll lead the way with the lantern."

Jo gave a weary nod, and Garrett realized she'd reached the end of her endurance. "Not much longer now," he offered by way of reassurance.

He circled her waist and easily lifted her onto the saddle. She rearranged her skirts and they set off once more. As they resumed their weary journey, the indigo horizon lightened enough he extinguished the lamp flame. The air was thick and damp, but no rain fell, and for that he was grateful. The path from the creek led them to the back of the house, and he paused on the freshly cut lawn.

Garrett caught sight of the porch and a trickle of apprehension stilled his progress. The back door stood open.

Jo slid off the horse, and he placed a restraining hand on her arm.

"Wait here," he ordered as he relit the lantern.

Without his gun, Garrett moved cautiously. He pressed open the door with one hand and lifted the lantern. His stomach clenched at the shocking sight. The entire room had been ransacked. Broken crockery littered the floor between piles of flour, sugar and salt. The overturned kitchen table and chairs blocked his path, and he sagged against the doorjamb.

He felt rather than heard Jo close the distance behind him.

"What happened?" she asked, craning her neck. "Oh, gracious," she said, her voice faltering.

Attempting to block her view, he turned and grasped her shoulders. "Let me check the rooms first. The people who did this might still be here."

"Why?" She stared up at him, her eyes wide and bewildered in the dim lamplight. "Why would the boys do this?"

"The boys didn't do this."

She shoved him aside and stepped into the kitchen, her hands on her hips. "When you find out who did, I get first go at them."

Garrett grunted his response and studied the ravaged room. The damage was malicious and angry, and he didn't for a moment believe the McCoys had been involved. He considered searching the outbuildings, but there was no place to hide except the barn, and the animals would be agitated if they had company.

Besides, if he left Jo long enough for the trip to and from the outbuildings, she'd search the house herself and he didn't want her stumbling into danger.

Though reluctant to leave her, even in the kitchen, Garrett needed the building searched. "Promise me you'll wait here?"

Looking dazed, she absently nodded her head. Garrett quickly toured the house, his rage growing with each room. The mattresses had all been slashed and feathers littered the floor. Even Cora's room had been tossed.

He soon realized the pillagers had fled, and the house was empty. He returned downstairs and found Jo kneeling on the littered floor, a broken plate in her hand, her expression stunned.

Garrett crouched behind her and gently wrapped his arms around her shoulders. "I'm sorry."

"It's not your fault," she spoke, her voice no more than a whisper. "I don't know anyone who would do this."

Even the Walbys, who'd been cruel with their words and their deeds, had never shown this kind of violence in their actions.

"I don't know, either."

The dish fell from her limp fingers. "I wanted our wedding day to be perfect."

Garrett fished out his pocket watch and checked the time. "It's six in the morning. Our wedding day ended at midnight. It's still perfect."

A sob shook her shoulders, and he couldn't recall a time he'd ever felt more helpless. He cradled her against his chest and brushed the tangled curls from her forehead.

Her body stiffened. "I can't make up my mind if I'm angry or sad."

"I'll find out who did this. I promise."

"I know you will." She sniffled and swiped the back of her hand across the pink tip of her nose. "I don't understand why someone would do this. It's so destructive, so hateful."

She clutched his hand and he realized she was ice-cold. Garrett chaffed her shoulders and nestled her against his warmth. "It's early and we're both exhausted. I'll rustle up some blankets and we can snatch an hour or two of sleep down here. I don't think they'll come back, but I want you close just in case."

After arranging a couple of makeshift beds in the dining room, Jo limped around the room, stepping over broken dishes.

"Sit," Garrett ordered.

"I can't. I can't relax."

"Let me help."

He lowered her onto the blankets and arranged the pillows behind her back, then tugged off her boots. Jo groaned. Encouraged by her response, he massaged the delicate arch of her foot with the pads of his thumbs.

"That's wonderful." She sighed.

He continued the gentle pressure on her other foot. Gradually her shoulders drooped, and her eyes fluttered shut. After tucking the blanket more securely around her shoulders, Garrett started the cleanup in the early dawn light. The lantern burned low and flickered shadows on the walls as he swept up feathers and straightened their scattered clothing.

The damage was targeted and personal. Done by someone who wanted revenge. Garrett had an idea who that person might be, but he couldn't reveal his suspicions without proof. If his hunch was correct, the troublemaker was guilty of more than vandalism.

Garrett was searching for a murderer.

## Chapter Twenty

Two days following her marriage, Jo lifted a bolt of fabric from the mercantile display and held the yellow calico before her in the mirror. She tilted her head to one side and made a face.

Mary Louise appeared behind her in the reflection. "We have a ready-made in the blue. I think that color would go much better with your hair."

"There's not enough gravy for this goose." Jo sighed.

The blond-haired girl lifted an eyebrow.

"Never mind," Jo added quickly. "I'll see the blue."

Mary Louise disappeared into the backroom.

With her family watching Cora to give the newly-weds time alone together, she and Garrett had spent the two days following the wedding cleaning up the house. They'd kept the damage a secret from the McCoys, since she didn't want to worry them. Despite her casual demeanor toward the incident, a sense of unease had permeated her days. Garrett had assured her they were safe, and she'd put on a brave face.

For two nights she'd tossed and turned, and she'd finally decided a trip into town was in order. Though school was out for the summer, Cora was studying with the teacher three mornings a week. Garrett avoided Jo at every possible opportunity.

Mary Louise returned holding a deep blue calico dress with blue, yellow and white flowers woven into the pattern.

"Try it on. The seams are only slip-stitched. I can have it finished in a day or two."

Without waiting for an answer, Mary Louise hustled her into the change room, where Jo struggled into the dress. Minutes later, a knock sounded on the door.

"Are you finished yet?" Mary Louise called.

Jo emerged from the room and smoothed the material over her stomach. "It's one piece. I never wear one piece."

"Maybe you should. You look lovely."

She guided Jo before the full-length mirror propped against a shelf of fabric bolts.

The dress was deceptively simple, a scoop neck with three-quarter sleeves and a deep V seaming at the waist. Jo turned from side to side. "It's not so bad."

Mary Louise lifted Jo's braid and draped it over the top of her head. "We could put this up with only a few pins."

Jo touched the side of her face. "What will people say?"

"You never struck me as the sort of person who wasted time on what other people thought."

Despite her quiet demeanor, Mary Louise had pinned Jo's braid around her head before she'd even thought of a suitable protest. Mary Louise fussed for another minute, then stepped back.

"That's better."

Jo glanced at her reflection again. She looked older, more sophisticated. Not foolish or silly at all.

Voices sounded from the store, and Mary Louise stepped before the door. Her face lit up, and Jo followed the direction of her gaze.

*David.*

Mary Louise fluffed her hair with both hands. "I have to see to a customer."

Jo quickly donned her serviceable shirtwaist and skirt and ventured into the main store. One look at David and Mary Louise together and Jo realized Garrett had been right. The two were sweet on each other.

David caught sight of her and flushed. "Garrett asked me to come by today. Do you know what it's about?"

"I think so. Why don't we have lunch?"

He stood in indecision, and Jo smirked. "Do you have a better offer?"

David cast a lingering glance at Mary Louise and slowly shook his head.

After they'd sat down at the Palace Café and the waitress had taken their orders, Jo frowned. "You'd best tell Caleb how you feel about Mary Louise."

David blanched. "Did your husband tell you?"

Her pulse stuttered at the title. That was the first time someone had referred to her as Garrett's wife. "Anyone can see by the way the two of you look at each other," she replied evasively.

"Nothing is settled yet. I can't marry unless I can support her. She wants to stay in Cimarron Springs, but there's more work for farmhands around Wichita."

"Garrett wants you to be his deputy."

David's face lit up like Christmas morning. "No fooling?"

"No fooling."

He threw back his shoulders and puffed out his chest. "I like the idea of that."

"Garrett is a good man. Don't let him down."

Tilting his head to one side, her brother squinted. "Did you do something different with your hair? You look older or something. Pretty."

Jo swatted his hand. "I hope you do better when you compliment Mary Louise." Her grin disappeared. "It still means you have to settle things with Caleb."

Her brother's face crumpled. "It's not going to be easy."

"The right thing never is." Jo rested her hand over his. "And the longer you wait, the harder it's going to be."

Garrett stood as Jo and David entered the room. He was suddenly conscious of the watermarks covering the battered desk he'd inherited from the previous sheriff. Glancing down, he caught sight of his loosened shirt-tail and surreptitiously tucked the beige material into his waistband.

His gaze lighted on David and lingered on Jo. She'd done something different with her hair. Instead of her usual, single braid, she'd wound the braid at the base of her neck. The difference was subtle, but pleasing.

Garrett circled the desk and scraped another chair into place. "Sit down, you two."

After they'd all gotten settled, he rubbed his face, wishing he'd shaved more carefully that morning. "I suppose Jo has told you what this is all about."

David leaned forward. "You need help."

"There are a lot of rumors floating around town, and business has slowed at the mercantile."

"People think Mr. Stuart shot Mr. Hodges?"

"Yep."

"What do you think?"

Garrett cast an uneasy glance at Jo. He trusted her, but he wasn't ready to speak about his theory just yet. "I have some ideas. But I need help."

As though on cue, Jo stood. "Why don't you two finish your discussion. I'll see if Cora is finished with the schoolteacher."

She swept out of the room and Garrett followed her progress. Since the marriage, he felt more estranged from her. They were testing the waters of this new relationship, carefully feeling for the boundaries. Too carefully. Their encounters were brittle and stilted. He didn't know how to keep his distance without jeopardizing their friendship.

"You were saying," David prodded.

Garrett startled to attention. "I need you to keep an eye on someone."

"Who?"

"Tom Walby."

David's eyes widened, and the younger man let out a low whistle. "You're in a real pickle, aren't you?"

Garrett thought of the evening ahead. Dinner with Jo. Small talk over the chores. His gaze drifting to her ripe, pink lips at every opportunity. "You don't know the half of it."

## Chapter Twenty-One

The next few weeks passed in relative peace for Jo. Her routine started at first light as she and Garrett rustled around the kitchen in companionable silence.

A gouge in the floor was the only evidence of the destruction from the night of their wedding, and Jo absently rubbed it with the tip of her boot. "How are you and David getting along?"

"Good. He's a hard worker. Smart."

Garrett had deputized her brother the week after their marriage and David had taken the sheriff's rooms above the jailhouse. Just as she'd suspected, the living arrangement with her new husband was similar to growing up with her brothers.

They treated one another like fellow boarders, each wary of disturbing the other patron. They took great pains to avoid encountering each other on the stairs or in the hall. There were no highs and lows, just the steady, polite talk of weather and the occasional outing with Cora. He'd been leaving earlier and earlier in the morning, and this time Jo wasn't letting him get away without talking to her.

She opened the pantry and searched the shelves. She

was certain there was a single jar of peach preserves hiding in the back somewhere. "I bet he's chomping at the bit for some excitement. We haven't had a fire or a shooting in weeks. Even Tom's been awful quiet."

"Yep."

Jo's curiosity peaked at his abrupt answer. "Maybe Tom has finally learned his lesson."

"Hope so."

She struggled with the lid on the jar of peach preserves. Garrett wasn't much of a talker first thing in the morning, but normally he didn't mind her idle chatter. "David said you had an idea who killed Mr. Hodges?"

"Suspicions. That's all."

"What about your cousin, Edward?"

"He landed an army contract from Fort Ryan." He plucked the jar from her stranglehold, easily popped the seal and handed it back. "Now that he's flush with cash again, he figures I'm a suitable guardian."

Jo smiled her thanks and set about making Cora's lunch. Growing up, she'd preferred being outside or in the barn caring for the animals. Lately, though, especially at times like this, she enjoyed the simple pleasure of sharing a quiet moment with Garrett.

Marriage was a lonely business. "Mrs. Fletcher said her husband has a milk cow he'd be willing to sell."

"That's a lot of work. There might be days when I'm gone, and I won't be able to help out."

Reaching for Cora's lunch pail, Jo considered his answer. "I bet Abraham could use some pocket money. Do you want me to ask if he'll come by once in a while for chores? I can pay him from my salary at the telegraph office."

"I have enough money."

While Jo didn't want to jeopardize this rare bout of

comfortable chatter, a question had been gnawing at her since the wedding. "Mrs. Fletcher said this was the first two-story house built in Kansas."

Garrett poured twin mugs of coffee from the blue enamel pot on the stove. "And she's wondering how a poor county marshal can afford such a fine house."

"Something like that." Jo felt her cheeks flush beneath his steady regard. "I told her to mind her own business."

"Empty houses sell cheap." Garrett passed her the steaming mug. "A drifter doesn't need much. I've built up some savings over the years."

"I didn't mean to pry. But I'm prepared to pay my fair share. Not enough for the house, of course, but I can help with expenses."

"You spend your money how you please. I've got enough to keep us set for a while." He named a sum that had her eyes widening.

Jo tittered nervously. "I can't believe you didn't starve. You can't have spent anything."

All her life she'd worried about money—the McCoys never had much. It was odd to think she'd changed her financial status simply by marrying. It felt like cheating. Then again, there weren't many chances for a woman to make money. And she definitely held her own with her share of the work and chores.

Jo sliced bread for sandwiches and slathered them with peach preserves. Behind her, Garrett knelt and retrieved his lunch pail from the bottom cupboard.

Their movements turned familiar, almost practiced, yet Jo felt as though she was playacting—like Cora and her dolls serving a make-believe tea party. There were times like this, when she felt as if her new life wasn't real. She could simply walk out the door and go back to her room at the boardinghouse and no one would even know the difference.

Jo shook her head. Cora would notice.

She glanced around the tidy kitchen, and her chest tightened. Freshly whitewashed cupboards and beadboard trim brightened the room, a perfect backdrop for the wedding gifts lining the shelves. Blue creamware pitchers, plates and opaque glasses stood beside the few brightly colored tins of spices she'd bought from the general store. On the walls, Garrett had hung the copper pots in a line by size. Jo figured that's why they got along so well. They both enjoyed order and routine.

He reached for the knife resting on the counter before her, and his arm brushed her shoulder. His hand drifted down and covered her fingers, and the air between them sparked like flint rocks. He reached his other arm around her back and gently crowded her against the counter.

Tucking his chin in the curve of her shoulder, he said, "You're cutting the slices too thin. Let me show you."

He guided her fingers over the handle of the knife and braced his other hand on the crusty loaf, then directed her motions.

"That's as thick as two slices." She laughed at the enormous cut he'd taken.

"You have five brothers. Surely you know a man needs more to eat than two thin slices of bread and a slather of jam."

Jo inhaled his dizzying scent. As large as the house was, living together beneath the same roof had driven them into closer and closer contact. It seemed inevitable they'd eventually be forced to touch each other.

He shifted and positioned the knife over the bread again. His skin was dark against hers and his hands coarse from years of labor. She'd never liked her own hands—they were rough and chapped and her nails never grew beyond the tips of her fingers. But next to Garrett's, they appeared almost delicate.

She wondered if she turned her head, would he kiss her. Her stomach tightened.

"Why are you smiling?" he said, his breath tickling her ear.

Embarrassed by the turn of her thoughts, Jo kept her attention focused on the counter. "What do you think about chickens?"

His chest rumbled against her back as he chuckled. "You're full of surprises, Mrs. Cain."

Blood rushed in her ears and she felt almost dizzy. She forgot sometimes she had a different name, but she liked the way he spoke it with his gravelly morning voice.

He carefully sliced another chunk of bread. "I like chickens. I like eggs in the morning. I like barn cats and watchdogs. Any other animals you'd like for your menagerie? How about a goat?"

"Absolutely not."

"What do you have against goats?"

"It's a long story." Jo smiled.

"What about sheep?"

"Definitely sheep. My pa would be so proud. His family raised sheep for wool back in Ireland."

"We'll knit the whole town sweaters for the winter."

"Even Mr. Stuart?"

"Especially Mr. Stuart. He doesn't have enough meat on his bones to keep him warm in the winter."

Garrett spun her around, pulled her into his embrace, and belted out, *"My wild Irish Rose, the sweetest flower that grows,"* in a low, pleasant baritone.

While she giggled, he whirled her through the kitchen in a clumsy waltz. *"You may search everywhere, but none can compare with my wild Irish Rose."*

Giddy with his infectious joy, Jo followed his lead. She'd never seen him behave with such abandon. They crashed into a chair and sprang apart. Smiling, Jo smoothed her hair. "You're usually so quiet in the morning, and here you are singing and dancing around the kitchen. What's gotten into you, Mr. Cain?" she said, mirroring the use of his name.

Appearing flustered, he reached for the overturned chair. "I don't know what came over me. Must have been all that talk of chickens."

He flushed, avoiding her gaze. Her lips tightened. While she'd enjoyed their spontaneous fun, Garrett appeared almost embarrassed by their shared enjoyment. Before she could voice her confusion, she caught sight of Cora at the top of the stairs.

"Did we wake you with our silliness?" Jo called.

The door closed behind her and Jo glanced over her shoulder. Garrett had fled. From past experience she knew he'd be quiet for the next few days. She clenched her jaw. If he was ashamed of her, he shouldn't have married her.

She recalled his words all those weeks ago—*I'm not capable of love.*

He'd lied to her.

She saw how he behaved with Cora, with his animals. He was more than capable of love. Which begged the question, why couldn't he love *her?* Though she'd vowed to let him keep his secrets, she didn't know how much longer she could take his changeable behavior.

She caught Cora's curious gaze. "It's almost time for your lessons. Why don't you get dressed."

Twenty minutes later Jo knelt before Cora and adjusted her collar. "It was nice of Mrs. Harper to help you with your numbers and letters over the summer. Are you enjoying your lessons?"

Cora clasped her hands. "I like it here. Maxwell is my best friend. I still miss my old room. I miss my mommy and daddy."

"Oh, baby." Tears pooled in Jo's eyes. "I'm so sorry."

"I like you. I like Uncle Garrett."

"I know. You can like us and miss your parents at the same time."

The little girl's brow furrowed. "Grandma said that, too."

"Grandma Edith is smart." Jo held out her hand for their morning walk. "She'd like you to stay overnight tonight." Her voice lowered. "Just between you and me, I think she's lonely. With David gone and the other boys spending so much time in the fields, the house is quiet. And Maxwell wants to show you his new dog."

The little girl grinned and eagerly nodded. Edith McCoy had fallen hopelessly in love with her new grandchild, and the feeling was obviously mutual. The two enjoyed their time together, and Jo encouraged the interaction. It brought them all together as a family. Cora needed plenty of love, and the McCoys had plenty of love to give.

Stepping outside, Jo glanced left and right. The street from their house curved right toward Cimarron Springs, and she adjusted her leather hat against the sun. While she'd made certain concessions toward a more feminine wardrobe, she wasn't giving up her gifted hat. The days were growing longer and hotter, though not intolerable just yet. Thankfully, a wet spring had turned into a stunningly beautiful early summer. The countryside bloomed with wildflowers and the creek bed swelled.

Garrett had offered to hitch the wagon for her, but she and Cora preferred the walk. By the time they arrived in town, a fine sheen of perspiration covered Jo's forehead.

She squeezed Cora's hand. "Tomorrow let's take the wagon. It's getting hotter than baking day."

Cora nodded with a grimace.

Jo left Cora in the teacher's capable hands, passed the boardinghouse and paused outside the marshal's office. Garrett felt something for her, she knew he did, and she deserved answers for his behavior. Gathering her courage, she lifted her hand, then paused midknock.

Bearding a lion in its den was never a good idea. If she confronted him before David, he'd turn defensive. She'd lived her whole life surrounded by men and had discovered a few things along the way.

She'd let Garrett work. But tonight, with Cora gone, they were going to talk. And this time she'd make certain he couldn't run away.

She'd glue him to the chair if need be.

## Chapter Twenty-Two

Mary Louise burst into Garrett's office, her face flushed. "They're fighting." She gasped. "And it's all my fault."

"Where?" he responded immediately.

"Behind the livery."

Garrett strapped on his gun and snatched his hat on the way out the back door. If Mary Louise was involved, it had to be the McCoy brothers. He followed the frantic woman to the corral behind the livery where Caleb and David wrestled in the dirt. Garrett fetched a bucket of water and doused the brawling pair. Coughing and sputtering, they sprang apart.

"What'd you go and do that for?" Caleb demanded.

Garrett tossed the pail aside. "You boys were making a mess. You want to tell me what this is all about?"

He already knew, but the two needed to work things out in the open with words, not fists.

The brothers exchanged a sullen glance. David broke away first, raking his hands through his hair.

Caleb glared at his back. "He stole my girl."

"She isn't a horse, son." Garrett raised an eyebrow. "It's not like he rustled her from the corral one night."

Caleb swiped the wet hair from his eyes. "He stole her just the same. She was sweet on me."

"She was being nice," David said. "That's how she is."

"What do you know? You don't love her."

David's arm shot out and he grasped a fistful of his brother's shirt. "That's not for you to say, is it?"

Garrett latched his hand around David's wrist and shook loose his hold. "Fighting isn't going to solve any of this." He encompassed the two in his question. "Has the lady made her choice known?"

Caleb aimed an accusing glare at his brother. "She's going for a buggy ride with David tomorrow. That don't mean she's sweet on him. She's probably just being *nice*." He bitterly drew out the last word.

David's face hardened. "You asked her for a buggy ride, too. What did she say?"

"She was busy." Caleb's face reddened. "That's all. That's why she couldn't come."

"She didn't want to hurt your feelings."

"You don't know that."

The two leaped for each other again, and Garrett held his arms askew between them. "This isn't going to be solved with a brawl. Why don't you two cool off."

David stalked away, and Garrett studied Caleb. He'd been paying close attention to Mary Louise over the past few weeks, and he was certain she'd chosen David. The two sweethearts were walking on eggshells, afraid of hurting Caleb.

Garrett swiped the back of his hand across his forehead beneath the brim of his hat. "It's time you moved on."

"How do you know? What has David said? Whatever it is, he's lying."

"It's not what your brother has said. It's how Mary Louise looks at him."

Caleb's face caved in defeat. "She just doesn't know me well enough. If he hadn't distracted her, we'd be together."

A sound caught his attention, and Garrett caught sight of David.

His battered deputy stepped forward and hung his head. "She's given me permission to ask her pa if we can court. She's already made her choice."

Garrett caught Caleb's stricken expression and waved David away. "Why don't you call it a day? Your brother needs a moment alone."

David hesitated for a moment, then dutifully turned away.

His heart heavy, Garrett propped his forearms on the top railing of the corral fence and stared at the brown earth stirred up by the brothers' fight.

He gave Caleb a few minutes with his thoughts before speaking. "There are two truths in life. You can't keep people from dying, and you can't make people love you. It's as simple as that."

"But if she spent more time with me, she'd know me better. She could sort out her feelings." The younger man's voice broke and he swallowed hard. "He stole her right from under my nose. My own brother. I trusted him and he—"

Garrett held up his hand. "I'll say it again. She's not a piece of chattel you can steal and steal back again. She's a living breathing person and she can make up her own mind. She *has* made up her own mind."

"Then why didn't she tell me?"

"I suspect she didn't want to hurt you."

"But—"

"Look, I know you're all torn up, but blaming David won't change anything."

A sheen of tears appeared in Caleb's eyes. "It's like someone ripped my heart out, and I'll never be whole again."

Garrett reached out a hand and gripped the younger man's shoulder. "It feels like that now, but it won't always. You're a fine man, and someday you'll find someone who loves you back. Don't settle for anything less. A one-sided love is like a poison. It eats away at you from the inside until you're just a shell."

"What does it matter? I already feel like I'm dying inside."

"You'll heal."

"How do you know?"

"I just do."

Garrett silently questioned his oft-repeated answer. The pain lessened, but did a heart ever truly mend? Or did a person carry around the reminders of the pain like a scar?

At least with one's heart, the scars were hidden.

Garrett caught a glance of the raw pain apparent in Caleb's mournful eyes.

Then again, maybe the scars of the heart were the most obvious of all. He wondered if his showed.

Jo sat in the sheriff's office and held her arm around a sobbing Mary Louise. She awkwardly patted the distraught girl's shoulder. "They've fought before. This isn't even the worst."

"I should have said something sooner." The blonde heaved in a shaky breath. "I just couldn't."

Garrett slipped through the door and he and Jo exchanged a glance. With a slight nod, she motioned him toward his desk. "I was just telling Mary Louise this isn't the end of the world."

The girl hiccuped. "It feels like it. Everything has gone wrong. Nobody is coming to Daddy's business anymore. Everyone whispers behind his back. They're calling him a murderer. Now the boys are fighting over me."

Garrett spread his hands along the table. "I'm doing what I can to find the killer. Hopefully, we'll have this case solved soon."

"I don't know what to do." Mary Louise blew her nose with noisy abandon into her lace-edged handkerchief. "It's even worse now that Daddy tried to buy all of Mr. Hodges's old stock at a discount. Everyone thinks badly of us."

Jo glanced at the sobbing girl. For such a beauty, she certainly didn't cry pretty. Her face had gone all blotchy and her frown disappeared into her chin.

Feeling like a first-rate heel for her uncharitable thoughts, Jo patted Mary Louise's hand. "Garrett will get to the bottom of what happened, won't you? Something will work out. Something always does."

"I hope so. Pa won't even talk about David, and I'll simply die if we can't get married. I love him so much."

Jo rolled her eyes. "You won't die."

The sobbing girl sprang to her feet and glared. "How do you know? You've never been in love. Everyone knows you two only got married because you had to!"

Jo sprang upright. "I know you're upset, but there's no need to be rude."

"You don't know what it's like. You've never even been courted!"

Mary Louise flounced out of the room and slammed the door, leaving them in stunned silence.

Garrett half rose from his seat, and Jo waved him down. "Let her go. She's young and in love."

Garrett fisted his hand on the desk. "That's no excuse for her behavior."

"It's all right." Jo stood and grasped the door handle. Her lungs squeezed and she desperately needed fresh air. "I'll see you at supper."

"Jo," he called.

She ignored him, scurrying along the boardwalk, her eyes burning. What did she know? Maybe Mary Louise *would* die if she and David couldn't be together. If *not* being in love hurt this much, Jo didn't want to know what the true emotion felt like.

A week after Jo's brothers' epic battle in the livery corral, Beatrice passed her deciphered message across the table and chewed on the end of her pencil while Jo reviewed her work.

Carefully checking each letter, Jo circled part of the translation. "You're still mixing up the *c* and the *y*."

Beatrice groaned as she accepted the corrected sheet. "I thought I got it right."

"Everyone gets those two letters mixed up at first. You'll get it. It just takes practice."

"I suppose."

Jo gave her hand an encouraging squeeze. "Don't worry. I was overwhelmed at first, too."

"Speaking of overwhelming." Beatrice perked up at the change of subject. "How is married life?"

"Well…" Jo carefully measured her answer. "Different than I thought."

"Different good or different bad?"

The office door swung open, interrupting her answer. Mr. Sundberg doffed his hat and ran a hand through his disheveled hair. "It's the missus. She's in labor, *ja*. Mrs. McCoy needs Jo."

The Sundbergs lived on a homestead just north of town. They'd emigrated five years ago, and Mrs. Sundberg pined for a baby. She'd lost three already, and Jo and her ma feared she'd never deliver a healthy child.

Dreading the answer, Jo spoke. "Where's the doc's wife? I thought she was helping out."

"Can't find her, *ja*. Must help. You."

A refusal balanced on the tip of Jo's tongue, but her ma wouldn't have called on her unless it was an emergency. "Bea, can you close up the office?"

"I'll take care of it," the older woman answered immediately.

Jo snatched a few belongings and followed the harried man outside to his wagon. The two-mile trip passed in strained silence. By the time Jo reached Mrs. Sundberg's bedside, the woman's brilliant blond hair hung damp around her face. She moaned and rolled her head from side to side on the pillow. She clutched her distended belly and grimaced.

Sensing the gravity of the situation, Jo snatched a rag from the bowl on the side table and made quick work of washing her hands. Mopping her damp forehead, Jo caught her ma's gaze. Edith gave an almost imperceptible shake of the head.

Her ma leaned closer and lowered her voice. "There's a complication with the baby."

Jo's heart sank.

# Chapter Twenty-Three

Garrett couldn't clear his thoughts. Caleb had thought Mary Louise the only girl for him, but Garrett was certain he'd find another love. How did a fellow know if he'd found true love? Was it possible to find that love more than once in a lifetime?

He kept picturing the look on Jo's face when Mary Louise had made her angry accusation. She'd appeared...defeated. And he'd done that to her. He'd taken the fire out of her heart with his distant ways. He'd talked himself into the marriage knowing it was wrong because he wanted her near.

He'd wrapped himself in ice as protection and had frozen her out in the process.

"Hey." David rapped on his desk. "Are you listening?"

Garrett bolted upright. "No. Were you talking?"

His new deputy rolled his eyes. "You've been daydreaming all morning. What's wrong with you?"

*Everything.* "Nothing."

Garrett rubbed the back of his neck. He couldn't get Jo off his mind. She must think him a first-rate loon after his antics the other morning. His feelings definitely felt like madness, but not like the madness of his father. His emotions were strong but not violent. More like forged steel than burning embers.

Not the black darkness he'd grown up with. He and Jo were friends before the marriage. He'd seen couples who acted almost as if they hated each other. Could you have love and romance with your best friend?

He'd never know unless he risked telling her the truth about his past.

David rapped on his desk again.

"What?" Garrett snapped.

"I've been following Tom Walby for days. He hasn't done anything out of the ordinary. Are you certain he's the culprit?"

Garrett checked his watch. "I called Tom in today. We'll put the pressure on him. Give him a chance to do the right thing. If we don't do something, there'll be a mob after Mr. Stuart."

The door swung open and Tom Walby stumbled inside looking as if he'd been dragged behind his horse instead of riding it. He collapsed onto the chair set before the desk and groaned.

Though his visitor was here sooner than expected, Garrett was relieved. He motioned for David. "Can you take notes while Tom talks?"

Understanding dawned on the younger man's face and he quickly retrieved paper and pencil from his desk opposite Garrett's.

Tom rubbed his face. "You know why I'm here?"

"I think so." Garrett tented his hands and kicked back in his chair. "Why don't you tell me what happened in your words."

"I didn't mean to do it." Tom's rough face screwed up in a grimace. "I was drunk."

"Didn't mean to do what? You'll have to say the words outright."

"I think I killed Mr. Hodges."

"You think or you know?"

"I was drunk." Tom repeated.

"Had you been drinking all day?"

"Most of it." Tom squared his shoulders. "There was a good crowd that afternoon and I'd been winning at poker. Those cowboys were full of money and the railroad boys had gotten their paychecks. They were buying us all drinks. Then I started losing." Tom grunted. "I don't remember much after that."

"Do you remember shooting the gun?"

"I don't." Tom swiped at his eyes. "When I woke up the next day, I had a shiner and my gun was short two bullets."

David's pencil frantically scratched across the page.

Garrett gave his deputy a moment to catch up before continuing. "You blacked out?"

"It's happened before."

"Why, Tom?" Garrett asked the question he'd always wanted to ask his own father. "The drink was bound to catch up with you. Why didn't you ever quit?"

The other man hung his head. "I don't know. I say I'm gonna quit. I make promises. To myself, to my wife. I go a day without drinking, sometimes more. Then, I don't know, something happens and I talk myself into coming to town. It's never going to be more than one. Never."

Garrett fought against the pull of time, keeping his thoughts rigidly in the present. "What about the shivaree at my house? That was you, too, wasn't it?"

"Yeah." Tom hung his head. "Mr. Stuart thought one of them cowboys was back in town. He was trying real hard to shift the blame. It was eating at me, you know? Because I knew Stuart didn't do it. I thought if your place was messed up at the same time, you'd blame the cowboys."

A low rumble of anger vibrated in Garrett's chest. "Was that the only reason?"

"Jo, too," Tom added sheepishly.

"You were sweet on her once, weren't you?"

"I didn't think she'd marry anyone. Ever. I guess I was mad when I found out the two of you were getting hitched. I married the missus just to show Jo someone else would have me. Jo was always too good for me anyway. Even in the eighth grade."

Garrett watched as David's eyes widened.

He'd been certain about the shooting, but the shivaree was only a hunch. "You've got a child now. You made a commitment. It's time you made peace with that. No matter what your reasons for marrying, it's your choice how you live your life each day. What you're doing isn't fair to any of you."

The day of the wedding Tom had been skulking around the edges of the festivities. The damage he'd inflicted on the house had been vicious, personal.

Tom cleared his throat and he dabbed at his brow with a dingy red handkerchief. "What's going to happen to me?"

"It's not up to me." Containing his anger, Garrett yanked the keys from his top drawer. "Your punishment is up to the judge. I'll keep you in the jail here. With no witnesses, I'm not certain how it will go for you."

"You'll put in a good word for me, won't you?"

"I gotta be honest, Tom, I'm not feeling all that charitable toward you right now. You killed a man and you can't even remember what happened. You took a life.

For all I know, it was self-defense. Mr. Hodges was known to have a temper. But you've lost all your credibility and I can't bring it back for you. Then you damaged my house. And on my wedding day, no less."

Garrett walked Tom back to the jail and locked him inside, then returned to the front office.

David sat in the chair, stunned. "You said the only proof you had was flimsy."

Garrett slid open his top desk drawer and fished out two bullets, then set them side by side on the dark blotter. "They look alike, don't they?"

David studied the bullets, rolling them over the leather surface. "Yes."

"This is the one that killed Mr. Hodges." Garrett brandished the warped metal cylinder. "And the other is from Tom's gun. I keep track of people who shoot first and aim later. Folks around here make their own bullets, and a lot of times you can tell who they belong to. Not always. But Tom's got a distinctive mold."

Garrett indicated three identical deep grooves on the side of each bullet.

David slumped in his chair. "Why did we need a confession?"

"Could have been a coincidence. No one saw anything. Tom doesn't even remember what happened." Garrett shrugged. "I didn't want to leave it up to chance."

"I still can't believe he had a crush on Jo." David frowned.

"You see what you expect to see. You don't appreciate the person she's become."

"Hey," Tom yelled from the rear of the jailhouse. "How about some lunch?"

David and Garrett exchanged a look.

"Next time, eat before you confess," Garrett called back, then leaned forward in his chair. "We'll set up something with the hotel for meals. It'll be double shifts until the trial. They might want him up in Wichita. It's murder, after all."

David scrawled something in his notes. "That solves all the crimes in Cimarron Springs."

"I got a telegram from Guthrie this morning." Except Jo hadn't delivered it. "They found the four cowboys who started the fire in the jailhouse. They've been arrested for cattle rustling." Why had Beatrice delivered the message and not Jo? The question had been eating at him all morning. "Yep. Everything is wrapped up neat as a pin." Garrett tucked the two bullets into his vest pocket.

He pictured Jo's once-lively green eyes, now dull with regret. He'd been a coward, and he'd made a real mess of things. The lies he'd told wouldn't clean up easy.

Jo rinsed her hands in a bowl and wiped them on a towel. After several tense hours, and though the baby had the umbilical cord wrapped around his neck, Mrs. Sundberg had delivered a healthy baby boy. Edith motioned for Jo and they stepped into the kitchen while the doc examined mother and infant. They took turns washing up in the sink.

Edith collapsed onto a chair. "I'm getting too old for this."

Exhausted and inexplicably cranky, Jo snapped, "Then why didn't you ask the doctor's wife, Mrs. Johnsen, for help?"

Ever since Mary Louise had shouted her accusations, Jo had been irritable and out of sorts. The words had echoed hollowly inside her chest. She had naively thought she'd grow closer to her husband with time and nearness. Instead, they'd grown further apart.

She pictured their future together. Two people in the same home, sharing the same name, and yet thousands of miles apart—speaking to each other across a chasm of stilted civility. How long could she live like that? How long before she turned so brittle a strong wind would break her into a thousand pieces?

Her ma huffed. "I didn't ask Mrs. Johnsen for assistance because she wasn't available."

Jo remained stubbornly silent. Garrett cared for her, she knew he did. She caught him looking at her when he didn't think she was aware. He kept his distance, circling further and further away.

"I'm scared," Jo whispered the admission, staring at her hands.

Her ma leaned forward. "Scared of what?"

"Of all this." Jo waved a limp hand in the general direction of Mrs. Sundberg's closed door. "What if that boy had died?" Jo choked back a sob. "Doesn't it ever bother you?"

Edith blanched. She opened and closed her mouth a few times. "Of course it bothers me."

"Then why do you do it?"

"Because it's my Christian duty. Because I feel good knowing I can help. Because…" Her voice trailed off as Jo's words finally sank in. "You really are afraid, aren't you?"

Jo swallowed around the lump in her throat. She hated this, hated feeling vulnerable. Truth be told, she liked having people believe she wasn't afraid of anything. She didn't want to admit her weakness.

Hiding had only driven a wedge between her and her ma, and she hated the lie. The hiding. "If I'm ever going to have children of my own, I have to stop delivering babies."

Emotions flitted across her ma's face—disbelief, remorse and finally understanding. She knelt before Jo and cradled her face in her hands. "Oh, gracious. I've been blind, haven't I? I never realized you were too young to understand." She studied Jo's defeated expression. "Is this why you never went courting? Is this why you married a man you hardly know?"

"Part of it."

And because she'd never found someone she was interested in spending her life with—until Garrett.

Her ma clutched her hands. "I thought you didn't want to be with me, that you were rejecting me. I've always been a little in awe of you."

"Me?"

"You're not afraid to speak your mind."

"But you always say the right thing."

"I say the correct things," Edith spoke earnestly, "because that's the easy way. You're brave enough to say what you feel even when it pains you. Like now." She stood and held out her hand for Jo. "This is why I do what I do."

Her ma pushed open the door, revealing the new family. Mr. Sundberg perched on the edge of the bed beside his wife, the swaddled infant cradled between them. They both looked radiant, stunned and overjoyed all at the same time.

Doc Johnsen latched his leather satchel as his wife caught sight of them in the doorway.

Mrs. Sundberg followed her gaze, and her face lit with a smile. "Would you like to hold him?"

Jo accepted the tiny bundle and stared in wonder at the sleepy new life. She'd held plenty of babies in her life, but never with the sense of awe she felt now. Something shifted in her chest. A door opened in her heart, and she felt a burst of light rush into it.

The child was perfect, beautiful and helpless. Each tiny finger was capped with a perfectly formed nail, a shock of dark hair covered the baby's head. That tug of emotion became an incessant pull. She wanted this. She wanted to be a mother.

For years she'd come up with excuses. Hidden herself away behind wide-brimmed leather hats and boys' clothes. She'd been afraid her whole life. Afraid of being weak. Afraid of wanting something she might never have.

The infant mewled, his tiny mouth working, and Jo reluctantly returned the swaddled bundle to Mrs. Sundberg. Her ma ushered out the bystanders and quietly closed the door behind her, giving the new family some privacy.

After exchanging a few words with the doc and his wife, Edith led her outside and held her hand. "I'm sorry, Jo. I should have paid more attention to your feelings and respected your wishes. I shouldn't have called on you today. I've been mule-headed. I realize that now. I saw things the way I wanted them to be, not the way they really were. Working with you as a midwife kept us close. I thought once you became a woman, my job was over. I was afraid of being useless."

"Like a hand break on a canoe?"

Her ma laughed. "Just like that."

As much as Garrett had been running hot and cold, holding back his feelings, Jo had been just as guilty. She'd been guarding a part of herself because she was afraid of being weak. She was afraid of having more to lose than Garrett. In their relationship, she'd been balancing the scales, only giving as much as she thought she could get in return, terrified of showing weakness, of losing the upper hand.

One of them had to give.

Edith touched her shoulder. "We're all afraid. Sometimes courage is merely the point when our need overcomes our fear."

Jo considered her ma's words. Unless one of them changed, she and Garrett would keep drifting apart. The day was still young enough for gathering some supplies for a picnic. It was time she gave him more than she received in return. No more balancing the scales of affection like a greedy banker.

She had to find her courage. And Jo knew just where to start.

"Ma," Jo said, her voice ragged with emotion. "Your job will never be over. I'll always be your daughter and I will always need your love and help."

Edith pulled her into a sobbing hug, and Jo returned the fierce pressure.

Being vulnerable was tougher than feigning courage, but it sure felt a whole lot better.

## Chapter Twenty-Four

Garrett snatched his saddle and tossed it over Blue's back. He tightened the cinch and then led the horse into the clearing. Hoisting one foot into the stirrup, a sound caught his attention. He turned and discovered Jo meandering up the driveway, blissfully unaware of the panic she'd caused.

He tossed the reins over the hitch and stalked toward her. "Where have you been?"

Her eyes widened at his tone. "Mrs. Sundberg had her baby."

"Why didn't you send word?" Garrett planted his hands on his hips. "I've been worried."

Jo halted. "Why didn't you ask Beatrice?"

A flush crept up his neck. "I was just heading back into town. In the future, let me know if you'll be late."

"Okay."

"Okay," he snapped back.

With the sudden release of tension, he fully absorbed her disheveled appearance and the dark smudges beneath her eyes. She appeared fragile, exhausted, and all his worries rushed back. "You scared me," Garrett reluctantly admitted.

"I said I was sorry," Jo grumbled. "What more do you want?"

"I'm sorry, too. Except I get mad when I'm scared."

"You'll fit right in with the McCoys," Jo grunted. "Once, Abraham stepped on a nail and he got so mad, he threw a hammer at the wall."

"And that didn't scare you?"

"He didn't throw it at me."

Garrett's heart continued pounding uncomfortably in his chest as he wrangled his emotions back in check. "Let's start over again."

"Agreed," she replied, her voice thick with exhaustion. "How was your day?"

"Fine. I guess I should ask about the baby," he added sheepishly.

"He's doing well now." Her lips trembled. "I didn't know what would happen. The baby had the cord wrapped around his neck. But Ma managed to save him."

Garrett wrapped his arm around her shoulders, and she sank into his embrace. "I'm glad you were there for her."

An air of melancholy surrounded her. She leaned against him, and he felt a swift, sharp relief at her show of trust.

"Actually, so am I." She linked her arm around his waist. "And Ma and I had a good talk."

Garrett let out a low whistle. "What about?"

"I'll tell you, but not now."

Hesitating, Garrett opened his mouth then changed his mind. "Fair enough."

He didn't understand the complexities of a mother-daughter relationship, and he respected Jo's privacy. Yet she'd always been open and honest with him, more than he'd ever given in return. Emotion shimmered in her expressive emerald eyes, sparking a pang of yearning. He had no right to ask her for her secrets when he'd guarded his own so fiercely.

They broke apart when they reached his tethered horse, and the heat of her touch lingered against his side. "You look exhausted. Why don't you wait inside while I take care of Blue."

"I'd rather hear about your day." She trailed him into the barn and opened the first stall door. She grasped the top slat, then rested her chin on her knuckles. "Word in town has it that Tom Walby's been arrested for Mr. Hodges's murder.

Garrett lifted the saddle off Blue with a grunt. "Word travels fast."

"Did he really kill him?"

Garrett met her sorrowful gaze. "That's how it appears. He doesn't even remember what happened that night. His day in court would have gone easier if Tom had come forward sooner."

Tugging off his gloves, he approached her, nervous at the soft reproach in her gaze. "I had to arrest him, you know that."

"I know." Tears pooled in her eyes. "There's no love lost between us, but I'm worried about his wife. His son."

"Tom can't change the past. He can only move forward."

She tossed him a cryptic smile. "I thought you said people didn't change."

"Can't a man be wrong sometimes?"

"We all get to be wrong sometimes," she answered enigmatically, then straightened her shoulders, throwing off the somber mood. "Say, do you realize we just had our first fight?"

Her announcement threw him off for a moment. "I guess so."

Jo shut the stall bar behind him. "That wasn't bad, was it?"

"You're right." He absorbed her words, hoping he didn't look as addled as he felt. "It wasn't."

Jo tilted her head. "You feeling all right?"

For the first time in a long while, he felt strong in spirit. He was addled, all right. "Great. I'm feeling better than I have in a month of Sundays. I'll finish mucking out the stalls and then I'll help you with dinner. Unless you want to rest first," he added quickly.

She'd perked up during the conversation, but he sensed she'd had an exhausting day.

"Nope," Jo replied. "I think I'm getting my second wind."

She sketched a wave and retreated into the house.

Mulling over the revelation, Garrett set about his chores. As he lifted another pitchfork full of hay into the milk cow's stall, his sense of bewilderment increased.

He'd spent their brief marriage walking like a man crossing grizzly country, tiptoeing around and dreading a confrontation. But they'd actually survived their first argument. Jo hadn't cried, and he hadn't yelled. All in all, the experience was nothing as he'd expected. For the first time since he'd made his hasty proposal, he felt more optimism than fear.

Staying away from her had been a good choice. In a few more months, when they had a solid foundation, he'd tell her the truth. First, he needed to foster their relationship without the distracting pull of attraction.

A sound caught his attention and he turned. Jo stood

in the open double barn doors, her outline silhouetted against the late-afternoon sun. She'd changed into a pretty blue calico dress with lace at the collar.

Garrett couldn't see her features and he shielded his eyes against the sun. She approached him, her steps more hesitant than usual, a basket hooked over her elbow and an unfamiliar red tartan blanket thrown over one shoulder.

"Is it suppertime already?" Garrett asked, brushing his hands together.

Jo held the basket aloft with both hands. "I thought we'd do something different tonight."

She tilted her head, and Garrett glanced behind him, feeling as if he'd missed something. "Like what?"

"A picnic."

"Ah, okay." He glanced down at his dusty clothes and Jo's neat dress. "I'll be right back."

Garrett stepped into the house, dashed upstairs, rinsed his hands and face in the washbasin and slicked back his hair. Cora was staying with the McCoys overnight, and he sensed a difference in Jo this evening.

He slipped into a clean jacket and considered changing the rest of his outfit, then reconsidered. He didn't want to keep her waiting. After a final assessment before the looking glass, he loped down the stairs and across the clearing toward the barn.

Jo lifted her head as he approached. "There's a lovely spot by the stream."

"Sounds perfect. I'll carry the basket."

With a shy smile, Jo handed over the burden. Garrett hooked the handles beneath his arm. On a whim, he stuck out his opposite elbow. To his surprise, Jo looped her hand through the crook. His chest swelled.

Though Jo normally charged ahead on any journey,

she kept the pace slow and measured. The summer days had lengthened, and the heat had given the late afternoon a lazy feel. A peaceful lassitude stole over him.

Nature had bloomed over the countryside, brilliant and unrestrained. As they neared the creek, sheltering trees rose before them, their leaves saturated with emerald-green.

Jo touched his sleeve with her free hand. "David caught up with me on my way home from Mrs. Sundberg's. That's how I found out about Tom."

"Your brother should have given you a ride."

"I wanted to walk. I needed to think. And of course I had to ask him about Mary Louise."

Garrett recalled how his deputy had been mooning around the office. "How is the courting progressing?"

"Excellent. He's ready for marriage."

"Her father won't be pleased."

"Nothing short of a fortune will please Mr. Stuart. But if Mary is content, that's all that matters."

"What about you?" Garrett asked, gathering his courage. "Are you content?"

She tilted her head, considering the question. "Cora laughs, and she seems happy and healthy."

Two spots of color appeared on her cheeks. She pointed out the site for the picnic and unfurled the tartan blanket draped over her arm.

The girl who'd boldly demanded his hand in marriage had disappeared, leaving behind this shy, beautiful woman. There was an air about her, a sense of hesitant determination.

Garrett helped arrange the covering. "Is this blanket new?"

The blush on her cheeks intensified, and his mood

soared. She'd bought the blanket specifically for this outing. That had to mean something, didn't it?

He set down the picnic basket, and Jo flopped onto the edge of the blanket.

She plucked a black-eyed Susan from a scraggly patch of wildflowers and twirled the stem. "David said Tom was sweet on me growing up."

"I told you so." Garrett raised his eyebrows, daring her to refute him.

Jo playfully chucked him on the arm. "Don't let it go to your head."

The sun hovered low on the horizon, blazing red behind a thin cover of clouds. Jo's hair fluttered in the breeze, pulled loose from its bindings. Instead of wearing her dark hair in a single braid down her back, she'd been twisting several braids in a knot at the base of her neck. He realized she'd been taking more care with her appearance lately and the result was breathtaking.

She'd always been beautiful and now she was stunning. Other people had noticed, too. With pride and not a little jealousy, he'd seen gentlemen tip their hats to her on the boardwalk. As much as he wanted the secret of Jo's allure all to himself, he liked seeing the townspeople react to the radiance he'd always seen, a beauty the folks around her had taken for granted.

He reached for a stray lock and tucked the soft strands behind the gentle curve of her ear. "You've been wearing your hair different. I like it."

"Thank you." She smoothed a stray lock, her movements jerky and self-conscious. "I guess I was afraid of trying something new."

Her announcement stunned him. "I can't imagine you being afraid of anything."

"You're the second person who's said that to me today."

He thought he'd been the only one in town who saw Jo, really saw the person inside, but he'd been just as blind as the rest of them.

She caught his gaze and smiled shyly. "Can I tell you a secret?"

"Of course."

*Secrets and lies.* How much of his life had been shaped by secrets and lies? He went through all the false motions—smiling when he was sad, laughing when he was angry and never telling anyone of his past. He was exhausted from hiding, exhausted from covering his true feelings.

Jo cleared her throat. "Remember when you asked me what Ma and I talked about?" She plucked at the weeds near the edge of the blanket. "We made our peace. I didn't like helping my ma with midwife duties. We had a big fight about it a couple of years ago. Everyone thinks I'm tough, but I'm not. I'm afraid of childbirth."

"That seems normal to me."

She absently braided several long, green stalks. "None of my friends from school are. They all have babies."

Garrett handed her a black-eyed Susan, and she delicately wove it into her chain.

"That doesn't mean they're not scared," he said.

"What are you afraid of?"

She needed his honesty right then, but he couldn't reveal his shame just yet, not when their budding relationship was this new and fragile. "I'm afraid of not being the man I want to be. Of hurting someone I love."

Jo stilled at the revealing admission. "What do you mean?"

"Nothing. I don't know." His gaze dipped to her lips.

Something happened then that he could not explain later. One moment he was revealing his deepest fear, the next moment she was wrapped in his arms. The evening sun warmed his back, and the air around them smelled deliciously of new leaves and freshly tilled earth.

Stirred by a depth of emotion he hadn't thought himself capable of, he surrendered to the foreign sensations. The embrace was right and good, a culmination of the feelings he'd kept rigidly in check since the moment he'd met JoBeth McCoy. *His wife.*

Nothing in his past had prepared him for the feelings rocking his carefully ordered world.

Realizing the enormity of what he was doing, he abruptly let go. Jo stared at him, her body still, not even breathing for a moment.

A shy smile spread across her face. "When I asked you to marry me last spring, you asked what would happen if I ever wanted children of my own."

"You said we'd cross that bridge when we got there."

"We're there."

His chest constricted. He knew what she was telling him. She wanted children. She wanted a real marriage. Garrett stood and stumbled back a step, putting some distance between them.

He was no better than any other addict. Like Tom Walby swearing off drink, he'd sworn to keep his distance. He'd broken that promise. "I can't. I'm sorry. But I just can't."

What if he hurt her? He'd promised himself he wouldn't touch her and he hadn't even kept that promise for a day—for an hour. He was a weak man, and weak men did not make good husbands.

"Why?" Jo demanded. "Is it me?"

"No, of course not." He raked his hands through his hair. "You're wonderful. It's me. I'm not the man you think of I am."

"Then who are you?"

Her words shot through him like a bullet. The question was deceptively simple, the answer needlessly complicated. He was a flawed man. No better than Tom. No better than his own father. He made promises to himself he didn't keep. Promises to his family he broke.

"I'm not the man you think I am," he repeated, his voice a jagged whisper. "I can't."

She deserved a whole man. And he wouldn't be whole until he made his peace with God, and with himself. Only then could he be a man worthy of Jo's love.

*Love.*

"Give me time." He dragged in a ragged breath. "Please just give more time."

As a cloud drifted over the sun, the radiance of the afternoon leached away. The budding confidence in Jo's eyes faded into a dull torpor.

A nauseating wave of self-disgust sent pressure pulsating behind his eyes. He'd done this to her. He'd robbed her of her confidence.

She stood and snatched the blanket, folding it in a disheveled square. "Never mind."

"No." He reached out a hand, and she flinched. He dropped his arm against his side. "There's something I need to do first."

She met his gaze, her chin set at a determined angle. "I know you have secrets. I thought I could live with that, but I was wrong. And it's not because I'm unworthy of your trust, it's because you're a coward."

He reared back as though she'd struck him. "I am a coward, but I can't change overnight."

She hugged the tartan blanket against her chest, her smile sad and tinged with defeat. "Ironic, isn't it? That's all we have together. Time."

Her voice was vulnerable, the small voice of a woman who'd wanted to please him and had been rebuffed.

A hopeless pall fell over him. He'd waited too long. He'd already run out of time with Jo.

## Chapter Twenty-Five

The following day, Jo sat at the telegraph office and seesawed a pencil between her fingers.

*Can't* or *won't*.

The words had been swirling around her head all morning. At least she'd learned one thing: rejection wasn't fatal. She'd faced her worst fears and come out only slightly worse for wear. She pleated her new navy blue calico between two fingers.

If anything good had come of her marraige, at least her ma had stopped ribbing her about her attire. Dressing nice wasn't so bad. And since she'd put up her hair, the grocer had ceased eyeing her as if she was going to nip an onion and run.

That definitely made her shopping trips less tense.

The 12:15 from Wichita rumbled into the station with a shrill whistle and a belch of steam. Jo stood and stretched. Her ma had said she was expecting a package today.

Edith had been awfully mysterious about the contents. Watching the passengers depart, Jo decided she needed a breath of fresh air. Or at least as fresh as the station permitted.

A smattering of passengers departed in a flurry of baggage, their feet disappearing in puffs of steam from the train's engines. With a jaundiced eye Jo watched as they sized up the town, holding handkerchiefs to their mouths against the dusty wind. No doubt grateful this was only a stop and not their final destination.

She was turning away when a tall gentleman caught her attention. After a quick double take, she launched herself at the unaware man. "Jack Elder!"

He stumbled back a step and tightened his grip. "How are you, JoBeth?"

Releasing her hold, she backed away. He hadn't changed much over the years. He was still tall and lean, his hair a touch grayer at the temples, and the lines on his forehead deeper.

She glanced around. "Where are Elizabeth and the boys?"

"At home. I had business in Wichita that finished up early. Thought I'd spend the night here."

"I can't believe Ma didn't tell me it was you. She said she was expecting a package."

"Well, I did bring a wedding gift." He tipped his hat. "Let me fetch it."

Jo shaded her eyes against the sun. Garrett had driven the wagon into town. He set the brake and hopped down. "Your ma said I should bring the wagon. Did you find this mysterious package?"

She kept her gaze focused on a point just behind his head. She wasn't going to let him ruin her day. "I did!" Jo exclaimed. "He's coming now."

She turned and discovered Jack leading two men carrying a slated crate. The crate tipped and the contents bleated. After the men set it down, Jo crouched before a stamp reading Live Animals.

She straightened and planted her hands on her hips. "It's a goat."

"I didn't bring the hat and coat, but—"

Jo playfully socked him in the arm and cast a glance over her shoulder. "That's our secret."

"I told you that you wouldn't end up like your aunt Vicky."

With another surreptitious glance over her shoulder at her unyielding husband, she held her index finger before her lips. "Shh."

Garrett cleared his throat. "We haven't been introduced. I'm Garrett Cain."

The two men exchanged a quick, single-pump handshake. "Jack Elder."

"I've heard a lot about you."

"Haven't heard much about you."

The goat in the crate bleated again. Jo grinned. "We'd best get back to the house. I'm sure they're all excited to see you."

The two men easily hoisted the crate into the back of the wagon. Jo lifted her skirts and scrambled onto the platform seat. The wagon dipped as Jack entered on her right, then dipped the opposite direction as Garrett alighted. Off balance, she slid across the seat, and they bumped hips.

"Sorry," Jo mumbled and sat stiffly upright.

She turned away and caught Jack's startled expression. No doubt he was curious about the strained relationship between two newlyweds.

*Time,* Garrett had said. She'd married a man who could never love her. She had all the time in the world.

Mustering a cheerful smile, she spoke. "I can't wait for you to meet Cora. She's five and the most precious thing."

"She'll be the same age as Maxwell and my littlest one. That's a handful."

"I almost wish she were. I'd know what to do. She's too well behaved for me."

Jack chuckled.

They chatted for the remainder of the trip, catching up on old news. Garrett sat beside her, his expression stiff and unwelcoming. When the wagon pulled before the barn on the McCoy farm, the McCoys swarmed. Jo caught up with her brother Michael and together they pried open the goat's crate.

Michael scratched his head. "What kind of present is that?"

"It's a joke."

Her brother shrugged. "I don't get it."

He wandered off, and Garrett knelt before the animal. "I don't get it, either."

Jo heaved a sigh. "I used to worry that I'd end up like my aunt Vicky. She never had children, but she had a whole herd of goats. Rumor had it she dressed them in flowered hats and coats at Easter."

"Nah. You'd dress them as soldiers."

Jo's smile buckled. She'd pinched her cheeks and bought a new dress, but he'd always see her as a tomboy. Her heart sank along with the last of her hope.

Cora dashed from the house. She enveloped Garrett in a hug, then offered another to Jo. "Michael says we have a goat. Does it have a name?"

"Nope. Why don't you pick one." Garrett grinned.

"Buttercup," Cora declared.

"It's an odd name for a boy goat." Jo considered the animal. "But I think it's perfect."

Cora skipped away, and the goat leaped after her. Together they cavorted around the yard.

Garrett touched Jo's arm. "Looks like Buttercup just might wind up in a coat and hat after all."

The words from the previous day hung between them. Her mood swung between anger and despair. She'd thought they could be friends. The attraction flaring between them prevented such a simple solution.

When she saw Cora, the obvious affection they shared toward one another, despair lanced her heart. They'd married to give the little girl a secure home, a safe future. Cora had blossomed beneath their care. If things hadn't turned out for Jo the way she'd hoped, she had no one to blame but herself for building her hopes on a rocky foundation.

She pulled her new bonnet over her head, shading her face. "I think I'll stay here tonight. You can go home if you want."

Hurt flickered in his eyes. Hurt and something she'd never seen before—doubt.

He swallowed, his Adam's apple bobbing. "I'll fetch you in the morning."

"I'll walk."

His shoulders sagged.

For a moment her resolve wavered. "Garrett."

He turned. Their gazes met and locked, and the tension pulsated between them. A thousand possibilities fluttered through her head, and she shooed them all away.

Jo ducked her head. "Never mind."

She'd given all she was prepared to give. He had to meet her halfway.

After Garrett's hasty departure, the next few hours passed in a distracted blur for Jo. Jack caught them up on news of his family, regaling them with stories of his three children.

Gradually, her family dispersed. Her brothers scattered for evening chores, her ma and pa disappeared out the back. Her parents did that sometimes. Walked by the creek in the evenings. Summer had turned and the days were long and hot. The sky clear and dry. Evenings by the creek were sometimes the only relief from the relentless heat.

Jo turned to her old friend. "When will you bring Elizabeth for a visit?"

His face lit up at the mention of his wife's name. "Soon, I think. You heard my brother is taking over the old Cole farm."

Jo nodded. "Reverend Miller said he's trying the land with cattle."

"It's not a bad notion."

"Why isn't he staying on your family's ranch?"

"Good question." Jack rested his forearms on the porch railing and leaned over, staring into the distance. "It's harder for some men, finding their place in the world. John is the youngest. He's got something to prove."

Jo stood beside him and rested her chin on her knuckles. "Men are odd creatures."

"So are women." Jack barked out a laugh. "I know it's not my business, but…"

He let his unspoken question hang between them.

Jo heaved a sigh. "We married for Cora's sake. He needed a wife. I was available." She twisted her mouth in a wry smile. "That's all there is."

"Oh, I think there's more. That man has something weighing heavy on his soul. I've been around long enough to see that much."

"I thought if we were together we'd grow closer. But the more I try, the more I feel the distance between us."

"There's something holding that man back. And I'd wager it has nothing to do with you."

"How do I change that? How do I make him see that we have a future together?"

"Be patient with him. It's harder for some people to trust. If that doesn't work, I'll knock some sense into him when I visit next fall."

Jo laughed. "If I thought that would work, I'd have the boys take care of it."

"He might not be able to change." Jack touched her hand, his gaze earnest. "Sometimes the things that happen to people in their childhood, in their past, changes them too much. It warps them and they can never grow straight again."

"You don't think people can change?"

"He has to want to change. You can't force him."

Her eyes burned, and she blinked away the tears. "I wish I'd figured that out sooner."

Jack turned and leaned his hip against the porch railing. "Marriage is hard work. But it's good work. Worthwhile. Put in the effort."

"I can't put in all the effort alone," Jo scoffed. She'd ignored the warnings from those who loved her most—her ma, her friends. She'd trapped herself in a loveless marriage and she had only herself to blame.

# Chapter Twenty-Six

Jo sucked in a fortifying breath. She took a step forward, then paused. Garrett had cleared the corral outside the barn and mended the fence. This morning he was working with his horse. He stood in the center of the corral and held the lead rope as the animal circled him.

He called out commands, sometimes with words, sometimes just with whistles and clicks of his tongue. The horse responded with lightning-fast precision.

Garrett wore his blue work shirt, the sleeves turned back. She stared at the corded muscles of his forearms and her pulse quickened.

She loved him.

She loved him and she'd pushed him too hard. That was her way. Full steam ahead with no thought other than victory. All she'd done with her dogged persistence was push him away. If she loved him, she owed him some space. Jack had urged her to be patient, and she'd decided to heed his advice.

She smoothed her skirts and plastered a serene expression on her face before calling his name.

He turned, and her determination wavered. She recalled their first meeting at the church, when she'd had pear blossoms in her hair. Even then she'd known she wasn't the sort of woman to attract a man like Garrett Cain. That knowledge hadn't stopped her from trying.

At her continued silence, he released the lead line from the horse's halter and crossed the corral. "Do you need anything?"

"Cora and I are going to the pond. Would you like to come?"

"Sure."

Jo exhaled a breath she hadn't even known she was holding. He rolled down his sleeves and buttoned the cuffs, then shut and latched the gate behind him.

Turning, she motioned for Cora. "He's coming."

The little girl skipped her way down the road, her blond curls shimmering in the sunlight.

Garrett took her small hand. "I don't know the way."

"Jo does," Cora declared proudly.

They linked hands as they set off for the road.

"Lift me," the little girl demanded with a giggle.

Jo and Garrett exchanged an indulgent grin over her head. On every third step, they hoisted their arms into the air, lifting the giggling little girl from the ground. They repeated the playful activity until Jo's arm ached.

She let go and rubbed her shoulder. "Enough." She laughed. "We should look for some rocks."

Keeping her hands above her waist, she waded through the dense brush toward the creek. She assisted Cora down the bank, and they sloshed through the water, their heads bent.

Garrett paused above them. "Why are we looking for rocks?"

"For skipping."

He joined them in the creek, then plucked a stone

from the creek bed and handed it to Jo. "Will this work?"

Squinting, she studied his find. "Nope. It needs to be like this."

She held up a flat, rounded stone.

"Got it," he replied, resuming his search.

Jo crouched next to him. "Haven't you ever skipped stones before?"

"Never."

She pressed off from her knee into a stand again. "It's too bad Abraham isn't here, he once got twelve skips off one rock."

"Is that good?"

"The best I've ever seen."

She forced herself to look away. If they were going to spend their lives together, she must foster the friendship. She'd feared from the beginning one of them had more to lose. Perhaps she'd even find a way for both of them to gain something.

As she struggled back up the hill, he took her hand. She steeled herself against the sudden rush of attraction.

Cora kept her proud stash of stones tight against her chest. "I've never skipped stones, either."

Upon reaching the small pond nestled in a shallow valley, Jo proceeded with her demonstration. She showed them how to flick their wrists, sending the stones skipping across the water. After several tries, Cora managed two skips.

She laughed and clapped hands.

Jo glanced at her husband as he crouched before his niece, pulling her into his embrace.

He'd only ever asked her for one thing. *Time.*

Marriage was work. But it was good work. Worthwhile.

She stood behind him, not quite touching. His request was a small enough thing to ask. She'd give him more time.

Garrett stood before the towering church doors. He felt as though he'd come full circle. This was where it had all begun between him and Jo. When he'd dropped his hat and she'd retrieved it. Their hands had touched, the feeling still lingered.

She deserved the truth, and he was finally prepared for the cost. Cora had grown fond of him, but his niece still preferred Jo. His cousin, Edward, had lost interest in demanding custody of Cora. The reason for their marriage had dissipated, and he needed another, better one. Garrett rolled his tense shoulders.

Everything was wrapped up neat as a pin. All he need do was screw his courage and tell Jo the truth.

Simple as that.

Reverend Miller opened the door, a question in his watery gray eyes.

Garrett cleared his throat. "I need a word."

The older man stepped aside and motioned him into the shaded interior of the cozy space. Without asking why, Reverend Miller led him through the smaller set of double doors into the church. They sat in the front pews facing the altar. Garrett braced his hands on his knees and hung his head.

The reverend touched his shoulder. "You can talk with God alone, or with me here."

"Stay," Garrett implored hoarsely.

He let the words flow. He spoke until his throat went dry. All the fears, all the horrors of his youth. Things he'd forgotten welled up in his heart and spilled over the side. The feelings tumbled loose, raging free as the dam within him burst.

A sob shook his body and he buried his face in his hands, letting go.

Reverend Miller rested his hands on his knees. "That's a heavy burden for one man to carry alone."

"Yes."

"And why must you carry this burden alone?"

"Because…because it's my shame."

"It's your father's shame. You were but a child. Would you blame Cora for her parents' death?"

"Of course not." Garrett shot upright.

"Then you must forgive. Forgive your father and forgive yourself." The older man leaned away and rested his forearms on the back of the pew. "I served in the war myself."

Garrett lifted his head in surprise.

"It does things to a man." Reverend Miller shook his head. "We'll never know what shaped your father. What drove him into such a black place."

"He stole my faith."

Garrett whispered a truth he'd only just realized.

"Forgiveness can restore that faith. Forgiveness and love."

"My mother should have left him sooner." Garrett spoke the words that had rotted his soul for years, eating away at him like a poison. "She should have been stronger for us."

Until that moment he'd never realized the anger sparking in his chest. "She should have been stronger."

"I don't fault your anger, son. As we grow, we come to realize those we love are flawed. My guess is that your mother did the best she could. She couldn't change your father."

"Why did he do it?"

There was so much more in the simple phrase, but he couldn't speak anymore.

"I can't answer that. I can only advise on matters of faith. Forgive them both. For being human. For being weak. Only you can heal the rift in your soul."

"But I can't forget."

"God does not require us to forget. You have a lovely niece who dotes on you. A beautiful wife who loves you. Take those gifts without the taint of hatred."

Garrett's heart stuttered. Jo didn't love him. If he told her the truth, she might never. He clutched his hat, bending the brim. He'd rather know if she could love him than live in a prison of his own making.

He loved her.

A moment of clarity cleared the fog from his brain. He'd driven away the people he loved from his life. He'd run from them, hidden from them, frozen them out—all because he was afraid of losing someone again.

And what had it gotten him? Fifteen wasted years that he could have spent with Deirdre. Five years he could have spent with Cora. He'd asked Jo for time when he'd wasted all of his. Instead of protecting himself, he'd created more hurt. For all of them.

His head throbbing, Garrett held out his hand. "Thank you."

The reverend took his proffered hand in both of his. "Forgive yourself first, son, and the rest will go much easier."

Garrett lifted his eyes toward the stained-glass window. Mary and Joseph held a swaddled Jesus in colorful, angled splendor. God had sacrificed his only son for the sins of mankind.

The reverend followed Garrett's thoughtful gaze.

"It is written in Ephesians. 'Be ye kind to one another, tenderhearted, forgiving one another, even as God for Christ's sake hath forgiven you.'"

His thoughts reeling, Garrett walked down the center aisle, leaving Reverend Miller alone. The moment he pushed open the double doors to the vestibule, the stench of cigar smoke hit him like a wall. The doors closed behind him.

Garrett stiffened and reached for his gun. The cold barrel of a pistol jabbed him in the ribs.

Bert Walby's dank breath puffed near his cheek. "Don't do anything stupid, Marshal."

Garrett raised his hands. "This isn't going to work," he said, keeping his voice low. He didn't want the reverend involved.

"Sure it is. If you don't help me, I'm going to tell the whole town that the man they entrusted to keep the peace is the son of a murderer."

Tensing, Garrett lowered his hands. "Then why do you need the gun?"

"Because I don't trust you." Bert fished in Garrett's holster and snatched his revolver. "We're going to the sheriff's office. The 10:15 to Guthrie is leaving in twenty minutes, and me and Tom are going to be on it."

Bert stuffed the extra gun into the front of his pants. Garrett pushed through the outside doors and blinked against the sunlight. A half-dozen people bustled along the boardwalk, too many to start something with Bert. He'd bide his time and wait until there were fewer bystanders.

Bert kept the gun beneath his jacket as they walked, his shifty gaze darting between Garrett and a couple, their elbows linked, passing them as they crossed before the mercantile. Garrett tipped his hat.

When they reached the sheriff's office, Garrett paused. Bert shoved him forward.

"Wait," Garrett ordered. "My deputy is young and green. If he thinks something is wrong he's just as liable to shoot me by accident. Let me get rid of him."

"You do that. But don't try anything funny. I'll kill you both."

Garrett nodded his understanding and stepped inside. David sat behind his desk. When the younger man saw him, he leaped to his feet, his expression flooded with guilt.

"I was just doing some paperwork."

"My desk is the best place," Garrett soothed. "Bert here wants to talk with his brother. Why don't you go see Jack Elder off."

David checked his watch. "I don't need to. I saw him last night."

"I have things under control here. Tell Jack it's always welcome having the assistance of a fellow lawman around."

David tilted his head to one side, then looked between the two men. Garrett held his breath. After a moment, David shrugged. "Suit yourself."

Garrett didn't exhale until the door closed. "Let's get Tom."

He snatched the circle key ring from the hook on his desk and led Bert into the backroom.

Tom sat up in bed when he caught sight of them. "What are you doing here?"

Bert waved his gun. "I'm busting you out. We're taking the train to Guthrie."

Tom shook his head. "It won't work. Even if we bust out of here, there'll be a posse waiting for us at the next stop."

"I got us some insurance," his brother declared. "I been trailing the marshal here. Figured I owed it to him after he had you and me followed. A man who goes to church on a Tuesday must have some powerful sinning to confess." Bert shoved Garrett forward. "The folks of Cimarron Springs have entrusted their lives to the son of a murderer."

Tom's eyes widened.

His brother cackled. "His pa shot his ma then killed himself. The marshal isn't gonna want anyone knowing that, are you?"

He jabbed Garrett in the ribs again. Garrett grunted.

Tom remained seated. "I'm still not going."

"You are the dumbest son of—"

"Not that dumb." Tom lifted his doleful gaze. "Since I've been here, I sobered up. I've been remembering bits and pieces of what happened that night. I didn't shoot Mr. Hodges. You did."

Bert sneered. "I was doing you a favor. We coulda opened the store across the street. Hodges was sitting on a gold mine of stock. We coulda bought it cheap." He spat at Tom's feet. "Who goes and confesses to something they didn't do?"

"I figured it must have been me. My gun was missing bullets…I'd been losing at poker to Hodges for an hour and then he wound up dead. I didn't know what to think." Tom's expression hardened. "You wanted them to believe I did it, didn't you?"

"Don't get yourself in a lather. I figured if they caught up with you, everyone would think it was an accident. You're always shooting off that gun."

Tom lunged toward the bars. "Get out of here. I got a wife and kid. I'm clearing my name and staying."

"You can't clear your name without ruining mine. Now let's get out of here."

"No." Tom sat back down and gripped the straw mattress. "I'm not like you. It's been eating away at me, thinking I killed someone. I'm not like you at all."

Garrett looked between the two brothers. So similar and yet so different. They'd been raised by the same parents, reared in the same town. Yet Bert had gone bad. Worse even than Tom because there was no going back for him.

Bert cocked the gun and leveled his hand at Tom.

The color drained from his brother's face. "You'd shoot your own kin?"

"You're too stupid for your own good, Tom."

He squeezed the trigger and Garrett lunged. The shot went wide. Garrett tossed the keys into the cell to give Tom a fighting chance and reached for the shooter. The move slowed him down. Bert leveled his gun at Garrett's forehead.

"Wait!" Tom hollered. "Don't kill him. I'll go with you."

He clumsily reached around the bars and jammed the key into the lock from the awkward angle. "You're right, I can't stay. We'll figure it out together."

Bert wiped the perspiration from his brow with the back of his hand. "That's better."

He flipped Garrett around and twisted his arm behind his back. Garrett cringed and arched his back.

Bert kicked him forward. "Get out there ahead of us, Tom. I'll follow."

Garrett was going to die. He knew it in his heart, in his soul. There was no way Bert was going to let him live. He thought of the morning he'd spent with Jo and cursed himself.

He'd lost his one opportunity to tell her he loved her.

*Time.*

He'd asked for time, and he'd just run out.

# Chapter Twenty-Seven

Jo hugged Jack Elder and stepped back. "Don't wait so long between visits."

"I won't."

"And give Elizabeth my love."

"I will." He glanced at someone behind her. "David?"

Jo spun around as her brother skidded to a halt before them. "It's Garrett."

At the panic in her brother's voice, her heart shot ahead three beats.

"He came into the jail with Bert Walby," David gasped. "The prisoner's brother. He told me to leave, but it was real strange. He told me to tell you that he appreciated the help of a fellow lawman."

Jack dropped his bags and began rummaging through the contents. He pulled out a pistol and spun the chamber, then stuck it into the back waistband of his pants. "You armed?" he asked David.

Her brother nodded.

"Do you think they'll come out the front or the back?"

"Bert came in through the front door. I'm guessing that's the way he'll leave."

Jack squinted toward the street. "All right. You circle around back, just in case. I'll watch the front."

Jo blocked their exit. "Give me the extra gun."

"No." Jack shook his head. "Absolutely not."

"I'm the best shot. He'll be holding Garrett as a hostage. That's the only reason he would have made David leave. I'm the best shot if there's an opening."

The men exchanged a look, and Jack reluctantly nodded. He handed her the gun, keeping his grip on the barrel. "Stay out of sight. If I see an opportunity, I'll give you the signal. When you fire, try to nick him, just for a distraction. I'll make the final shot."

Her mouth dry, Jo nodded.

David circled the row of connected buildings toward the rear of the jailhouse. She and Jack dashed down the street. Jack cleared the boardwalk of people while Jo crouched behind a rain barrel and leveled her gun toward the door. She hadn't told Garrett she loved him because she was afraid of spooking him. What if it was too late?

An eternity passed before Tom stepped out. He glanced left and right, his expression stunned. Garrett came next, his arm twisted behind him at an odd angle. Bert cowered behind him.

Garrett scanned the street and for a moment Jo thought he was looking at her. Then his gaze slipped away. She breathed a sigh of relief.

Bert caught sight of Jack and stopped short. "Out of my way, or I'll shoot the marshal."

"You won't get far without a hostage."

"Far enough."

"You willing to take that risk?"

Jo aimed her gun.

Bert yanked Garrett to the right, searching the deserted street as he calculated his odds.

Jack gave her the signal, a slight shake of his hand. Jo fired.

Garrett shouted and went to his knees, clutching the wound at his thigh.

Jack fired almost simultaneously.

Bert jerked. He glanced at his chest, astonished by the growing bloom of red covering his white shirt. His knees buckled and he collapsed onto his back, his eyes staring sightlessly at the clear blue sky.

Jo emerged from her hiding spot and crouched before her wounded husband. "Are you all right?"

"I'm fine," he replied, his expression rife with amusement. "You shot me, didn't you?"

"It's only a flesh wound." Jo pressed her hand against the bleeding.

He twisted to the side and unfurled his blue bandanna from his back pocket. She quickly tied it around his thigh.

Jack leaned over her shoulder. "I told you to nick the bad guy, not the hostage."

Jo grimaced. "My way was better. It gave you a clearer shot at Bert."

She glanced over her shoulder and realized Tom was sobbing over his dead brother. Her heart ached at the sight.

Jack stepped before her and blocked her view. "Let's get your husband inside."

He hooked his arm beneath Garrett's shoulder. Doc Johnsen, drawn by the commotion, followed them, his bag in his hands. Jo trailed behind the three.

Since the holding cell was the only place for Garrett to lie down, they shuffled him into the back.

The next fifteen minutes passed in a blur as Doc Johnsen sterilized the wound and added a few stitches.

The handsome, blond-haired doctor smiled at Jo. "Remind me not to get on your bad side. If you'll shoot your own husband…"

Jo scowled and crossed her arms over her chest. "He'll live?"

"He'll live."

Garrett motioned at the doc. "I need a moment with my wife. Alone."

The doc nodded. "Don't walk unless you absolutely have to." He adjusted his hat and closed his satchel. "Don't put any strain on that leg. I'll be back in a week to take out the stitches."

After he left, an unnatural quiet permeated the room.

Suddenly shy, Jo blurted, "Are you sore at me for shooting you?"

"Nope."

She grinned.

Garrett frowned. "I'm furious with you for putting yourself in danger." His soft voice blunted his harsh words. "You're the bravest woman I've ever met."

"No." Jo held his hand to her chest. "I haven't been very brave during our marriage. I didn't want you to reject me. I should have let you marry some pretty girl who would always know the right thing to say, but I was selfish. I wanted you for myself."

"Hey," he spoke sternly. "No one gets to speak badly about JoBeth Cain. Not even you."

She blushed. "Let me finish. When I realized you were in danger, I died a little bit inside. I love—"

"There's something I have to tell you."

He placed two fingers against her lips. "Don't finish that sentence until I've said my peace."

Jo sucked in a breath. Whatever happened, she was prepared to face the truth.

"I lied to you." Garrett drew himself into a seated position as Jo perched on the edge of the bed. He tried not to let the disappointment in her expressive face way-lay his confession. "My parents didn't die from small-pox. My father killed my mother and turned the gun on himself."

She clutched his hand tighter against her chest, and her heartbeat quickened beneath his fingers. "He wasn't a well man. He'd served in the war. He'd been wounded. He drank to ease the pain and when that didn't work, he turned to laudanum. He started having hallucina-tions. He thought my mother was an enemy soldier. He couldn't live with what he'd done."

Her mouth worked. "Did you see—?"

"No," Garrett hastily replied. "My sister and I were at school. A neighbor heard the shot. He found my fa-ther babbling like a wild man. He left to fetch help. I guess. I guess it was too much."

"You said you worked on the docks after that?"

"Deirdre was eighteen. We tried to live on our own for a while. It didn't work out. We stayed with my moth-er's uncle after that. And my cousin."

"Edward? The one who wanted custody of Cora?"

"Yeah. He didn't have much use for me. It was diffi-cult…on my aunt and uncle. I looked too much like my father. My uncle and I fought…" His voice trailed off. "I should never have become a lawman." He laughed humorlessly. "It's not such a big deal if a blacksmith has a murderer for a father, but a lawman is held to higher standards."

"Garrett…"

"I don't know what will happen when the town council hears about my past. I don't know if I can keep my job. We'll go someplace. Maybe I can apprentice as a blacksmith after all."

He smiled encouragingly, but tears welled in her eyes. His heart sank. "You know, never mind. You deserve better. We'll get an annulment. I'll—"

She mirrored his earlier gesture, pressing two fingers against his lips. "I'm sorry you thought your father's actions would change the way I feel about you. What he did makes me ache inside for you. For your family."

Garrett closed his eyes against the memories. "I was terrified of being like him. Then I saw Tom today. His brother wanted him to escape, but he couldn't. They're brothers, but they're different. Tom didn't have it in him. They'd faced the same difficulties and chosen separate paths. I'm different from my father."

"I know you are."

"I knew I loved you, but I couldn't tell you until I made my peace with God. I'd blamed Him all my life. I thought I'd been singled out for punishment. But then I realized I was only punishing myself. I didn't want to lose anyone I loved again, so I drove them all away. You changed that. Once I forgave my father, it was like I forgave myself."

She offered him a watery smile. "I love you, too."

His throat worked. "Are you certain? Because if my past is too much for you, I understand. If we have to start over, it'll be hard."

Jo snatched his coat lapels and fisted the material in her hands, jerking him upright until their noses were a hairbreadth apart. "If you leave me, I'll shoot you. Again."

Garrett grinned. "I believe you."

He cupped the back of her neck and kissed her. The past melted away, and he felt new, reborn.

She pressed her hands against his chest and frowned. "Your leg must hurt something fierce. You should be home where you can rest."

Garrett brushed the pad of his thumb over the faint scar on her cheek. "Not until I get this right." He sucked in a fortifying breath. "I'm sorry I lied. I've loved you since the moment you wrapped that snake around your arm. You're brave and honest and I can't wait to wake up in the morning just so I can see you." He paused. "You bring light to my world. You helped restore my faith in God. In myself."

She launched herself into his arms and hugged him tight. "That's all I ever wanted to hear."

"Then I'll say it to you every day for the rest of your life. I love you."

## Epilogue

He didn't show it, but Jo knew her husband was nervous. She squeezed his hand. "Whatever happens, we'll stay together."

Cora and Maxwell played marbles in the dirt beneath the sun. In light of his past, Garrett had offered to tender his resignation. The town council had met in the empty schoolhouse to discuss the matter.

Jo didn't figure the council had any reason for voting him out, but Garrett felt it was important, and she respected his wishes. They were waiting outside the schoolhouse while the decision was made.

Following the shooting, they'd buried Bert in the small cemetery outside the church. Tom and his wife had left for Oklahoma City soon afterward, with Tom declaring his need to start over.

David stepped out the door, and Garrett stiffened beside her.

Her brother winked at them and sketched a wave. "They're letting me keep my job."

Garrett stood and shook the younger man's hand. "I'm proud of you. Proud to have had you as my deputy."

Before David could reply, Jack Elder emerged. He approached Garrett, and Jo held her breath.

"I don't know whether you'll think this is good news or bad news."

Jo fisted her hands.

"They want you for five more years."

She jumped to her feet. Garrett stood beside her and caught her around the waist.

Keeping his arm around Jo, Garrett shook Jack's hand. "Thank you for everything. I hope to meet your wife and children one day."

"Might be sooner than you think. Elizabeth is beside herself with worry. My brother, John, set off on his cattle drive and we haven't had word in a month. She'll be up here soon to scold him herself when he arrives."

Cora tugged on her skirts. "I beat him. I beat Maxwell at marbles!"

Maxwell stood and dusted his trousers.

Her husband sighed. "You have to be on your toes around these ladies."

"I'll try again next Sunday when you come for supper."

Garrett groaned. "Your pa already asked me to balance the gate again."

"You adore my family," Jo said.

"Almost as much as I adore you." He moved his lips closer to her ear. "I thank God every day for bringing us together."

"Me, too," Jo replied simply.

Despite all the tragedy in his life, the shadows in his eyes had abated as his faith had grown. And she never tired of the way he looked at her.

As though he saw who she really was, even with her faults, and loved her all the more.

"Say." Jo pressed a kiss against his cheek. "You said I gave you a gift on our wedding day, but you never told me what it was."

"Peace. You gave Cora and me peace," he continued, ignoring their rapt audience. "Our family is the greatest gift I've ever received."

Tears pricked behind her eyes. She'd set out to win the marshal's heart, and he'd gone and turned the tables on her.

\* \* \* \* \*

Dear Reader,

From the moment JoBeth McCoy appeared in *Winning the Widow's Heart,* she demanded her own story. Jo is feisty and independent and always speaks her mind—except when it comes to her feelings. I couldn't wait to give Jo a hero who saw her true beauty and spirit. Someone who would show her that her vulnerabilities could also be her strengths. I found the perfect match for my spirited heroine in Marshal Garrett Cain, a man with a kind heart and a shadowed past.

Sometimes people ask me where I get my ideas. Here's my secret—the characters write their own stories. I simply corral their adventures within the pages of a novel. I've grown to love Cimarron Springs and the cast of characters who clamor around my head, each begging for his or her own adventure.

Thanks to each of you who take time from your busy schedules to write a kind note and let me know you appreciate my stories. I treasure each letter and email.

Wishing you many blessings,
*Sherri Shackelford*

## Questions for Discussion

1. Even though Jo and Cora are very different, they have an immediate affinity from the start of the book. Why do you suppose they are drawn to each other?

2. Many people in Cimarron Springs insist on treating Jo as a tomboy instead of a lady. Why do you suppose it's difficult for people to change their first impressions of one another?

3. Cora forces Jo to examine her life in a new light. What are some of the things Jo discovers about herself?

4. Garrett is worried that once people discover his past, they will judge him based on his father's actions and not his own. Do you think his fears are justified?

5. Jo changes her appearance as the book progresses. When does pride in one's appearance transform into vanity?

6. Although Jo's mom is skeptical of the marriage, she shows her support by gifting Jo with cowboy boots on her wedding day. Do you think Jo understands the significance of the gesture?

7. Jack Elder refers to marriage as "worthwhile work." Do you agree or disagree? Why?

8. Why is it important for Garrett to secure the town's approval of his marshal status after he reveals his secret? Do you think his insistence is necessary?